Heiress
to a Curse

ZANDRIA
MUNSON

MILLS
BOON

For my wonderful husband and my pooh, Christopher.

First published in Great Britain 2011
by Mills & Boon,
an imprint of Harlequin (UK) Limited,
Large Print edition 2011
Harlequin (UK) Limited, Eton House,
18-24 Paradise Road, Richmond, Surrey TW9 1SR

© Zandria Munson 2010

ISBN: 978 0 263 22380 4

Harlequin (UK) policy is to use papers that are
natural, renewable and recyclable products and made
from wood grown in sustainable forests. The logging
and manufacturing process conform to the legal
environmental regulations of the country of origin.

Printed and bound in Great Britain
by CPI Antony Rowe, Chippenham, Wiltshire

In walked the gargoyle.

He was gasping as if he'd been racing against time itself. The sleek muscles of his chest were glistening, and his long hair hung dripping over his shoulders. At the back of her mind, past the fear and desperation that jerked every nerve ending she possessed, Alexandra realized that he had probably flown through a thunderstorm.

His glare went straight to her, then to the scattered items of the chest on the floor. "How did you get in here?" he growled.

She'd been right! Marius was harboring the creature. Slowly she stood, the sound of her heart drumming in her ears.

He extended a hand. "I will not harm you. Please, you must come with me."

Alexandra's attention drifted to the blood-stained bandage on his arm. And the leather tie that held it in place.

"Marius?" she whispered.

Dear Reader,

Heiress to a Curse is the first novel in the *Hearts of Stone* series. My inspiration for this book came from two directions. One, my love for romance and for dark and dangerous alpha males. *Winks*. And two, my desire to be original. It seems everyone is trying to write the next great vampire novel. Although I have nothing against vampires, I just needed to think outside of the box.

I've found there are so many other creatures that one can make, shall we say, *alluring*. I chose gargoyles because I've always been fascinated by the ancient stone statues that sit quietly, monitoring our mundane routines from their vantage points. From this idea I was able to fashion the Drakon clan.

While writing this story I took every opportunity to visit places that would keep me in the right frame of mind. I wanted the scenes and characters to leap from the pages and tamper with the senses and emotions of readers. One of my most memorable experiences was visiting a haunted site in Michigan called the Paulding Light. There's nothing like creeping through a dark and misty forest at 1AM on a cold September morning to get my creative juices flowing. I didn't see any ghosts that night, but I did gain a wealth of inspiration.

Please enjoy Marius and Alexandra's love story. I hope these characters bring you as much excitement as they did me.

Happy Reading!

Zandria Munson

Prologue

16th Century, Romania

Lord Victor Drakon stood at the foot of his wide, four-poster bed as he watched his wife in repose. Her tall and elegant frame was entwined with the many furs that covered the bed, while the lovely wealth of her hair lay splayed about her face. She was beautiful and equally as gentle hearted and he loved her dearly. From the moment he'd first spied her picking flowers on his land, he'd loved her. She held no title and she wasn't of noble birth, but she was pure and her love was sincere.

He'd gone against propriety, against his family's wishes, and severed his betrothal to Lady Vivian Dancescu to claim this woman as his own. She was his heart, his life and his love.

Moving closer, he gazed upon her face, bathed

in the flickering glow from the hearth. She sighed then, her soft breath fanning the stray tendrils that had fallen near her lips.

He leaned over her and gently drew away the black curls. "My sweet Amelia," he breathed.

A sudden knock sounded at the door. It was his messenger, no doubt. He'd been waiting for news of Lady Vivian. After learning of his covert marriage to Amelia, the lady had been consumed by rage, hacking off her hair and publicly cursing the day of his birth.

He, however, didn't hold himself accountable for her ill feelings, for he'd tried desperately to reason with her. They'd been forced into their betrothal as children—a union that was to join the wealth of two powerful houses. There was no love between them and thus, he'd offered her freedom. He'd proposed a sizable fare to appease her wounded pride, but she was a greedy and self-righteous woman; it was his lands she desired. And so, he'd been left with no choice but to summon the chancellor during the silence of the early morning to perform the ceremony that would join him and his beloved Amelia.

He quickly donned his cloak and opened the door. His manservant stood on the other side, panting and covered in soot. "The Lady Vivian, my lord, she is dead," the man informed him.

"What do you mean, dead? Surely you jest!"

"No, my lord. She took her own life."

The blood drained from Lord Drakon's face and a sudden feeling of guilt overcame him. "How?" he asked.

"She burned herself alive, my lord. Even now fire consumes Elburich Castle."

Lord Drakon's nostrils flared as he inhaled a pained breath. Why anyone, most especially the gentle-bred Lady Vivian, would choose to end her life in such a horrific way was beyond him. "And her family?" His voice trembled.

The messenger's head lowered. "They were all sleeping. Everyone perished in the flames."

Lord Drakon spun away from the door and ran his fingers through the thick mane of his hair. Had the woman gone mad? To end her life was one thing, but to do so without the slightest consideration for her own family was another.

Was he to blame for her crime? Had his rejection driven her to insanity? *No,* he told himself. Her actions were the result of her own lust for greater wealth. No, the only one to be blamed was her.

A shrill cry resounded from the window of his bedchamber, shattering the solemn moment.

"Lord Drakon, I curse you!"

He exchanged confused looks with his messenger and they hurried toward the open shutters. Below, a woman stood bearing a torch. She was garbed in a heavy cloak that permitted only a shadowed view of her face.

"I curse your house and all who dwell within!" she continued.

"Who is she?" Lord Drakon asked.

"The witch Necesar. She was cousin to Lady Vivian."

By this time, Amelia had awakened, and she slipped from the bed, draping the heavy coverlet around her. "Victor, what is it?"

He hesitated for a moment. "Lady Vivian's cousin," he replied.

Again the voice of the woman below rang out. "You rejected my cousin to take a common woman to your bed! Her heart was slain by your insult and now she is dead, taking her beloved household with her!"

"It was not her heart that was slain, but her pride!" Lord Drakon called in return.

"You are one to speak of pride when you have

disgraced yourself and sullied your family's name. Tell me, when you lay with your peasant bride, do you see Vivian's face? Do you feel her pain?"

"Go home, woman!" he barked. "The hour is late and my patience runs low."

"I do not fear you," she snarled. "My beloved cousin bestowed a task upon me and I shall not fail her. You and your house shall suffer as she has. Your souls shall be stripped from your flesh and even the sun will betray you. Curse upon you, Lord Drakon, and curse upon your kin."

"Silence!" he shouted, consumed by rage now. "Leave this place, you wretched witch."

She stripped the hood of her cloak from her head, revealing a mass of silver hair. "My death will not end your torment. You and your generations to follow shall bear the same fate. Darkness will be your prison and you shall pray for death, but it will flee from you."

Lord Drakon turned to the man at his side. "Go below and cease this heresy. Give her a horse and send her on her way."

The messenger nodded and left to do his bidding. Lord Drakon maintained his post at the window as the woman continued her ranting.

Deep within him, fear kindled, for he'd heard of the power of the witch Necesar. Her spoken word was potent, like the venom of a serpent. Yet could one possess such power that she could curse an innocent man and his entire house? Would God allow such a thing?

Amelia appeared at his side, her beautiful features ashen. "Why does she speak so?"

He draped an arm about her, drawing her to him. "Lady Vivian has taken her life. The Elburich Castle has burned to the ground and everyone inside has perished."

"Oh, dear God," she gasped.

Beneath them, the sound of hooves emerged as three armed men on horseback, one with a mare in tow, moved to circle the witch.

Necesar continued as if they'd never come upon her. "For an eternity you and your children will be feared by all men and you will be hunted like beasts! The world will change, and as the vines come creeping to shroud the walls of your castle and the trees grow so dense that you cannot see beyond them, you will remember this night and what was lost in it."

One of the men advanced upon her. "Be silent, sorceress!"

She continued. "Five were those who perished, and in five winters darkness will be brought upon you. From thence, for five centuries will I be your constant torment. And when this time is spent, the one whose love you rejected will claim the body of my descendant and gain her vengeance."

With an angry growl, the horseman dismounted and drew his sword. "Be silent!"

She fixed the horseman with an unblinking stare. "Your wife is only two moons from giving birth," she stated.

Slightly taken aback, the horseman halted his advance.

"You will have a son. He will be born beneath the sign of Aquarius. He will be in your image, but his eyes will be taken from him. Born into darkness, he will never see your face."

"I am warning you, witch," the horseman growled.

"Your young wife, in her grief, will fall into madness."

"Silence!"

"For an eternity you shall dwell in this castle…."

Her words were cut short as he thrust his blade

into her abdomen just as Lord Drakon's protest echoed over the courtyard.

"No!" he shouted. But it was too late. The blade passed through her slender frame.

Necesar gasped, her eyes turning to the balcony. "Remember this night well, Lord Drakon, for it marks the beginning of your eternal torment." With that she collapsed to her knees.

Lord Drakon turned from the window and raced down to the courtyard. He pushed aside the horseman who remained above Necesar, staring in disbelief at what he'd just done.

It seemed that time slowed as Necesar's gaze roamed the faces of each individual present. She fell onto the dirt, her breathing slow and labored.

Lord Drakon moved to her side, stripping his cloak from his shoulders and draping it over her. He eased her head from the cold ground. The last thing he'd wanted was to see her slain, witch or no witch. The night had already claimed too many souls. He hung his head. To think that something as pure and simple as love could brew such a tragedy saddened his heart.

A flash of silver toppled from beneath the cloak and onto the hand he had positioned beneath her head. Necesar's amulet, with the Dancescu crest.

He reached out to retrieve it, for she should die with the symbol of her family near her heart. Necesar suddenly snatched his arm in a painful grip. She held on to him, her eyes deep and penetrating. He could only return her unnerving stare, for he found no words to appease the pain he saw there. Then, as silent as the drifting of ashes, her eyes closed and she breathed no more.

Chapter 1

New York City, Present Day

Alexandra Barret tilted up her head toward the warm water that streamed in steady waves down her naked body. She ran her hands along her wet hair, smoothing the long and heavy mass against her scalp. Over the sound of the shower, she could hear the television in the background. It was 8:00 p.m. The familiar voice of the news reporter beamed with excitement as he relayed the latest development on the Central Park sightings.

With her eyes closed, she reached down and shut off the water. Her pink terry robe, which had been draped over the towel rack, was quickly donned, then she wrapped a towel around her hair and padded out of the bathroom. A single lamp on her bedside table cast a dull glow about her

New York apartment. She sat on the edge of the bed and began to towel dry her hair.

"The eyewitnesses state that the creature resembled a pterodactyl with a reported wingspan of about twelve feet," the reporter continued. "This new sighting brings the count to five during the last month. Authorities have been hard-pressed to find any clues to aid in their investigation. I'm Anthony Newman with KB1 News."

The corny tune of a car insurance commercial filled the room. She stood and walked toward a small table in one corner of her room. Notes and photographs lay scattered upon it. She often brought her work home and her latest assignment was a story about the people affected by a series of mysterious fires in the Hyde Park community. At twenty-eight she was a successful features writer at one of the biggest heralds in New York, the *Daily Sun*. But where others relied on their interrogation skills to complete a task, she depended on a more mysterious talent.

Ever since she was a child she'd been gifted with a rare sight. At first it had been limited to her dreams, in which images had appeared to her, often seemingly meaningless. A few days later, she'd realize they were glimpses of events that had occurred. She'd never been able to predict the future, but with the added ability of tapping into others' emotions, she was often able to make accurate guesses, enabling her to complete assignments with uncanny insight. This ability propelled her to the top of her field.

Briefly, she skimmed through the photos then moved toward her dresser. She shook her hair out and gazed at her reflection in the mirror. She picked up her comb, a fancy silver and ivory family heirloom, and ran it through her long dark curls.

My gypsy.

That's what her father had always called her. Michael had been American and her mother, Marciela, Romanian. Her father had been a journalist. He'd met her mother thirty years ago while doing a story on Romanian folklore. It had been love at first sight. Within three weeks of their meeting, Marciela and Michael were wed. They'd remained in Romania for a year, but after Marciela's father had died Marciela and Michael decided to emigrate to the U.S. As her parents' only heir and the last of the Dancescu bloodline, Alexandra had inherited the entirety of her family's estate.

Alexandra put down the comb. Nearly two

years had passed since the accident. She missed
them sorely. Tears welled in her eyes and she exhaled a shuddering breath. She wasn't going to do
this to herself again. Her parents wouldn't want
her moping over their untimely deaths. They
would want her to move on and find happiness.

She switched off the television, stepped out
of her robe, climbed into bed and turned off the
lamp. The room was completely enveloped in
darkness except for a narrow bar of light that
spilled in through the window. She stared at it for
a moment, feeling the hairs rise at her nape. She
had the oddest sense that she was being watched.

She sat up slowly and glared through the glass
door. A few seconds skipped by and she sighed.
She really had to stop getting herself worked up.

She returned to her pillow and gazed at the ceiling as she tried to banish the thoughts she'd awakened. It wasn't long before her lids grew heavy
and her eyes closed as she slipped into a restless
sleep.

Marius Drakon perched on the metal rail of the
small balcony outside the seventh-story window,
his attention fixed on the form of the woman
on the bed. He'd been following her for several

days, and if all his father had said was true, then she was the last of the Dancescu bloodline. As his family had come to learn, the witch Necesar had been reincarnated throughout the centuries within the bodies of her descendants. There had been occurrences when her abilities had manifested within them when confronted by members of his clan, but Necesar had never gone out of her way to make her presence known. With the death of this final descendant—which he'd come to deliver—his family would be set free of their five-hundred-year-old curse.

He shifted his weight, his massive wings spreading to beat against the night air. He'd gladly volunteered to leave his Romanian castle and venture into the West to seek out the one woman who stood between him and freedom. He yearned to taste her blood on his lips. It would be sweet, like fresh air drawn into drowning lungs. No more would the shadows be his home at night and stone his prison by day. No more would he be damned—a gargoyle cursed to walk the earth for eternity.

From his vantage point, his gaze raked her body. She lay on her back and slept soundly. The pale sheets clung to every curve, outlining her femininity.

For months he'd envisioned killing her, a faceless descendant of the witch Necesar who'd cursed his family so many years ago. He'd never expected her to be so lovely. He remembered the softness of her face. She was young, too. It was a pity she had to die.

Years ago his parents had gone to every sorcerer and witch on every continent and had learned the true nature of the curse and what was necessary to end it. Every descendant of the witch Necesar had to be dead, and the last must die on the equinox and within the restrictions of a sacred ritual. It was imperative that the curse end this year, on the equinox, for the end of the Spring Equinox would mark the end of Necesar's five-hundred-year possession of her descendants' bodies—and another spirit would be allowed to take her place. The spirit of Lady Vivian Dancescu.

That could never be allowed to happen. From his father, Marius had learned that the deviant and malicious Lady Vivian wouldn't be so idle with Necesar's power at her disposal. His family—and perhaps, the world—would be damned as she exacted her revenge on the Drakon family and acted upon her greed for wealth and power.

Tonight, beneath the new moon, the Spring Equinox had begun and so, tomorrow, for the first time in one year, Marius would walk the daylight as a man instead of hardening into stone. He had twenty-eight days to carry out the ritual. Guided by the lunar sequence, each step would have to be completed individually before the next new moon. Before the first quarter, she would have to extend to him an invitation of trust, welcoming him into her home. By the full moon, a lock of her hair would be required. Before the waning crescent, a drop of her blood must be drawn. And finally, on the eve of the new moon, he would be permitted to slay her.

The fire raged on. The cries within the castle had ceased long ago, yet she stood there in the saffron light of the holocaust that lit the early morning. Villagers raced about with pails of water drawn from the lake as they fought to extinguish the flames.

She'd lost someone this night. She wasn't certain who, but there was a throbbing pang in her heart and she was consumed by grief.

Something slipped from her fingers and fell to the soft earth beneath her. She bent to retrieve it, then held it up to the light. It was a silver amulet much like the one she owned: the one that had been passed down through her family for generations.

Her fist clenched the object and anger seeped into her heart to replace the grief. Smoke burned her eyes and swept into her lungs with each ragged breath she inhaled. She would have her revenge! His name hovered before her in a haze of scattered thoughts. She closed her eyes, trying desperately to recall it.

Lord Victor D—

Alexandra's eyes flew open. Sweat beaded her forehead and her breathing came in short gasps. She'd been dreaming again—the same nightmare that had plagued her for years. Every time, the dream was the same: a beautiful woman, garbed in a velvet gown, walking calmly into a castle that was completely engulfed by flames. Alexandra could always hear herself screaming, trying desperately to stop her, but each time she'd failed. The woman's cries were always the last thing that filled her subconscious before she woke up.

The torturous dream had been the first manifestation of her gift. When she was younger, she used to try to stay awake to avoid the mayhem that might await her at sleep's threshold.

As her gift progressed, she'd begun to have difficulty venturing into crowded places, as she would be bombarded by images and emotions from those around her. Her parents had done a fair enough job of making life easier for her. She'd been tutored at home and provided with therapists and prescription medication, which had served to diminish her experiences for a time. Her mother had always tried to comfort her, telling her that her gift was something to be cherished and embraced. She'd told stories of women within their family who'd also had this talent. But considering the countless psychiatrists who'd described her condition as a rare case of psychosis and the fact that her own mother hadn't possessed any of the psychic traits, Alexandra had always been skeptical.

As she'd gotten older, she'd gained better mental control and could block out the imagery and emotions enough to fully function in everyday life, though she'd always been reluctant to date. There was no way to get close to someone without revealing some degree of her talent, and being rejected for being weird was painful. But she was tired of being alone, and a virgin.

Ring! Ring!

The sound startled her and she groaned, pulling the sheet over her head. Today was Sunday. Who the *hell* was disturbing her at this hour? The ring chimed again and she reached onto her night table, feeling around until she found the phone then bringing the receiver to her ear.

"Hello?" The dial tone greeted her.

She sat up as she realized it was her doorbell ringing. Tossing the receiver aside, she slipped into her robe and hurried to the door. The bell sounded two more times before she spied through the peephole. Her best friend, April, stood on the other side, looking quite impatient.

Alexandra unbolted the door and swung it open. Before she had a chance to say anything, the other woman swept in.

"Do you know how long I've been standing out there?" April asked.

Alexandra closed the door then headed toward the kitchen. "Sorry. I'm just tired." She opened an overhead cupboard and reached in for a bag of coffee beans. "I haven't been getting enough sleep lately."

April seated herself on one of the counter stools, crossing her long, slender legs. "Still having those nightmares?" she asked.

At five-foot-seven, April was an inch shorter than Alexandra and a year older. She also worked at the *Daily Sun.*

"Yeah." Alexandra sighed. "And those pills Dr. Peters prescribed aren't helping. I think I need a stronger prescription."

"What you need is to get out of this apartment. When was the last time you did something fun?"

Seating herself on the stool opposite April, Alexandra slumped over the counter. "I think you're right," she agreed.

"Of course I'm right! You've been working too hard. Oh, and speaking of work, did you see my Friday article?" She reached into her shoulder bag and pulled out a copy of the *Daily Sun,* tossing it onto the counter. "It made front page."

The newspaper landed next to Alexandra's head with a *flop* and she looked up, reading the bold black letters that comprised the headline.

Winged Creature Sighted for Fifth Time in Central Park.

April turned the paper sideways so that they both had a correct view of the image. "Some guy was filming his kids when the thing appeared. He managed to get a few shots. It's not a good picture, but it's proof that something is out there."

Alexandra looked closer at the picture, which showed a huge dark shadow with wings. "It's a wonder I haven't spotted this thing. I have a perfect view of Central Park from my bedroom window."

The coffee machine bell went off. April hopped off her stool, waving a hand for Alexandra to remain seated. "I'll get it."

She smiled her appreciation then returned her attention to the article. "A pterodactyl? I heard the same thing on the news last night. Thanks." She took the mug from April.

April retook her seat. "Yeah, but I don't think it's a dinosaur." She took a sip from her own mug. "I mean, such things don't just appear out of nowhere, especially not in New York City."

"Well, what do you think it is? You're the one following the story. Have you come up with any conclusions yet?"

April looked pensive, her sleek brows furrowing together. "Either it's an elaborate hoax, or some government experiment gone wrong. Anyway, enough talk about work. It's Sunday. Right now you need to get cleaned up. There's this huge fundraiser luncheon starting at twelve, and we have to be there."

Alexandra regarded her with suspicion. "When have you ever been interested in any fund-raisers?"

"Well…" She stood, adjusting her short chiffon dress. "Ever since I learned that this one is collecting money for scholarships and that all the powerhouses of this city will be in attendance, many of whom are eligible bachelors." She checked her hair and makeup in the mirrored finish of the toaster.

"I should've known." Alexandra laughed.

"Oh, and speaking of eligible bachelors, have you met your new neighbor yet?"

"New neighbor?"

"Yeah, I spotted him with some boxes while I was standing out there. He's moving into the apartment next door, and he's *gorgeous*." She took Alexandra's hand and pulled her from her seat then proceeded to drag her toward the front door.

On tiptoe, April spied through the peephole.

"He's there again!" she said, then motioned for Alexandra to take a look.

Alexandra followed suit and caught the blurred image of a tall man standing near a pile of boxes in the hall. A flutter of excitement danced in the pit of her belly. The only other male resident on her floor was shy Mr. Winston, who preferred the company of his eight cats to that of a woman.

"I can't believe someone is finally moving into 13A. It's been vacant forever," she commented, feigning indifference.

She continued to watch him and wished her hazy peephole was a proper spyglass. She could see only his obscured image as he lifted what appeared to be a crate of books from the top of the pile. He paused suddenly and turned, his eyes riveting to her small vantage point.

Alexandra gasped and spun away from the door. "He saw me!"

April raised a brow. "Please. You're behind a door," she scoffed.

"I know, but he looked right at me—well not at *me,* but at the peephole." She grimaced when she realized how ridiculous her claim sounded.

April folded her arms with a sigh. "Do you see what I've been telling you? You need to socialize." There was a brief moment of silence then a smile crept to her lips. "And I know just how to get you started."

Alexandra's eyes widened and her mouth fell open in a silent protest as the other woman reached for the knob and pulled the door open. Alexandra froze, acutely aware of the tall figure glaring at them. She was going to kill April the first chance she got!

April flashed a smile then turned to the man, offering him the same gesture. "Good morning," she chirped.

"Good morning." He nodded.

She flounced into the hall and began chattering away. "My name is April," she said, extending a hand. "I'm only visiting, but you'll see me around often."

"My name is Marius Drakon." He accepted her proffered hand. "It is a pleasure to meet you."

Alexandra remained in the doorway. She couldn't help but notice how deep and rich his accented voice was—like smooth, warm chocolate spread thickly over fresh fruit. She pulled the folds of her robe tighter when his eyes moved to her.

April motioned for her to come closer. "This is Alexandra, your new neighbor."

"Hello." Alexandra gave him a quick smile as she accepted his hand.

"It is a pleasure," he said quietly.

Lean fingers enclosed her slender ones. The heat he exuded was electrifying.

April's initial assertions were all too correct—the man was positively gorgeous. He was tall, and she was forced to incline her head to meet intense, slate-gray eyes that appraised her with an undeterminable emotion. He wore a white gauze shirt and black pants, and his long dark hair fell loose over his broad shoulders. He seemed groomed into old money, and he wasn't wearing a ring.

Silently, Alexandra cursed herself. It wasn't every day that she encountered such a man, and today of all days she just had to be barefoot with her hair in a wild cascade from a restless sleep. She could feel his eyes trailing over her, assessing. It was almost as if he could see right through the pink terry that covered her slender curves.

"You have an accent," April commented. "Where are you from?"

A rise of discomfort enveloped Alexandra

as Marius's attention remained fixed to her. Strangely, she was becoming quite aware of her nakedness beneath her robe. Her nipples began to tingle and harden and she was grateful that the thick material adequately concealed their betrayal. It seemed like minutes lapsed before his silver stare finally left her.

"I am Romanian," he supplied at last. "I have only just moved to the United States."

April's smile brightened. "Romanian, wow, so is Alexandra. You two have something in common already," she informed him. "Maybe you guys can discuss it over coffee sometime. She has lots of free time, you know. She is single, after all."

Alexandra shot April a deadly look. "Well, my mother was Romanian and my father was American," she said to Marius with a strained smile. "And I would love to tell you the story of their meeting sometime, but right now we have to get ready for a fundraiser."

"Nice meeting you." April waved and shut the door.

Once they were securely out of sight, Alexandra turned on her. "What is wrong with you?" she asked in a harsh whisper. The woman was her best friend, but God, she could be embarrassing!

April regarded her with an incredulous expression. "I should be asking you that question!" she replied in a similar tone. "You had that tall, handsome hunk out there practically drooling all over you, and all you could do was stand there like some mute pigeon! Then, when I try to help things along, you run?"

Alexandra spun away and stalked to her bedroom. "Well, forgive me if I'm not inclined to make dinner dates with strange men in my robe. And he wasn't drooling," she countered. She wouldn't allow herself to believe that she was so physically stunning that she'd taken the man's breath away—especially after just rolling out of bed.

April was hot on her heels. "Are you kidding? Did you even see the way he was looking at you? He could barely take his eyes off you."

"He was probably wondering when I last combed my hair," she said, sliding open the door to her closet. "How could you do that to me, April? Do you know how embarrassing it was to have him see me this way?"

April placed her hands on her hips. "What

are you talking about? You look…" She paused, wincing a little. "Well, we had to act quickly. There was no time to be concerned with appearances."

With a groan, Alexandra disappeared into her closet. The man was beautiful, yes, but that wasn't enough. So before she got herself all wound up weighing the potential for a relationship with him, she'd need to learn more about him.

"If it bothers you so much, then the next time you meet him, we'll have to make sure you look your best," she said.

"The next time?" Alexandra yelled from the closet. "I hope there isn't a next time!"

"Oh, come on. It wasn't that bad. And besides, you can't avoid him forever. He lives next door."

"Can we just change the subject?" Alexandra emerged holding two dresses. "Blue or lavender?"

"Lavender."

Alexandra nodded. "Great. Now I'm going to take a shower." She tossed the lavender dress across the bed and headed for the bathroom. "And not one more word about Mr. 13A from you."

"Fine!" April shouted after her.

Alexandra closed the bathroom door and stared

at her reflection in the mirror. She wasn't getting any younger, she told herself. Perhaps it was time she put some of her inhibitions aside. Her new neighbor was gorgeous and possibly interested in her. It would be a shame not even to try to get to know him.

Chapter 2

Marius remained in the entryway of his new apartment long after the door across the hall slammed shut. The image of the woman called Alexandra—the woman he'd been sent to kill—remained in his mind. He'd been hard-pressed to take his eyes from her, for she'd looked even lovelier than she had the night before. The shadows had deftly hidden the sleek lines of her face—a straight and regal nose that was befitting her lineage, long feathery lashes and soft, pouting lips. She was beautiful.

He'd noted that his mention of being Romanian had drawn her attention, and rightly it should have. Romania had been her home once, some five hundred years past. Her curious hazel eyes had reflected no knowledge of this. Instead, a gentle and honest nature had become apparent. And something more—strength, and a silent beckoning that oddly, he felt the urge to explore. It was hard to believe that behind those alluring pools lurked the presence of the witch Necesar.

Sometime in the early evening, while he was unpacking a set of two-hundred-year-old books, he heard a soft cry and a thud. He opened the door of his apartment and was surprised to find Alexandra on all fours in the middle of the carpeted hall, gathering packages of shredded cheese, shrimp and fresh parsley that littered the floor around her. A small, pink cat toy that lay a few feet behind her was the obvious culprit of her misstep.

"Mr. Winston and his *damned* cats," she grumbled a second before she realized that she was no longer alone. Slowly, she turned her head toward him. "Hello," she said with a pained expression.

"Good evening," Marius returned, his gaze coming to rest upon her rear.

A wave of heat surged through him, and the muscles of his jaw tightened as he attempted to tame the carnal urge that was rising within.

Alexandra sat up quickly and adjusted her dress. "I hope I didn't disturb you," she said, tucking a lock of ebony hair behind an ear. "I just returned from the grocery store and didn't watch where I was going."

"No, you did not," he replied before moving forward to assist her.

With a few deft movements, her grocery bags were repacked. He stood and extended a hand to her, noticing a brief hesitation before she placed her fingers in his. She had soft hands, delicate and smooth—a lady's hands. He wondered if the rest of her was just as delightful and defied the urge to dip his gaze into her exposed cleavage.

"I'll take them in," he offered as he picked up her bags.

She didn't respond immediately. Wariness flickered in her eyes. She was wise to be cautious, too. She had every reason not to trust him, and it had nothing to do with the fact that he was nearly twice her size and could crush her slender frame with his bare hands. Last night the Spring Equinox had begun, and should she invite him in, she would start the process that would end in her death.

"Thank you," she said at last and removed her keys from her purse. "Come in."

She opened the door and as he crossed the

threshold, victory raced through him. Was it so simple? Would his task be so easily accomplished?

Alexandra motioned toward the countertop. "You can put them right over there, thanks."

He did as she asked and then turned to look at her. She appeared uncertain, and he wondered what she was thinking. Could she see beyond his facade? Did she suspect his true identity?

"Would you like to stay for dinner?" Alexandra blurted out.

Marius's brows raised a measure. Quickly he made his expression impassive. The last thing he'd expected was an invitation to share a meal with her. He tried to convince himself that it wasn't the softness he sensed in her eyes, or the gentle incline of her head, or the indelible image in his mind of her naked body that urged him to accept. Instead, it was the need to assure himself that she was indeed the last of her bloodline. He would glean information from her, and once he'd learned all he needed to know, he would leave.

He offered her a subtle smile. "What are you preparing?"

"A seafood casserole. It's my special recipe," she told him.

"Then I would be delighted to stay and have dinner with you." His attention fell to her ripe lips as they curved into a brilliant smile.

"Great," she said. "Just give me a few minutes to change."

She tossed her keys onto the counter and disappeared into her bedroom. When the door shut behind her, Marius focused his attention on his surroundings. The decor was of a contemporary style with a sprinkling of Romanian influence. A large tapestry that hung on the wall of her dining room caught his eye. He sauntered toward it, recognizing the depiction immediately.

He could almost feel the chill of the wintry mist that was settled over the ground, smell the pungent odor of moist earth and decaying leaves that rose from the lake that he knew lay just beyond the frayed ends of the textile. It was Elburich Castle in its prime. Now, it was a vacant ruin that howled with the ghosts of its past.

Marius inhaled softly. Alexandra had returned. Her entrancing fragrance drifted into the room to assail his senses. "You are a collector?" he asked without turning around.

There was a brief moment of silence before her composed response came. "No. That has been

in my family for generations. It depicts a Romanian castle in the twelfth century," she said as she
moved to stand beside him. "It belonged to my
mother."

"Do you know the name of this place?" He
turned his attention to her and drank in the view
of her slender form clad in a clingy velour hoodie
with matching pants. Something within him
stirred. It was more than the carnal wanting that
had harassed him earlier. It was a need to learn
more about her.

"No," she replied.

Their gazes locked in an unconscious mating of
intense attraction. He found himself drawn into
her stare, unable to look away. She was so lovely.

"I should start dinner," she breathed softly.
"Would you like something to drink while you
wait? Some wine, juice, coffee maybe?"

"Some wine would be fine, thank you."

She nodded and flashed him a hesitant smile
before moving to the other side of the countertop
that divided the kitchen from the dining room.
There she busied herself with the task of gathering the ingredients for her casserole.

Marius's attention strayed to the tapestry one
last time. All he could hope for now was free-

dom, and there was only one way to bring that about. He knew what he had to do.

"Red or white?" Alexandra asked as she held up two bottles of wine.

"Red," he responded somberly.

She nodded and popped the cork on the wine bottle, pouring him a glass. "I think I'll have some, too. So, why did you choose to move to New York?" she asked.

Marius accepted the glass. "It is a big city with much opportunity. I thought it would be a good place to live."

"Me, too. I've only been here for about a year. And you're right, it is a good place to live. There's a lot to see and do." She strapped on an apron.

He took a sip of the wine. "Where did you live before coming here?" he asked, seating himself on a stool.

"Washington, D.C. I was born there and lived there all my life." She turned away to rummage through a cupboard.

Marius noted the perfect curve of her rear beneath the pants. With her transfixing eyes and curvaceous frame, he was hard-pressed to remind himself that she was his enemy.

She returned to the counter with a baking pan. "I landed a great job here, so I moved."

"Do you have family in Washington? Brothers or sisters?"

"My mom and dad were the only family I knew, except an aunt on my father's side. After they died, I needed a change." She paused. "It was hard, leaving everything I had ever known, but without my parents, there was nothing to stay for."

A brief silence lapsed between them.

"How old were they?" Marius asked with sincere interest.

She kept her eyes averted. "Mom was fifty-two and dad was fifty-eight," she replied solemnly. "Mom wanted us all to spend the summer in Bucharest. It was her first time back there in almost twenty-seven years. She and Dad went ahead, and I was to follow a week later." She paused, obviously blinking back tears. "They never even made it to the city. Somehow, Dad lost control of the SUV they'd rented and went off the road."

Marius experienced a pang of remorse, for it had been his family who'd caused the accident. And it truly had been an accident. They'd believed that Alexandra's mother, Marciela, was the final descendent of Necesar. His clan had just begun planning her mother's death to coincide with the next Spring Equinox. They had been surprised to learn that Marciela was returning to Romania to sell her family's estate, especially after so many years of maintaining it. Against Lord Drakon's wishes, several of the clan members had gone to look upon the individual who barred the way to their freedom. It was along the highway to Bucharest that Alexandra's father had caught a glimpse of one of the gargoyles and in a panic had lost control of the vehicle.

Devastation had spread quickly through the Drakon clan, as it had seemed their final hope for restoration had been shattered by Marciela's early death. However, it had taken them only a few weeks to learn that there was one remaining descendant of Necesar. And thus, here he was—the bearer of Alexandra's ill fate.

"Would you like some more wine?" she asked, obviously trying to change the subject.

"Please."

His gaze strayed to her face as she leaned over to refill his glass. He could tell that she suppressed much of her feelings. If it was as she said and she had no one, then she had no shoulder to cry on. Strangely, he found himself filled with the need to reach out and draw her into his arms. His father had warned him to expect cunning and deceit, but that was not part of the woman who stood before him. No one, not even the heiress to a curse, deserved to suffer alone.

Chapter 3

Dinner had gone amazingly well, Alexandra surmised a few nights later as she lay in bed. Her usual thing would have been to thank her new neighbor for his assistance then bid him a good evening, but April's criticism had replayed in her mind, and she knew it would have been a sin to allow him to slip away without even trying to get to know him a little. And she was certainly glad that she had. She'd really enjoyed herself. Marius Drakon wasn't only very appealing to look at, but he also possessed the degree of wit and intellect she craved in a male companion.

Of course, all that talk of her parents had left her feeling a bit embarrassed and alone. She wasn't sure why she'd bared herself to him that way. She didn't like talking about the deaths of her parents with anyone. On the surface, the pain had eased, but the hurt still lurked deep inside her heart.

Marius had listened intently, and after she'd finished her sad story, they'd debated history, particularly that of Romania. Alexandra had always been intrigued by the legends and mysteries surrounding the place. Marius had proven to be quite knowledgeable about the subject, to the point where he could name all the kings in order of succession.

His mind captivated her as much as his tall and lean body did. He exuded wisdom and absolute masculinity. She grew hot just thinking about him, and a sudden image of his powerful form pressed between her thighs flashed in her mind. An unwanted breathlessness assailed her.

With an impious groan, she rolled onto her back, squeezing her thighs together in a vain attempt to subdue the rapidly spreading heat that seemed to emanate from her most intimate place. Silently, she scolded herself for allowing her thoughts to wander in that direction. She'd known him only a few days. Although he'd given her no reason, she felt the need to be wary of him. Something dark lurked behind those beautiful eyes, yet she feared that was the very thing that most attracted her to him.

With a sigh, she reached onto her night table for her bottle of prescription sleeping pills. She slipped one into her mouth and, after a thought, took another. If she wanted to get any kind of sleep tonight she was going to need some additional help. The double dose worked quickly and within minutes she was falling helplessly into the world of dreams.

Marius flexed his hand over the hilt of the fourteen-inch Romanian knife. He stood at the foot of Alexandra's bed, legs braced and massive wings erect as he gazed down at her. After completing the first step of the ritual so effortlessly, he'd found no need to delay the second. He'd come to harvest a lock of her hair.

She slept soundly with the sheet at her waist and entwined about her slender legs. The room was dimly lit by the street lights spilling in through the window, yet he could see every satiny inch of her naked body. His eyes devoured her, taking in the soft and ripe curves of her breasts, hips and thighs. She was perfection.

Regardless of his efforts to remain focused on

the task at hand, he felt himself swelling with desire. He couldn't discern why she had such an effect on him, for during his many years of life, he'd seen and had some of the most beautiful of women. There was just something about Alexandra—something that called to the more primitive nature within him.

Shaking himself, he moved to stand at the side of the bed. He would do it quickly—she wouldn't even awaken from her sleep. His gaze crept over her a second time. Such a waste, he thought. A woman like her was every man's dream—she was made for loving. Another surge of desire shot through him and his grip tightened on the hilt of his knife. He should be done with this task before he lost himself to witless thinking.

He lifted a long tendril of ebony hair from the spill that covered her pillow. It was soft, weightless gossamer threads of shimmering silk. One quick flick of his blade and the smooth length fell away from the lock that remained in his hand. Carefully, he placed it within a leather pouch at his waist.

In her sleep, Alexandra sighed softly. A flash of silver between her breasts caught his attention. She wore a small amulet attached to a rope chain.

With the tip of his blade, he lifted it then took it between his fingers to examine the outline of the falcon at its center. The symbol was unmistakable, for it had haunted his family for hundreds of years; it was the Dancescu crest.

Slowly, he replaced the amulet against her chest, his fingers grazing her soft skin. His hand lingered in that spot, gently circling the circumference of the heirloom.

Again she sighed, her full breasts rising and falling with the effort. Marius stilled and his gaze crept back up to her face, fixing upon her lush lips. She was so enchanting. He would taste her just once before leaving.

He placed the blade to the right of her pillow and lowered his hard mouth to graze her lips in a tender kiss. When he withdrew he noted that his pulse had quickened and his breathing was slightly labored. And what was worse, he yearned to taste her a second time. Before he could justify this desire, his head fell again, bringing his lips against hers with increased intensity.

Alexandra groaned beneath him and her lips parted to welcome his hungry kiss. He devoured her, tasting every inch of her mouth. When her soft, wet tongue grazed the tip of his own, he retracted as if seared by hot iron.

What vile witchery is this? The woman is intoxicating!

Blood surged through his veins and he could feel his manhood strain against the material of his pants. With a predatory growl, he dipped again and his mouth found the delicate curve of her neck and shoulders. In her sleep she gasped, her soft breath warm against his ear.

Marius worked his way along her shoulders then found the ripe mounds of her breasts. His fanged mouth enclosed one at a time, sucking greedily while his large, clawlike hands moved to encircle her slender waist.

With a wanton cry, Alexandra arched from the bed, offering herself to him. "Yes," she breathed. "Please, don't stop."

With this encouragement, Marius traced a path of fiery kisses down her flat midsection. A haunting voice at the recess of his mind screamed at him and he knew he should take heed and cease this blasphemy, but it was too late. His self-control had fled and he could think of nothing save possessing the soft and beautiful woman beneath him.

He spread her legs wide then slipped his hands beneath her rear, lifting her off the bed. He took only a moment to gaze upon her smooth softness before his mouth descended upon her hot, moist core. He ate greedily, his studded gargoyle's tongue thrusting deep as he drank of her sweet nectar. Tender flesh began to writhe beneath him in shameless and suggestive undulation, urging him to complete his onslaught.

He lifted her higher, allowing his tongue deeper invasion into her secrets and a moment later, her entire body began to tremble with a climatic orgasm.

Marius fought to catch his breath. He couldn't understand what had just happened. He'd come with only one task in mind, yet somehow he'd found himself driven to touch and taste her. Even now he battled the urge to pin her where she lay and appease the ache in his loins. He'd allowed himself to be weakened by her, his enemy. He was unworthy of the Drakon title.

She dreamed of a sensuous heat that engulfed her, seeping in and out of her mind and body. She was helpless against it and could do nothing but succumb to the intense pleasure it offered.

Alexandra screamed. She spread her thighs wider and arched higher off the bed as she welcomed the shuddering release. She felt herself being lowered back down and she abruptly realized that this was no dream. Her eyes flew open and her moan of pleasure quickly became a shriek. Thinking only that she needed to get away, she rolled off the bed and landed on the floor.

The broad shadow that was crouched at the foot of her bed glared at her with fiery eyes that reflected a deep and burning passion. It rose slowly and the spill of the moonlight fell over it.

Alexandra was rendered motionless. The creature was unlike anything her mortal mind could conjure. His face and body resembled those of a man—he was tall and powerful like the Greek gods she so loved to read about—he wore only a fitted pair of black pants that clung to his lean waist and sculpted thighs, and boots of the same foreboding hue complemented his attire. Yet, he was no man, for horns crowned his head and great wings guarded his back. *Is he a demon?*

With a savage growl, the creature snatched his blade and fled through the open door and into the night.

Had what she'd seen been real? Her heart was racing, and her trembling fingers found their way to the wet and throbbing place between her thighs. One thing was certain—she'd experienced an intense orgasm. A gust of cool night air flooded her room, lifting the sheer drape, and she shivered. She was also certain that the glass door had been closed. Something or someone had climbed in and assaulted her while she slept.

Still trembling, she grabbed the phone off the night table and began to dial the police, but paused before her fingers could engage the third digit. What would she tell them? That a demon had just invaded her seventh-story apartment and given her great oral sex? She hung up and dialed her psychiatrist instead.

Chapter 4

The next morning Alexandra was still unsure if what she'd seen had been real or some sort of twisted dream. She'd decided to keep the experience to herself, at least until her 7:00 p.m. appointment with Dr. Peters. Instead of dwelling on it, she poured herself into her work. The story on the mysterious Hyde Park fires still needed to be finished.

She sat behind her desk and began sifting through the countless photographs and notes that she'd collected over the past two weeks. Her mind immediately began to race, its performance no doubt fueled by last night's events. Images and words began to flash within her thoughts. She snatched a pen from her desk and began scribbling down everything she saw.

Alexandra was about to leave her desk to follow the leads she'd obtained from the photographs when her attention was drawn to the plasma TV, mounted on the wall, that broadcasted the news during the day.

"In Pennsylvania, the body of a female was discovered in an abandoned building early yesterday morning." The reporter spoke somberly. "The partially decomposed corpse has been identified as twenty-seven-year-old Trish Gooding, who has been missing since last Tuesday. This murder brings the count to three within the Union City area, and detectives have concluded that it is the work of the Penn State Serial Killer."

Alexandra's heart felt heavy. She didn't understand how an individual could be so callous as to regard human life as nothing but a tool for his amusement. How could a man's conscience allow him to snatch a young woman from her home, rape her, torture her and kill her?

She was about to turn to go when an image on the TV made her pause. A photograph of a young girl.

"In other news, twelve-year-old Mady Halman went missing on Friday evening," came the reporter's voice. "She was last seen a few blocks from her home in the South Bronx area."

Alexandra froze as blurry images flashed before her eyes. The reporter's words were lost in the heavy drumming of blood rushing to her brain. She could see Mady, walking in the park. A tall man, his face obscured by a hooded sweat-shirt, talking to her. Taking her. Then darkness. Blood. Pain. A young girl's screams. Then the uncanny image of Trish Gooding, fleeing for her life.

Alexandra gasped as she came abruptly back to the present. She was shaking and the breath had been snatched from her lungs.

It was as if she'd been standing right there, watching it all take place. She'd felt the child's pain. Mady was alone, crying for her mother and receiving only silence in return. The Penn State Serial Killer had kidnapped that child, and he was going to kill her.

Alexandra knew what she had to do. She couldn't wait for her certainty to be confirmed. If there was a chance to save that little girl, then she was willing to take it. She hadn't been able to save her own parents, but she'd do everything in her power to save this little girl.

With hardened resolve, she headed toward the editor in chief's office.

"Come in!" came Mr. O'Reily's reply following her knock.

Alexandra entered to find him perusing a pile of articles on his desk. He shot her a quick glance over the rim of his glasses. "Barret, what can I do for you?" he asked.

She braced her hands on his desk and fixed him with a determined look. "I want the Mady Halman story."

"That's breaking news, not a feature. And I assigned that one to Thomas already." He refused her without taking his eyes from his work.

"Then reassign it. I want it."

He looked up then, his eyes narrowing. Alexandra knew that her behavior was out of character, for she'd never made a fuss about getting any particular project.

He reclined in his chair. "Are you done with the feature on the victims of the Hyde Park fires?"

"Well, no, but I'll finish it before the end of the month. I just want this story."

"I can't have you working two stories at once and I need that Hyde Park article completed by Wednesday," he told her firmly.

Alexandra sighed in exasperation. "Look, I'll get it done and have it on your desk by tomorrow if I need to. Just give me a chance. I need to do this."

His eyes focused on her. After what seemed like an eternity of silent assessment, he nodded. "Fine, but if you don't have the Hyde Park article on my desk by Wednesday morning, I'm pulling you out."

She nodded with a smile. "Thank you, sir." All she needed was enough time to locate Mady.

"You're not crazy, Alexandra," Dr. Peters said from behind his desk. "You were just hallucinating because you overdosed on the medication I ordered."

Alexandra frowned up at the ceiling. "It all seemed so real." She was curled up on a leather chair with her shoes off.

"That's what hallucinations are like," Dr. Peters continued. "It's very hard to distinguish one from reality. What you shouldn't have done was taken that additional tablet."

"I know," she groaned. "But lately my nightmares have become so vivid. I can't seem to get enough sleep."

"I understand that, but what you did was very dangerous. You should've simply come to me," he scolded.

With a sigh, Alexandra looked at him. He was a small man in his early sixties and he wore wire-rimmed glasses that made him look like an owl.

"You're right," she agreed. "But I still don't undertand how taking one extra tablet could cause me to visualize something like that. I mean, I usually dream of castles and fire. So, why am I hallucinating about this creature?"

The doctor clasped his fingers together on his desk. "There is a logical reason for that, I'm sure."

She sat up. "Like what?"

"Well, if you consider all the hype surrounding the recent Central Park sightings of a mystery creature and your proximity to that location, I daresay that you're transferring suppressed fear into imagery," he said.

Alexandra thought for a moment. It sounded logical, except that she entertained no fear where the mysterious Central Park sightings were concerned. She respected Dr. Peters's opinions, but there was no way she was going to allow him to inject emotions into her mind. If she'd been hallucinating, it was definitely not due to fear. "And what about the orgasm?" she asked.

He pushed his glasses up on his nose. "Well, what you experienced is actually quite common in both men and women. It's called a nocturnal orgasm or better known as a wet dream."

When she fixed him with a look of skepticism, he continued. "Alexandra, you must understand something. The mind is very influential. If you believe something is happening to you, then naturally your body will respond. So, having an orgasm during a dream or hallucination isn't un-heard-of."

She didn't respond. Instead, she sat there in a contemplative trance as her thoughts returned to the previous night. Dr. Peters was a wise man and everything he said seemed to make sense, yet she couldn't bring herself to believe that what she'd seen had been only a figment of her imagination. There were just too many indications that something or someone had indeed visited her during the night.

Dr. Peters stood and came to the front of his desk. "Alexandra, you really must try to forget this," he said as he seated himself on the lac-quered oak finish. "I know what you're thinking and the answer is *no,* you're not crazy. I'm certain it was the overdose that initiated this experience." When she turned attentive eyes on him, he continued. "What you need now is a warm bath and some rest and I promise you, as long as you follow my instructions, you'll be fine."

Dr. Peters's words replayed in Alexandra's mind as she stepped out of the taxi. He was right; the idea of what she'd seen was a little far-fetched. This was New York City and strange things happened every day, but to think that there was a creature out there that visited lonely women in their beds at night was preposterous.

She glanced at her watch. It was 9:00 p.m. already and the dark streets appeared all but deserted. She reached into her saddlebag and pulled out a file and flipped to the address page. Mady Halman's picture greeted her, the girl's sweet smile and innocent eyes tugging at her heart.

"I'm going to find you," Alexandra promised softly as she replaced the file in her bag.

She shot a glance about her. The South Bronx definitely wasn't the kind of place she wanted to frequent. Rows of identical, graffiti-covered apartment complexes lined both sides of the street and garbage littered the sidewalk.

She entered the building where Mady lived and was met by a foyer that reeked of urine and marijuana. She made her way up the dimly lit stairway, skipping over soda cans and cigarette butts. Somewhere on the first floor a door slammed and she could hear shouting. A baby started crying.

Alexandra's heart pounded. She'd only seen places like this in movies and on the news, but she knew exactly the sort of riffraff that frequented them. She quickly counted the numbers on the apartment doors until she found the one she was looking for.

She knocked softly and a moment later the muffled voice of a woman greeted her.

"Who's there?"

Alexandra focused on the peephole, for she was certain she was being observed from the other end. "Hi. I'm looking for Ms. Veronica Halman. I would like to speak with her concerning her daughter's disappearance."

There was a brief silence, then the sound of a set of locks being released. The door opened a crack and a woman looked out from behind the chain.

"I'm Veronica Halman. Who're you?" She was

a middle-aged woman with a humble face that was etched with lines of grief.

Alexandra offered her a smile. "I'm Alexandra Barret. I'm a reporter for the *Daily Sun*. I just need a few minutes of your time, please."

Her request was met by a look of exasperation. "Another reporter? I'm not doing anymore interviews. I've talked with so many people already, and no one has any idea what happened to my baby. So please, if you're not here with something to tell me, then leave."

She was about to close the door, but Alexandra placed a palm against it, stalling her effort. "Please, Ms. Halman. I only need to talk to you for a few minutes. I can help you," she pleaded. "I can help you find Mady."

She tried to appear confident, but inside fear and uncertainty dominated her. Making promises based solely on her visions was terrifying and guilt inspiring.

Ms. Halman eased the door open a measure. "Help me how?"

Alexandra wasn't certain if she should reveal that she possessed a psychic ability that only of late seemed to be getting stronger. Most people didn't believe in such things and now that she'd gained Ms. Halman's attention, she didn't want to risk losing it. But what other choice did she have?

"I'm…a psychic. I've seen Mady in a vision," Alexandra responded. "She's alive, and I promise you that I'll do everything I can to see her returned safely home."

A glint of hopefulness mingled with doubt reflected beyond the worry in the other woman's eyes.

"Look," Alexandra continued. "I know this isn't something you hear every day, but I promise you, I'm authentic and everything you share with me will remain between us."

Ms. Halman stared at her for a moment then eased the door shut. Alexandra could hear the chain being released and when the door reopened, Ms. Halman stood to one side and motioned for her to enter.

"Thank you," Alexandra said as she slipped into the apartment.

The living room was small but neatly kept. A worn floral sofa was positioned against one wall, and on the other, a television set sat on a wooden stand. A toddler was seated in front of it, watching a cartoon show. He turned wide eyes on her and Alexandra sent him a smile as she stepped around him.

"You say you've seen her? Where is she?" Ms. Halman asked anxiously.

"I'm not sure, and that's why I need your help," Alexandra replied, noting the dark circles around the woman's eyes. She wouldn't dare mention that her vision had revealed Mady being taken by a man she suspected was the Penn State Serial Killer. Ms. Halman obviously had enough to contend with.

"Just tell me what to do. Please, have a seat."

Alexandra complied as she removed a file and a small notepad from her purse. "I know this is hard for you, but please bear with me. I'm going to ask you a few questions. This information is important, so I need you to tell me everything you can. Is this the most recent picture you have of your daughter?" She slipped the photograph from the file.

When Ms. Halman nodded, she placed it on the table and continued. "I saw Mady walking. Where was she going?"

She cleared her throat. "It was Friday, around 4:30 p.m. Mady'd just finished her homework and she asked me if she could play with her friends in the park and I let her go alone." She paused to dab at her eyes with a handkerchief.

"Which park? And what route did she take?"

"Brook Park. It's only a few blocks from here, and we always take the main road. I usually walk with her, but her brother had a fever that day and I let her go alone."

Alexandra knew what it was like to lose someone dear. "It's not your fault," she said empathetically. "Sometimes we don't know when bad things are going to happen."

"I'm her mother. I should've been protecting her." She dabbed at her eyes again.

Alexandra fought the tears that burned her eyes. She saw herself in this woman, this mother. The pain she'd experienced when she'd lost her parents had been unbearable. She'd tormented herself, wondering *what if.* Yet no amount of wondering could have changed what had already taken place. This was different. Mady was still alive. She could feel it. And she knew that she could possibly prevent her murder.

"Ms. Halman, may I borrow an item that belongs to Mady, something dear to her?"

Curiosity registered in the woman's eyes. "Something like what?"

"Anything that she loved."

The other woman thought for a moment then nodded. She reached into the pocket of her house-coat, pulling out a gold charm bracelet. "I bought this for her on her twelfth birthday. She loves ani-mals." She passed it to Alexandra.

Accepting it, Alexandra noted that each little charm was shaped like an animal. "Thank you."

Ms. Halman forced a smile, her eyes brim-ming with tears now. "The puppy is her favorite. I couldn't afford a real one, so I was sure to get that charm attached." She hung her head then, her body shaking as she sobbed silently.

Alexandra couldn't help herself. She placed her notepad aside, slid toward the other woman and wrapped her arms around her. There were just no words to ease such a pain. All she could do was hope that she could keep her promise.

When Ms. Halman regained her composure, she sat up to wipe her eyes. "I'm sorry," she apol-ogized. "It's just been so hard. I've always prom-ised myself that I would do whatever it took to protect my children. That they'd never have to suffer through what I did."

She met Alexandra's questioning look. "Thir-teen years ago I was working the night shift at a local diner. While walking home one morning, I was attacked and raped." She looked away. "I became pregnant, and nine months later Mady was born. They never caught the guy. Somehow I managed to survive through it all. I even got married and had my son, though his father and I are separated now."

Alexandra's heart sank in her chest. She couldn't imagine suffering through something like that. "I promise you, Ms. Halman, I'll do whatever it takes to bring your daughter back," she assured.

"Thank you." She gave Alexandra's hand a squeeze. "Please, excuse me for a moment."

She stood and headed off toward what Alexandra assumed was the bathroom. She sat there, looking at the bracelet in her hands. Her eyes drifted closed as she tried to channel her mysterious ability. She didn't really expect anything to happen, as she'd never been able to summon her visions, but it didn't hurt to try. She didn't notice the toddler moving toward her.

"Hi," came his small voice.

Alexandra opened her eyes and a smile crept to her lips. "Hello. What's your name?"

"Peter, and this is Muffy." He held up a straggly, one-eyed stuffed rabbit.

"Well, hello to both of you."

He smiled. "Are you the police?"

His question caught her by surprise. "Oh, no, I'm just…a helper."

"Are you gonna bring Mady back?" He waited, his eyes wide with innocence and anticipation.

A great sadness tugged at Alexandra's heart. With the police having no solid leads, she was the best hope for saving Mady. Her eyes fell once again to the charm bracelet in her grasp. "Yes, I'm going to bring Mady back."

Chapter 5

Impatiently, Alexandra looked down the busy street, spotting the bright yellow hood of a cab making its way toward her. "Taxi!" she cried out, waving a hand.

The vehicle zipped by without even pausing. Two subsequent attempts rendered the same result. With a sigh she began walking up the street in search of a better location to catch a cab. She noticed a sign for Brook Park and decided that she'd stop there for a few minutes. Mady's charm bracelet, which she'd fastened onto her wrist, hadn't evoked any visions, but being in the location of the abduction just might stimulate her psychic ability.

And so she shrugged off her navy, pin-striped blazer that matched her knee-length pencil skirt, draped it over her arm and headed in that direction.

She'd only walked a short distance when an image a few feet in front of her forced her to slow her pace. It was the silhouette of a preteen girl, wreathed in an apparition-like glow. Instantly, Alexandra knew that she was having a vision, although she'd never had one quite this vivid before. Her guess was confirmed when the girl turned to look at her. Alexandra froze as vacant pools locked onto her. It was Mady Halman. Her face was impassive, yet Alexandra sensed a deep sadness that called out to her.

Mady turned then and began walking in the direction of the park. Regaining her composure, Alexandra followed. After about a block, the image raced across the street, passing through the ongoing traffic, and Alexandra was forced to stop at the curb. From where she stood she could see Mady moving along the sidewalk. A van appeared then, and a man stepped out. The man from her vision.

Alexandra took a chance and wove her way through the traffic, but by the time she crossed the images were gone. She looked up and down the street and caught the tail end of the van turning a corner. Quickly, she raced in that direction, turning the corner and running halfway down the alley before she came to an abrupt halt. It was a dead end and there was no sign of Mady or the blue van.

"Hey, lady, can you spare some change?"

The voice startled Alexandra and she turned to face the man who'd spoken. He wasn't alone. The three men who barred the entrance of the alley were tall and disreputable in appearance. They wore layers of dirty clothing, and she could smell their stench even from a few feet away.

"Sorry, I have no money," she said, offering them a nervous smile. "I think I've made a wrong turn. If you gentlemen would excuse me, I'll just be on my way."

"Oh, no, you don't," said the shorter of the trio as he sidestepped to block her path. His tanned skin was covered with smudges of dirt and his straggly blond hair fell forward to shield half of his narrow face.

"Careful, Weasel," another man spoke. "We don't want to scare the little lady, now do we?" He was completely bald and his skin was as dark as midnight. He smiled, flashing yellow teeth.

The man called Weasel laughed. "I ain't scaring

her, Bubba. She just needs to do what we ask her to and she'll be fine."

The third man advanced a step and with a quick flip of his wrist, he produced a pocket knife. "And if she doesn't, we'll cut her!" He leered.

Alexandra's heart drummed in her chest when the man holding the knife took another step toward her. He looked more forbidding than the others with his towering height, pale skin and the tattered patch he wore over his left eye. She shot a frantic look down the alley. Two solid walls of brick surrounded her on either side, and no doorways offered hope for help. The only way out was through them.

Bubba turned to the man on his left. "Put that thing away, Scratch. I'm sure we won't need to do any harm. This little lady isn't gonna give us no trouble, isn't that right, missy?"

She took a step backward, clutching her studded saddlebag. "I told you before, I don't have any money," she said, trying to mask the slight tremor in her voice.

"I don't have any money," Weasel mocked in a distorted voice. "We heard you the first time, broad. We just don't believe you. All dressed up in your fancy suit, smelling real good, and you expect us to believe you don't have any cash? What are you, some kinda social worker or something? Well, I've got some special needs you can attend to." He was moving closer now, circling her slowly.

Alexandra stiffened, holding her breath as his gaze traveled from her black wedges up her slender, stocking-clad legs to the smooth curve of her hips in the formfitting skirt, her narrow waist and the slightly revealing V-neck of her ruffled blouse.

When his eyes snapped back up to meet hers, he wore a sadistic grin. "Hand over your purse!"

Slowly, she slipped her designer handbag from her shoulder and passed it to him. She was shaking all over, for she knew that they would find nothing in it to appease their greed. She'd been in a rush to leave her apartment that morning, and she'd failed to pack her wallet. All she had was a MetroCard and a few dollars, barely enough for a taxi home.

Weasel snatched the purse from her and his accomplices gathered around to inspect their bounty. The zipper was yanked open and he rummaged through the pockets, discarding anything he thought useless. Her cherry lipstick, followed by her address book and then her notepad, hit the gravel. When he pulled out her mini tape recorder, he tossed it to Bubba, who held it up for inspection.

"I think we can get a few bucks for this," Bubba commented.

Scratch leaned over to look at it, as well.

Alexandra was grateful for the diversion and she eased to the left as she calculated the distance to the main street. She could make a run for it. She would probably get caught, but at least she'd be near enough to scream and hope that someone would hear her.

Without a second thought, she swung her blazer over Weasel's head and gave him a firm shove, sending him stumbling into the others.

Not even looking back, she raced toward the ongoing traffic as fast as her heels would allow. She heard an angry growl and then the heavy thud of footfalls behind her. In the next moment, a punishing hand grabbed her arm and she was yanked violently around. The sleeve of her blouse ripped and she was propelled to the right, where she slammed into the brick wall and fell to the ground.

Recovering quickly, she looked up to see

Weasel tossing her shirt sleeve aside and storming toward her. She tried to scramble away, but was promptly blocked by a pair of long legs. Scratch stood above her, turning the knife around in his hand.

"I guess you don't like your pretty face." He sneered.

Weasel came to stand beside him. "I think we need to teach her a lesson." He reached down to twist a lock of her hair about a grimy finger.

Alexandra tried to push his hand away. "Don't touch me!" she screamed.

"Man, shut that bitch up!" Bubba, who was still rummaging through her purse, barked.

Scratch squatted next to her, bringing the knife dangerously close to her face. "Make another sound and I'll cut you, I swear I will."

His fetid odor engulfed her and she was forced to hold her breath. Her heart was racing. Only once before had she been so afraid, when she'd gotten the news of her parents' deaths and she knew she was all alone in the world. Yet she'd survived that, and somehow she'd survive this.

With a laugh, Weasel grabbed her right arm and brought her wrist to his gaze. "Now ain't this pretty," he snarled as he snatched away the charm bracelet.

Alexandra sucked in her bottom lip to avoid crying out as the gold chain cut into her skin.

He held it up to the dim light. "I bet I could get a few bucks for this." He bit into it before stuffing it into his pocket.

"Please," Alexandra began softly as she tried to ignore the sharp point of the knife that hovered near her cheek. "That doesn't belong to me. If you want money I can get some for you, but please, I need that bracelet."

The two men near her erupted in laughter. Scratch traced the smooth edge of the knife against her jawline. "Did you hear that, Bubba? The broad is trying to bargain with us." He laughed. "Says she'll give us money if we give her back her bracelet."

Bubba tossed Alexandra's handbag aside. "What money? All she has in here is twelve bucks," he said as he recounted the bills.

Weasel walked toward him. "*Jeez,* is that all?"

"Cell phone," Bubba replied as he passed the lavender, rhinestone-encrusted object to him.

Left alone with Scratch, Alexandra turned

frightened eyes onto him. He leered at her. He seemed to thrive on her fear.

"I bet you got some valuables under your clothes," he said as he trailed the knife along her neckline. "There's only one way to find out now, ain't there?"

The tip of the blade slipped beneath the top button of her blouse and with a tug, it popped away. The upper half of her top fell open.

Alexandra's breath caught when, with a grin, he positioned the knife under the second button. Desperation flared though her. She wasn't about to sit still and allow this dirty bastard to violate her. She grabbed a handful of dirt and gravel and tossed it into his face.

The retaliation came as a surprise and Scratch fell over, screaming from the pain in his one good eye.

"The bitch tried to blind me!" he shouted, drawing the attention of his accomplices.

Alexandra was about to jump up and make a run for it when a loud thump came from somewhere at the rear of the alley. The earth beneath them vibrated and the lid of the big, rusty Dumpster slammed shut. All eyes turned toward the shadows.

"What was that?" Bubba asked.

Weasel shrugged. "How the hell should I know?"

Using the wall for support, Alexandra stood slowly. She shot a glance to the exit of the alley and when she looked back the three men were approaching her.

Scratch, who was squinting, retrieved his knife from the ground. "I'm going to teach you a lesson, bitch!" he spat.

Another sound emerged from the rear of the alley, making them pause a second time. It was a low and ominous growling that was like nothing Alexandra had ever heard before.

"Man, what *is* that?" Bubba asked again.

The noise grew louder and a large figure loomed in the shadows.

Weasel took a step backward. "Maybe a dog," he suggested nervously.

"Man, that ain't no dog," Scratch said.

"Then what is it?"

The dark figure flew from the ground into the shrouding darkness overhead, rattling the fire escape. Incredulously, Alexandra blinked her eyes. The thing had moved quickly, but the brief moment in the light had been enough for her to recognize it. And if she'd seen correctly, then the thing that stalked them was the very creature that had visited her the night before. But…how could it be? She'd been hallucinating, right?

Her three assailants stumbled backward with their gazes turned to the sky. "Where'd it go?" Weasel shouted.

"I don't know," Bubba replied as he pulled a short knife from his pocket. "But if it comes down here, it's gonna get what it's looking for."

Scratch kicked angrily at the gravel. "Come out!" he taunted. "Show yourself so I can cut your throat!"

Before the last word spilled from his lips, loud vibrations from the fire escape echoed through the air and the shadow sprang forward, disappearing again into the overhead darkness.

Weasel retreated a few paces. "What the hell!" His eyes were wide and fear danced within them. "Did you guys see what I just saw? That thing has wings!"

The low, guttural growls persisted and in the next moment, the creature leaped from the shadows, coming to land before them in a huddled position. Slowly, it rose like a demon emerging from the pits of hell, its wings spanning a full length of about twelve feet, its long tail slashing the night air.

Alexandra stood frozen with her back pressed against the wall. She couldn't believe her eyes. The creature was just as she remembered him, tall, powerful and beautiful. For an instant, his transfixing eyes set upon her and a shudder racked her body. Hours ago those penetrating eyes had draped her with lust and blazing desire. Hours ago he'd spread her thighs wide and tasted the very core of her womanhood, when she'd shuddered with a climatic release that would've put a wanton to shame.

A scorching heat made its way up her legs and down her breasts, coming to unite in that soft place between her thighs.

Her present danger was forgotten and all she could think was that the creature was real—flesh and blood and not a figment of her imagination!

Marius flexed his wings, assessing the situation.

The three men stumbled backward another step. "Hey, it's too early for Halloween!" The one called Scratch sneered.

"Man, I don't think that's a costume," Bubba

said as he and Weasel staggered away another few paces.

"Oh, yeah? Well, watch me cut that ugly mask off his face!" Scratch poised himself for a fight, his fingers flexing over the handle of the knife. "*C'mon,* you weirdo freak!"

With slow, confident strides, Marius advanced upon them, his gaze pinned to the man wielding what appeared to be an arrowhead. He'd been following Alexandra when, from the roof of an apartment building, he'd spotted her turning into an alley. By the time he'd discreetly found his way to the roof overlooking the alley, the three men had trapped her. An unexplained rage had filled him as he'd witnessed Alexandra being thrown against a wall. Then when the largest of the trio had brought the tip of his weapon against her chest, severing her button, a new anger had possessed him—the very anger that flooded him now. He told himself that it was due to the fact that the Lunar Ritual had already began and should something happen to her before its completion, his family's curse would be sealed for eternity.

The man called Scratch charged, his knife held high for the anticipated assault. Marius turned his attention toward his assailant just as Scratch swung his blade. Marius caught the man's arm, but not before the sharp point slashed his chest. His eyes narrowed on the thin film of blood forming where it had made contact and a deep growl reverberated within his chest. His grip tightened on the thief's wrist and the weapon fell from the man's fingers.

Scratch let out a loud, agonizing cry that was cut short when Marius snatched him off his feet by his throat. Holding him high, Marius regarded him with distaste. He was of half a mind to snap his neck and end his repulsive existence, but he hadn't come to New York to start a laundry list. The man was insignificant. With an aggravated growl, he threw the thief toward the Dumpster, where Scratch hit the brick wall and fell unconscious to the ground.

"Let's get the hell out of here!" Weasel exclaimed, and he and Bubba turned and fled.

Slowly, Marius approached Alexandra, who remained motionless against the wall. He paused when he came within a few feet of her, his wings folding. His gaze drifted to her full mouth, parted so sweetly as she took small gasps of breath. Her blouse remained open where the button had popped away and he could see the smooth mounds of breasts that he knew were ripe and soft. Yet lust didn't beset him, for he also caught sight of the red bruises on her forehead and wrist. The knowledge that those men had done this to her rekindled his anger and he wondered how he could feel protective toward someone he intended to kill himself.

She feared him—he could see it in her eyes, smell it even—and she was wise to do so. Yet he was tempted to assuage her worries—to tell her that she needn't be afraid. He considered the hilarity of such a gesture. He stood before her, a monstrosity, a beast, a prince of hell—to expect her to simply dismiss his appearance was insanity. Then there was the fact that she was his enemy, that before the passing of the Spring Equinox, her blood would be on his hands.

A moan followed by the scurrying of rats sounded from beside the Dumpster. The thief was coming to.

Marius shot a look over his shoulder then returned his attention to Alexandra. "Leave this place," he growled.

Feeling torn by emotion, he spread his wings again, shrouding her in darkness. Their gazes locked for an instant, hers reflecting unspoken gratitude, among other things. Time seemed to pause in that brief moment, preserving the torrent of sensations between them.

He turned away and took to the air, soaring into the night sky.

Chapter 6

"Ouch!" Alexandra exclaimed.

April stopped wiping the small bruise on her forehead to glare at her. "Now let me get this right. While you were walking in the South Bronx, three men tried to mug you, but you were saved by a man with wings and a tail?"

Alexandra, still grimacing slightly, nodded. "Yes, and he had horns, too. And fangs."

April's face twisted into a pained expression. "And this creature came to your bed last night and went down on you?"

Alexandra nodded a second time, and when April fixed her with a look of concern, she sighed. "I know it sounds insane, but it happened. I mean, look at me—what other reason would I have for being bruised and missing a shirtsleeve?"

April moved around the couch and sat on the edge of the coffee table facing Alexandra. "It's not that I don't believe that some guys tried to mug you. You shouldn't have gone to that neighborhood alone in the first place. What did you expect? I think you've suffered a real hard blow to the head. Are you sure you don't want to see a doctor?"

Alexandra jumped up from the couch. "No, I don't need a doctor! I know you don't believe it, but do you honestly think I would make up something like this? The visions? The creature? Trust me—it would take a much harder blow to my head before I start hallucinating about things like that."

With a torn expression and a heavy sigh, April slumped onto the couch. "I want to believe you, but listen to yourself. How can you get upset with me for being concerned? I'm sure if I was the one ranting, you'd respond the same way."

Alexandra walked to the window of April's apartment. She parted a space in the blinds and peeked out. It was late, but traffic still swarmed the streets below. Her gaze traveled up the buildings to scan their towering peaks. She was looking for *him*.

Alexandra had gone to April because she really didn't have anyone else to turn to and she'd been too afraid to go home. The other woman had patiently listened to her frantic recount of the events in the alley and then had offered to accompany her to the police station to file a report. Alexandra had declined, of course. With no witnesses and no solid evidence, she would come across as a raving lunatic. April's offer to take her to the hospital was also declined. Alexandra felt fine physically. It was her mind that was in a state of frenzy.

"I'm sorry, April. I'm overreacting," Alexandra apologized, feeling guilty. "It's just hard to believe that even you don't think what I'm saying is the truth."

"Well, I *want* to believe you, but I just can't imagine something like that lurking in alleyways or creeping into women's beds at night, especially not in New York."

"You're the one working on the story, for God's sake!" Alexandra tried reasoning. "Don't you think that there's a remote possibility that this thing is the mysterious shadow that's been haunting Central Park?"

April's face contorted. "I write articles about it,

but I don't actually believe that there's something out there. Well, nothing like *that,* anyway."

Alexandra let the blinds snap back into place. "I don't want to argue about it. I know what I saw, and I know I'm not crazy. Right now I just need to get some rest before my head explodes," she said.

"Well, you're welcome to stay here tonight," April said.

"Thanks." Alexandra smiled at her friend and crossed the elegant living room to the bathroom.

She turned the light on and looked at herself in the mirror. She wasn't badly bruised, but then that was the least of her concerns. For now, she had to find out what the creature was, where it had come from and why she seemed to be the focus of its attention. And, more important, she had to find another way to connect with Mady Halman. The bracelet was gone, but she'd seen enough to start an investigation of her own. She didn't know how she was going to tell Mady's mother that she'd lost the bracelet, but finding Mady was more important.

The next morning, Alexandra borrowed some of April's clothes for work. She matched a tweed sleeveless dress with a blue blazer to mask the bruises on her wrist. To hide the small grotto on her forehead, she combed a sweeping bang over it. She really didn't have the time or the patience to answer any questions.

Later, she sat at her desk in the busy newsroom, completely oblivious to the noise and activity around her. She'd acquired a list of all the blue Mercury vans registered in the area and was comparing it to the lists of registered sex offenders in both New York and Pennsylvania. It was a tedious task, especially without a name to go on, but if there was a match, she was determined to find it.

She was so engrossed in her work, she didn't see April approaching her desk until her friend tossed a copy of a rival newspaper in front of her. "Look at this," she said.

Alexandra looked up at her. "What is it?"

"Just read it."

She looked at the heading.

Central Park Mystery Revealed!

Below the bold letters was a large and overly exaggerated illustration of a winged creature that looked more like something from a horror film than the thing she'd seen. Alexandra quickly skimmed the article. It was an account of what had happened in the alley the night before, only the thieves had tactfully omitted the part where they had been trying to rob her.

"Those dirty bastards!" she gasped.

April leaned over her desk. "I'm sorry for not believing you. It's just…"

"It's okay," Alexandra interrupted her. "No need to explain. I don't know if I would've believed myself, either."

"No, it's not okay. You're my best friend. I should've at least given you the benefit of the doubt. I really am sorry," she apologized.

Alexandra offered her a reassuring smile. "Stop beating yourself up about it." She returned her attention to the front page. "It says here that the creature attacked them while they were rummaging for food. Those lying scumbags!"

"Is that really what you saw, Alexandra?" April asked with a daunted expression. "It looks like something from a bad dream."

Alexandra's brows puckered and she looked over the picture again. "Well, this drawing is a bit gruesome. It had wings, a tail, horns and fangs and its face was somewhat distorted, but it looked like a man."

"Do you think it could've been some kind of costume?" April speculated.

She shook her head. "No. The way that thing jumped around, it was totally not human. And I told you, it flew away. There's no way some guy in a suit could've pulled that off."

April's eyes brightened and she snatched a pen from the mug on Alexandra's desk. "Wow, you must've been scared to death. And you say this thing came into your apartment a few nights ago? Tell me everything," she said as she pulled out a notebook.

Alexandra looked at her friend, uncertain of how to proceed. By this time she was pretty sure that the creature was following her, but she wasn't sure why. She really didn't feel comfortable revealing more until she learned exactly what was going on.

"I'm sorry, April. I can't. Not yet, anyway."

April raised an eyebrow. "What do you mean you can't? You have a perfect eyewitness's point of view. This is going to make the front page, not to mention that the *Daily Sun* will be the only paper with this account."

Alexandra shook her head. "No, I just can't.

There are some things I need to find out before any of this gets out."

"Oh, come on!" April retorted. "Do you remember the time I flirted with that district attorney and persuaded him to give you the information you needed?"

"Yes, but this is different. I seem to be a target for this creature, and I need to know why." At April's displeased look she sighed. "Look, please try to understand. And you have to promise that you won't print anything I told you."

April was silent. She glared at her, tapping her pen against the notebook. Alexandra knew that stubborn expression, for she'd seen it countless times before.

"Please, April. Will you promise?"

April rolled her eyes and sighed. "Fine, but only if you promise to tell me everything—and I mean from start to finish—as soon as you're ready."

"Agreed." Alexandra smiled.

Alexandra didn't go directly home after work. She went to the New York Public Library. There was too much on her mind, and she needed to know what the creature was and what he could possibly want from her. The only thing she had to aid her in determining his origin was the way he'd been dressed.

His attire had been rather sparse, but she remembered the leather bracers that had encased his wrists. They'd looked like the accessories of knights and archers of another time. She also remembered the weapon he'd carried. Although she'd only gotten a quick look at it, it very well could have been a medieval knife.

She headed straight for the section on medieval legends and folktales and plucked a thick volume from the row.

"*Medieval Myths* by Percy Langston," she read aloud as she flipped open the book.

She began turning the pages, skipping through sections on werewolves, vampires and dragons. She read each heading and examined the illustrations for any likenesses to the creature. She froze when she came to a drawing. It wasn't a large one, but it immediately sparked a sense of recognition within her. The thing stood on the rampart of a castle wall. It looked to be the size of a man, with horns protruding from its forehead, claws, ragged wings and a great lashing tail. Its face was contorted in a fierce growl, its daggered teeth bared and menacing. It was like looking at a snapshot of the Central Park Creature—only the one that had saved her was beautiful.

His long inky hair, coupled with the shadows of the night, had shrouded most of his face, but what she'd seen had been enough to imprint his features in her mind. She remembered a chiseled jawline, a straight and hard mouth, a regal nose and intense eyes that had penetrated her very soul. An image of his head between her thighs flashed in her mind, and she remembered the feel of his strong hands clenching her backside as he'd thrust his tongue into her throbbing body. She'd never imagined a pleasure quite so extreme.

A wave of heat washed over her and she shook herself, returning her attention to the book before her. The paragraphs below the illustration described gargoyles as beings of the night—beings that were doomed to spend eternity guarding castles and holy places. Their fate was punishment for sins committed during another lifetime. They were grotesque creatures that shunned the daylight with such vehemence that they became stone beneath the sun's rays.

She slumped in her chair. Could it be that he was a gargoyle? That somewhere in New York City, he was frozen at the apex of some skyscraper, waiting for darkness? Was he a protector, as the book claimed, and if so, then why did he choose to protect *her* of all people? Or perhaps his services were random and he scouted the city for those in need. It was plausible, but it still didn't explain why he'd come to her bedroom. *Maybe he's a perverted gargoyle.*

With a sigh, she stood. Her attention was drawn to the window. About one more hour of daylight remained. If her assumption was correct and the creature was a gargoyle, then it was only a matter of time before it broke free of its stone confinement. Her doors would remain locked from now on, but she'd be ready if it found her again. She pulled the small digital camera from her purse and checked the settings. She'd also have her proof.

Chapter 7

Alexandra slipped on her second teardrop pearl earring. She stepped back to appraise herself in the full-length mirror in the corner of her bedroom. The dress she'd chosen was just right for the occasion. It was a black halter in satin that sported a modest neckline, but clung suggestively to her curves. She was heading to the Annual New York Police Ball. Apparently April had made the acquaintance of one of the department's top detectives and had obtained a few invites. Alexandra's main purpose for the evening was to locate the chief inspector of the forty-seventh precinct of the South Bronx and approach him about the Mady Halman case. She was determined to convince him to tell her what evidence the authorities had and to relay what she'd learned from her vision. She wasn't sure how she was going to gain his compliance, but she needed help. She realized that now.

The doorbell rang and she looked about frantically for her black beaded clutch. Bradley Applebee had arrived. He was a senior reporter at the *Daily Sun* and Alexandra had asked him to escort her to the ball. There was, of course, someone else she would have loved to have on her arm— her new handsome neighbor. After meeting Marius, every other man she'd come into contact with seemed to pale in comparison: too short, too thin, too...not Marius. But the man was nowhere to be found. She'd buzzed at his door and spied through her peephole with absolutely no luck, and so, regrettably, she'd made other arrangements.

She told herself that she should wait for Marius to make the next move anyway, but the temptation had been too great. His image was a constant visitor with her, slipping in unannounced between the other thoughts that plagued her.

Snatching up her clutch from the bed, she quickly checked the lock on the sliding door. The gargoyle hadn't surfaced again since that night in the alley, but she wasn't about to take any chances. She didn't need to come home to find the thing waiting for her in the shower. As much as she wanted to get a picture of it, she'd prefer to snap it with some distance between them. There was no telling what the creature wanted and she didn't intend to find out while she was naked in her bathroom.

When she opened the door, her breath caught in her throat. Bradley looked quite handsome without his glasses on. He was part Japanese and had the most adorable eyes that twinkled when he smiled. He wore a black and white tux that fit him rather nicely and his glossy black hair was combed to one side and so stiff that it looked as if it had undergone a session of cryotherapy.

"Hello," he greeted. "Wow, Alexandra…you look beautiful!"

She flashed him a smile. "Thank you. You don't look so bad yourself."

When he continued to stare with his mouth half open, she motioned toward the small bouquet of flowers he held. "Are those for me?" she asked.

"Huh? Oh, yes!" He handed them to her. "I bought them from that florist on the corner. I wasn't sure what color you would wear, but I guess that doesn't matter because you won't be taking the flowers to dinner with you anyway.

I mean, you would have to leave them here…in water. You know, so they won't wilt."

Alexandra nodded slowly. "Thank you, Bradley. They're lovely. I'll put them in some water now. Why don't you come in for a moment."

He followed her and closed the door. "Nice place."

"Thanks." She opened an overhead cupboard and pulled out a vase. "These will brighten up my kitchen."

"I was thinking red tulips instead of yellow, but yellow is my favorite color." He laughed softly. "When I was little all my stuff was yellow. Even now I buy lots of yellow, right down to my underwear!"

Alexandra looked up. "Uh…okay." She blinked. She was wondering if she'd made a mistake asking him out. He was an attractive man, but kind of a dork. Now that she thought about it, she'd never really had an actual one-on-one conversation with Bradley. They worked together and saw each other every day, but she really didn't know that much about his personality. To her, he'd always been the smart, quiet and good-looking senior reporter with the tight butt. Well, one date would do no harm.

She finished slipping the flowers into the vase then picked up her clutch. "Are you ready?" she asked, feigning more enthusiasm than she was feeling.

Bradley nodded and swung the door open for her. "Ladies first!" He smiled.

They were halfway through the foyer of her apartment complex when the entrance door opened and in walked Marius Drakon. Alexandra saw him immediately. With his towering height and broad frame, he couldn't be missed. The mere sight of him made her breathless and a sudden feeling of embarrassment enveloped her. She wasn't sure why. It wasn't as if they were romantically involved or had established some kind of emotional commitment or anything. Yet, strangely, it was there, creeping over her to stain her cheeks.

She slowed her pace as she came within a few feet of him. "Marius, how are you?" she asked with an uneasy smile.

His gaze swept over her. "I am well. And you, Miss Barret?" His tone was polite, but there was an obvious coldness radiating from him.

"I'm fine," she answered.

Damn, but she'd underestimated how alluring

the man was! He was dressed as if returning from work—suit, tie, briefcase—and he looked exquisitely handsome. His steel-gray eyes combed her again, a slow and sensual perusal, and she felt a tingle crawl up her spine. What did it mean when a man looked at a woman that way? What was he thinking? He had a way of making her feel naked. It was as if, with his eyes, he could read into her soul, caress her body and make love to her all at once. And this intrigued her!

Her nipples hardened against the satin bodice of her dress and she knew it didn't go unnoticed.

Beside her Bradley cleared his throat then extended a hand. "Hi. I'm Bradley Applebee." He deepened his voice to a baritone.

Marius shot him a look then dropped his gaze to the proffered member. It took him a moment before he accepted it. "It is a pleasure," he said with a lack of emotion.

Alexandra tucked a stray curl behind her ear. "Bradley, this is my new neighbor, Marius. Marius, Bradley and I work together at the *Daily Sun*," she supplied uncomfortably.

Marius looked at her, his gaze assessing. "I see," he said quietly.

"We're just heading to an annual police ball,"

she added quickly. "I'm working on a story and there are a few people I need to speak with who will be in attendance." She wondered why she felt obligated to produce an excuse.

He nodded, but said nothing. An uncomfortable silence fell into place as they continued to stare at each other. Alexandra noticed that there was a shadow of a beard along Marius's firm jawline. It made him look rough and dangerous, even in a suit and tie. Yet his eyes were tired—they held a heavy weight, as if the burden of the world was upon him.

A light caress on her arm drew her attention and she met Bradley's questioning look. She'd actually forgotten the other man was standing there.

"Alexandra, we have to get going," he said with a hint of impatience.

She glanced from one man to the other. "Oh, of course." Then back to Marius. "Traffic is terrible this time of day and we don't want to get stuck."

Marius nodded. "Very well. I hope you two have a lovely evening. Now if you will excuse me, I have some business to attend to." He didn't wait for a response. Instead, he slipped between them and stalked toward the elevator.

Alexandra watched him go and fought an urge

to follow. She would much rather spend the evening with him. Marius Drakon had awakened something new within her. In the past she'd sometimes found herself wanting intimacy, but it was never something a little vibrating silicon couldn't remedy. But now that she'd met Marius, she found herself craving much more than a quick fix. She wanted to feel strong hands on her, caressing her body and touching her in forbidden places. She imagined what it would be like to kiss him—intense, no doubt. He'd pull her close, their gazes would lock and passion would overtake them. Marius was definitely mesmerizing, but she wondered if he was relationship material. She knew it was dangerous to entertain such thoughts without knowing more about him, but she couldn't help herself. The man was just too *damned* sexy!

Heavy gray clouds covered the expanse of the night sky and thunder rumbled overhead. A storm was coming. Marius could smell the pungent odor of the rain that drifted on the light breeze. He inhaled deeply, drawing it into his lungs, hoping it would cure the twisting ache in his belly.

The thick glass of the skylight he peered through wasn't enough to hamper his keen gargoyle senses. He could hear the soft tunes of the live string quartet rising from the large ballroom below, and he could see clearly each occupant as they danced and laughed in social splendor. But his attention was fixed to only one. Even from this angle Alexandra looked enchanting. Her long gypsy hair was contained in a loose pin up with stray curls falling around her face, and the dress she wore only served to remind him of the tempting figure she hid beneath it. Tall, slender and very graceful she was as she whirled around the dance floor with her date.

He'd noted that she'd not worn a bra this evening. He was still trying to understand why it bothered him so much to see her in the arms of another man and missing an undergarment.

He would add this matter to the ever-swelling list that had kept him pondering for days. After leaving her in the alley that night, he'd been consumed by confusion and guilt and had secluded himself in an old church in a remote area. Now, two days later, he'd been awarded no answer. He could only speculate that his intense attraction to her was due to the ritual he'd commenced. He and Alexandra had somehow become connected amid the tangles of the deep sorcery.

His attraction was false, he knew, yet there was nothing he could do to abate his cravings. He wanted to be the one holding her seductive body close to his, smelling her soft fragrance and listening to her delighted laughter. He should be the one to return her safely to her apartment with perhaps a parting kiss or a gentle caress that would lead to a night of lasting pleasure. Oh, how he wanted to pleasure her—to spread her perfect thighs and again feast upon her charms before filling her soft body with his need.

That initial taste of her was a much regretted mistake. He should have simply left her that night in her bedroom. But he'd gone against all he'd been taught, disgraced himself and his family, and now she was in his blood—a vile, yet so sweet poison. He wanted to be a part of her world, as pathetic as it seemed with its senseless routines and unnecessary complications. He wanted her. And he was expected to kill her.

The song ended and Alexandra broke away from Bradley. She was flushed. After three dances in a row who wouldn't be?

She snatched a glass of champagne from a passing waiter and downed it with one gulp. Another tune was striking up and Bradley appeared at her side.

"Shall we, my lady?" He affected a sweeping bow.

Alexandra's brows puckered. The man was determined to keep her to himself all night! "I'm sorry, Bradley. My feet are too tired," she said with an exhausted look.

"C'mon. The night is young! We have kingdoms to conquer!" He laughed.

She frowned at him. "Are you drunk?"

Again, he laughed. "No. Well, maybe a little. I'm drunk on your beauty. Now dance with me."

Despite her disbelief, she smiled softy. "I see." She set the empty glass on a nearby table. Bradley was definitely tipping the scales.

"Was that a *yes?*"

"No. It was an 'I see' and my answer is *no,* Bradley. If I dance to another song I'm going to collapse."

He looked disappointed. "Okay. Would you like to sit together, then? Or take a walk somewhere? Or we can view the art display that's set up in the adjoining ballroom."

She stifled a pained expression. All she needed was a few moments to herself, if only to clear her head. She hadn't come there to frolic all night. She had business to attend to. "I'm sorry, Bradley." She placed a gentle hand on his arm. "I'm really too tired. I just want to sit for a while. Alone."

He pursed his lips in a half frown. "Okay, fine." He sighed. "Let me know if you need anything. I'll be right over there."

She nodded with a smile. "I will. Thanks."

When he finally turned around and ambled through the crowd, she breathed a sigh of relief. Alone at last, she slumped in the chair nearest her and massaged an ankle. A glance at her watch revealed that she had another three hours to go before the end of the event. She had yet to speak with the chief inspector overseeing the Mady Halman case. Her eyes found him at one end of the ballroom. Since his arrival, Inspector Cantrell hadn't spent one moment alone. Women hovered around him, flirting relentlessly or waiting their turn for a dance. Now he stood in a circle of his peers, sipping wine and laughing heartily.

Alexandra decided that if she was going to approach him, her time had come. She stood and made her way across the room, making sure that she stayed far out of Bradley's line of vision. She waited until Inspector Cantrell turned to place his empty wineglass on the tray of a passing waiter before introducing herself.

With a determined look, she extended a hand. "Inspector Cantrell, hi, my name is Alexandra Barret and I'm a reporter for the *Daily Sun*."

His eyes flashed with approval as they trailed the length of her. He reached out slowly and accepted her hand. "Hello. And to what do I owe this introduction?" he asked with a subtle smile. He was a tall man with broad shoulders and a suave demeanor.

She returned his smile. "I understand that you're overseeing the Halman case. I just need a moment of your time to relay a few new developments."

"Ah, I see. You want an interview. And here I thought you wanted to steal me off to the dance floor."

Alexandra played along. "Perhaps we can do both," she said.

Inspector Cantrell inclined his head. "I see no reason to refuse." With that he led her to the center of the floor and slipped an arm about her waist. "So you're covering the Halman story?" he asked as they began a graceful waltz.

"Yes, and I've interviewed a few eyewitnesses who said they saw a girl fitting Mady's description near Brook Park on the day of her disappearance," she lied. She'd already resolved to fabricate a story because she knew that if she dared to mention her visions, her claims would be instantly discredited.

The inspector's eyes narrowed on her. "My men did a sweep of that neighborhood and came up clean. Where did you find witnesses?"

"Well, I went to the park and interviewed a few of the parents and kids there. One child said she saw a girl who looked like Mady talking with a man the day she went missing."

"Did anyone actually see the girl being taken?"

Alexandra was briefly tempted to affirm his statement, but she wasn't about to fabricate a witness she couldn't produce. "No, there're no actual witnesses to an abduction, but the child was able to provide a description of the man. He was tall, thin, wearing a gray sweatshirt, and he was driving a blue van. Are there any suspects who match that description?"

She waited, hoping she'd piqued his interest enough to release some pertinent information.

With a pensive look he shook his head. "No,

there aren't, but I'd like to speak with the child who gave you the information. Perhaps if we got a sketch of this guy…"

"That won't be possible," Alexandra said, her mind working to find a plausible excuse. "She didn't see his face," she added. "And I doubt I could find her again."

The inspector gazed at her as if he knew she was hiding something. "Then I'm afraid the description you've given me is next to useless, unless a suspect turns up fitting that profile. There could be a hundred men in the Brook Park area like the one you've described."

Alexandra nodded solemnly. "I know." Silently she scolded herself for not being able to learn more from her vision. "May I ask how many suspects you do have in this case?" She tried her luck.

A wan smile crept to his lips. "You can ask, but I'm not at liberty to answer. Until I have conclusive evidence, the identities of all suspects will remain confidential."

"So…are there any sex offenders living in that area?"

The song ended and they came to a stop. "Let me worry about that, Miss Barret. I suggest you stick to your reporting and leave the police work to the police," he said firmly. "Now would you do me the honor of sharing another dance?"

Alexandra would have declined, but she was halted by a piercing cry that filled the room. Her eyes immediately found the source of the exclamation. A middle-aged woman stood at the center of the ballroom with her head tossed back as she gazed up at the skylight. Her eyes were wide and she trembled.

An older man stood at her side wearing a worried expression. "Carmine, what is it, love?" he asked. "What did you see?"

She brought a gloved hand up to her throat. "A face, Nigel! A hideous face!" she exclaimed.

Gasps filled the room and heads tilted back in anticipation of catching a glimpse of the face.

Nigel looked skeptical. "Are you sure, dear? Perhaps you should sit down." He took her arm and began to guide her to a vacant chair.

"I don't see anything," said a lady in a blue gown.

"Neither do I," added her companion.

Similar comments hummed throughout the room. Alexandra looked to the skylight. She could see nothing, yet only one thought circulated

within her mind—the gargoyle. Fear and anticipation drummed through her. Had he followed
her here?

A man wearing an array of colorful insignia
passed through the anxious guests. Alexandra
recognized him as Andrew Wagner, the New
York police commissioner.

He approached the terrified woman. "Carmine,
Nigel, what's going on here?" he asked as he
clasped his hands together on his protruding abdomen.

"My wife said she saw a face through the glass
up there," Nigel replied.

Wagner followed his gaze. "A face? Up there?
That's impossible!"

"I know what I saw, Andrew! It was hideous,
not human at all!"

The commissioner turned his attention to her.
He looked sympathetic for a moment then sighed.
"I'm sure there's nothing up there, ma'am. We're
on the tenth floor, and sometimes the light from
other buildings can play tricks on your eyes," he
said reassuringly. "Or it may have been caused by
a distorted reflection of the clouds."

Murmurs moved through the crowd as they absorbed what he said.

"What if it was that horrible Central Park Creature?" one woman asked.

Her conjecture was met by an outburst of gasps and nervous whispers.

Wagner lifted his hands to quiet them. "All right, settle down everyone!" He had to raise his voice to be heard. "That is highly unlikely. So far there's been no actual proof that this Central Park Creature exists."

Mumbles of agreement filled the room and he continued. "I assure you that there's no reason for alarm. Now, if I'm not mistaken, there's a buffet over there that's just brimming with food and fine wine. So, why are we all standing around looking up at the ceiling?"

Laughter erupted and the crowd began to disperse. Alexandra stood where she was, unable to move for fear that she would miss a glimpse of the gargoyle's face. She had no doubt that the creature was up there, looming somewhere in the darkness. All the hairs on her nape were standing on end and an uncanny sensation coursed through her. She needed to know for sure; she had to see him with her own eyes.

She wasn't aware of Inspector Cantrell excusing himself or of April approaching.

"Alexandra, you okay?" April's gentle touch on her arm forced her to look away from the sky-light.

"Uh, yes. I'm fine," she replied with a distant look in her eyes.

The expression on April's face told her that she wasn't convinced. "You don't think that creature is really up there, do you?" she asked softly.

Alexandra gazed at the skylight again. "I don't know."

"Well, you can take that look off your face. You're not going up there."

She smiled innocently. "I wouldn't dream of it."

"Good. Now where's Bradley?" April shot a look around the room.

Alexandra motioned toward the dance floor. "Over there. He nearly danced me into the next life and I had to get rid of him."

They both turned to look at him as he perfected his moonwalk on the dance floor.

April laughed quietly. "This date, I'm sure, you'll never forget." A strapping man dressed in a tuxedo joined them then. "Oh, you remember Detective Beckford from the fundraiser, don't you?" she asked with a smile.

Alexandra extended a hand to him. Of course

she remembered him. How could she forget? He was a tall, dark chunk of rich chocolate, just dripping with sensuality. He was also the captain of the NYPD Special Missions Squad. With his muscular frame, chiseled features and a smooth bald head, he seemed ideal for the job, too.

Detective Beckford accepted her hand and smiled, displaying perfect teeth. "How do you feel about being rescued from all this? April and I were thinking of going to that new lounge, the Fluid Palace. Want to join us?" he asked in his deep voice.

Alexandra's gaze strayed to the skylight again. "Sure, why not?" She offered them a smile.

April's eyes lit up. "Great. There's a live jazz band playing there tonight. It'll be fun."

"Yes, but we'd better see Bradley home first."

April nodded. "You're right. I'll tell him it's time to leave." She turned and sashayed her way to the dance floor, no doubt knowing full well that Detective Beckford's eyes would be on her.

Alexandra shot the man a glance, and sure enough his gaze was locked to the ripe curve of April's backside in the long red strapless gown. Alexandra took that moment to inch around him and out the wide, arched entryway. She had absolutely no intention of going anywhere. Agreeing to go to the lounge with April and her date had been a necessary distraction to get her friend away from her long enough so that she could slip away.

She entered the hall and looked for a stairwell to the roof. She spotted the small black and white sign above a doorway at the end of the hall. She paused when she stood before the door. Her heart drummed against her breasts as fear mounted within her. She wanted answers, and the only way she was going to get them was by confronting the gargoyle.

It was dark save for the subtle glow of the hexagonal-shaped skylight. Marius remained silent as he watched Alexandra ease open the door to the roof. His keen gargoyle senses had alerted him to the footsteps ascending the stairway, and he'd concealed himself within the shadows. He wanted to know why she was coming to him when others would have fled.

Even in this dim light she looked radiant. The wind was in his favor as it swept around her, unpinning her long hair and raising the tail of her dress to allow him small glimpses of her slender legs. Desire rammed through him as he remembered how she'd spread those legs for him. Never had he seen a woman so passionate, and to think she'd been asleep. To have her twisting in his arms, alert and receptive to every heated kiss, every caress and every hungry thrust would certainly be satisfying.

"Who are you?" she asked. "Why are you following me?" She couldn't conceal the trembling of her hands.

The wind whipped long, black tendrils of hair around her face and shoulders. It carried her fragrance—that sensual odor that was hers alone. His nostrils flared as he inhaled it deep into his lungs. She was moving closer now, so close that if he reached out, he could snap her neck with one swift movement. Or he could force her into the shadows and satiate the lust that was burning in his groin. Either way, no one would hear her screams.

"I read about your kind," she continued. "It's said that gargoyles were once men who were cursed as punishment for crimes they committed." She waited.

So she'd done some research. It was a pity her books didn't speak of an ancient curse or its end result. Had she learned her true identity and the fate that awaited her, he was certain she would never have come to him.

When no response came, she moved a few paces forward. "But it's believed that they can regain their humanity by performing good deeds—like protecting others."

Lightning flashed then and Alexandra froze. She blinked. Marius knew that she'd seen him in the brief illumination. He could hear the frantic pounding of her heart as she waited for another flash that would confirm what she'd just glimpsed.

It came, and the ensuing rumble of thunder masked her gasp of fear. She stumbled backward. "Why are you following me?"

Slowly, Marius left the shadows and came to tower above her. She was a fool if she thought she could communicate with him or trust him not to harm her.

Alexandra retreated a few more steps when he advanced. "What do you want from me?" she breathed.

His fiery gaze seared a path down her slender frame and he wondered if she wore anything beneath the satin dress at all. He felt himself swelling with desire at the thought of stripping the gown from her and sinking into her tight body.

His slow strides forced her back another few steps. He would have reached for her, but the door to the roof suddenly swung open and April and her date raced through, both coming to an abrupt halt when their eyes fell upon him. April screamed loudly, drawing Alexandra's attention.

Alexandra sent them a desperate look. "You have to get out of here!"

April's eyes were wide and she looked frantic. "Oh my God! Get away from that thing, Alexandra!" she cried.

The tall man at her side reached into his coat and pulled out a handgun. "Back up!" He aimed his weapon at Marius. "If you move one muscle I'll blast your brains out!"

Marius eyed his new opponent. He knew of guns and the damage they could inflict. While his brothers favored such weapons, he preferred the old ways. He reached one muscled arm over his shoulder and drew his broadsword. His grip flexed on the hilt and a growl escaped him. He didn't respond well to orders, and he didn't like being threatened. Yet he knew that this was neither the time nor the place for a decapitation. The last thing he needed was to be hunted. He had one purpose in the city and that was to kill the Descendant.

His gaze zeroed in on Alexandra. In a few days the moon would be full and then he would be able to complete the final step of the Lunar Ritual. The time didn't matter yet, for he wasn't quite ready to end her life. There were a few things he wanted to do to her first.

April's companion had eased his way to Alexandra's side. "I said back the hell up!" he shouted, his gun still aimed at Marius.

Without taking her eyes from Marius, Alexandra stepped to her right. "Beckford, put the gun down," she pleaded.

Lightning flashed.

He shook his head. "If this thing moves, I'm blasting it away. Now you women get inside and get help."

April was too frightened to leave her post at the door. "Alexandra, let's go!"

Marius realized that he would have to continue this another time. There were too many witnesses. Already what had transpired was enough to start a manhunt. With an irritated growl, he leaped into the air and took flight. There was a clicking sound as the gun was cocked.

"No!" Alexandra screamed, lunging at the officer just as he fired.

The loud *bang* echoed over the sound of the traffic and Marius noticed the stream of blood on his left bicep before he felt the sting. He'd been wounded, but the bullet had passed all the way through. The injury caused him no concern, for not only had the curse enhanced his family's senses, speed and agility, but is also enabled them to heal quickly.

Out of range at the top of an adjacent skyscraper now, he gazed down at the scene he'd just left. He couldn't fathom why Alexandra would try to save him. Had she been trying to return the favor? Or was all he'd sensed in her before— a kind heart, a gentle nature and honesty—true? Strangely, he felt the need to learn more about her before he did something he would regret for many years to come.

Chapter 8

Alexandra listened intently to the distraught young woman before her, and a great wave of anger and sadness tore through her. She knew this woman. Her name was Vivian, and Alexandra cared deeply for her. But Vivian had been disgraced and now she sought Alexandra's help in avenging her honor.

"I hate him!" Vivian spat, her beautiful face streaked with tears. "You must help me."

She moved to sit next to Vivian, who was curled in a fetal position on the bed. "Be still, child." She placed a comforting hand on Vivian's shoulder. "He will pay for what he has done. Ask it of me and it shall be done."

Vivian sat up slowly, her sobs momentarily

abated. "I want him dead," she gritted out. "I want his entire house dead."

She stared at Vivian in disbelief. Never had she harmed another, let alone taken a life. And here she was being asked to terminate an entire household.

Vivian must have read her reluctance, for her tears began anew. "How can you not do what I request after this man forced himself on me, filled my belly with his spawn then took that peasant whore to his marriage bed?" Vivian gripped the lacy folds of her dress, ripping it as she emitted a tortured wail.

The look in Vivian's eyes was unlike anything she'd seen before. Hazel pools flashed with an incensed madness, and the woman's chest heaved as she fought for breath. There seemed to be only one way to heal Vivian's wounded heart. She knew what she had to do—exact vengeance upon this man and his entire household. She wasn't one to take a life, but she would see to it that his sin caused him an eternity of grief.

The alarm clock chimed loudly. Alexandra awoke suddenly, traces of the dream lingering in her mind. The events of her nightmare had been different for the first time in her life—this time the young woman had been given a name, and although she hadn't been forced to witness Vivian walking mindlessly into the blazing castle, she'd felt the same searing anger. So consuming had it been that even now she felt the dissipating prickles of its intensity. She also wondered if Vivian's suicide had been related to the wrong done to her.

She sat up slowly and realized that she was still wearing her evening gown. After returning home, she'd been too emotionally and physically drawn to do anything other than collapse on her bed and fall into a restless sleep.

Memories of the chaotic night she'd had came rushing into her mind. She'd left the roof in an attempt to make a hasty retreat, knowing full well that the place was already swarming with police and reporters. April had cornered her before she could escape and had grilled her relentlessly for every detail. Unwillingly, Alexandra had told her everything, anything to get out of there. Then, with much difficulty she'd been able to convince April to keep her name out of the whole thing. She'd actually bribed April with the prospect of getting a close-up picture of the gargoyle for a future article. But she was willing to bet that the entire ordeal was plastered on the front page of every newspaper in New York City by now.

And what would they say? *Reporter Prevents Capture of Central Park Creature!* Or better yet, *Reporter Caught in Secret Rendezvous on Rooftop with Creature!*

She groaned again. She wouldn't be surprised if every journalist and newscaster in town was waiting outside her building for an interview. Just to be sure, she pitched out of bed, unlocked her sliding door and stepped onto her balcony. The street below was congested with its usual early-morning traffic, but there was no sign of any stampeding paparazzi.

She breathed a sigh of relief—was it too much to hope that her part in the night's events had gone unmentioned? She bit her lip and headed for the front door—her morning paper should be waiting for her by now.

The last thing she expected to find when she opened the door was Marius Drakon. As she bent to retrieve her newspaper from her threshold, she noticed his form in her peripheral vision. She could do nothing but glare at him, for she was well aware of her appearance. This was the second time they crossed paths where she didn't look her best. On this morning she just had to be sporting a crumpled satin evening gown that he'd seen her in the night before, a wild twist of bedraggled hair and smeared mascara.

He stood leaning against his own doorjamb, regarding her with half-lidded eyes. She wondered what he was thinking in that gorgeous head of his.

"Good morning," he greeted her.

Alexandra blinked, feeling silly. "Uh, good morning."

"Looks like you had a very interesting night." When she fixed him with a confused look, he held up a copy of the *New York Herald*.

From where she stood, Alexandra could read the bold title on the front page.

Central Park Creature Terrorizes Police Ball!

She tried to mask her trepidation as she moved toward him and quickly skimmed the article. Her pulse slowed when she finished reading the last line. She looked up to see Marius watching her. Her cheeks pinked when she realized that, in her excitement, she'd snatched the newspaper from his hands.

As if he could read her mind, he offered her a

half smile. "Did you see this infamous creature?" His voice was low, very absorbing.

She found that she couldn't take her eyes from him. "Yes, but just a glimpse," she lied.

The last thing she needed was for Marius to learn that the gargoyle had taken a special interest in her and that she'd probably saved him from being captured. If Marius thought that she was some kind of closet Goth who went around cultivating relationships with weird beasts, she was sure his interest would stray elsewhere.

"And?" His stare was insistent.

She blinked at him. "And what?"

"Does he really look the way the newspapers describe him?"

"Actually, he doesn't. He seems more of a man than a monster." She became thoughtful. "It was just the look in his eyes. He seemed sad, lonely and maybe even a little confused. I almost felt sorry for him."

He watched her quietly for a moment before speaking. "You gained quite a bit from a mere glimpse," he commented.

"Well, I'm very perceptive," she told him.

A silence lapsed between them. Alexandra knew that she hadn't been imagining the disappointment in Marius's eyes when he'd spotted her with Bradley. He was such a mystery to her—a dark and sensual mystery.

She told herself that she was a fool for wanting to know more about him. The man had disappeared for three whole days without an explanation—not that he was obligated to provide one, but his absence could mean that he was in a relationship. And if he was, she needed to know.

His gaze dipped to the wrinkled bodice of her gown, and Alexandra was reminded of her appearance. She handed him the newspaper. "Thanks. It was nice chatting with you, but I really have to get cleaned up now."

"It was nice talking with you, too," he said quietly.

She nodded and turned away, then after a thought, faced him again. "You know, I was going to invite you to attend that ball with me, but when I couldn't get in touch I asked Bradley," she said as lightly as possible.

Marius smiled. "I am sorry I disappointed you. I had to leave the city for a bit."

"Oh." She nodded impassively. Honestly, she didn't know what she'd expected him to say. He owed her no explanation about his whereabouts.

"Well, I do have to get going now." She glanced at her watch.

When he said nothing, she turned and headed back to her door.

"Alexandra," Marius called when she was about to enter.

"Yes?"

"Have lunch with me."

Alexandra blinked. *Are you kidding? How do I know you're not in a relationship? How do I know you're not married with kids?* "Sure." *Good God! I don't have anything to wear!*

Pelos was a cute little Greek restaurant in the downtown area. Marius sat opposite Alexandra at a table near a wide glass window. She looked beautiful in a soft coral dress, and he found it difficult to take his eyes from her. Behind his curiosity lay a dark and dangerous yearning. Last night he'd come so close to taking her. Never had he desired a woman so. Even now he tried relentlessly to douse the flames that burned within him.

"Go ahead, try it." Alexandra laughed.

Marius glared reluctantly at the uncooked shellfish on her plate. "It's not prepared." He stated the obvious.

She laughed again. "Of course not. That's how it's eaten. Now go on. Give it a try."

When he stared at her, she grabbed a spoon and scooped an oyster from its shell then brought it to his mouth. "Open wide."

His eyes darted around the room and he caught a few smirking couples watching them. "Alexandra, people are staring," he informed her.

"Of course they are. They're wondering why you're so afraid to eat this delicious oyster."

"I think the word *repulsed* would better fit my present mood."

She shook her head. "I just love the way you say things. Now come on, give it a try. It may look unpleasant, but it's really very good. Mmm." Her pink tongue darted out.

His attention shifted to her lips. He had better ideas for that mouth.

"Come on," she urged again.

Marius met her encouraging gaze and sighed. With those wide hazel eyes fringed with thick and curling lashes, she could probably get him to eat a four-day-old rat corpse if she tried hard enough.

"Very well," he said at last, and reluctantly opened his mouth.

Alexandra leaned closer and slipped the oyster in. Then she sat back and waited for his reaction. And so did the two couples observing them.

Without chewing, Marius forced the repulsive glob down his throat, nearly gagging in the process. He chased it with the remainder of the wine in his glass then dabbed his mouth with his napkin.

"Well?" she asked expectantly.

"It was...interesting." He didn't bother looking around when he heard the soft giggles in their immediate area.

Alexandra wore a beautiful I-told-you-so look that made her cherry lips pucker and her eyes twinkle. Surprisingly, the embarrassment he knew he should be experiencing didn't surface. Instead, a subtle mirth took its place. It was the gentle look she gave him that made him feel unashamed.

"You are so charming. How is it that you're single?" The thoughts spilled from his mouth before he could contain them.

The question was obviously unexpected, but she managed to maintain her composure.

"Enough about me," she said. "I want to know more about you."

A few seconds ticked by before he inclined his head. "As you wish. What would you like to know?"

"Well, to start off, how is it that you came to be in America? Romania is a long way away."

"Business," he said simply. "I am an antiques dealer and I am considering starting my own business here. I have been supplying several of the major antiques stores here in the U.S.A. for some time now, but I am ready to settle down with my own store."

She took a moment to absorb what he'd said. "I see. And did you come alone? I mean, do you have any family here?"

He smiled knowingly. "If you are trying to ask me if I am in a relationship, the answer is no. I have family here, but I traveled from Romania alone."

She nodded and flashed him a subtle smile. "Tell me about your family. Do you have any siblings? Are your parents alive?"

Marius experienced a brief moment of guilt; the last thing he should be doing was discussing his family with his enemy. He took a sip of his wine.

"I have two older brothers and yes, my parents are alive."

"You're the runt of the litter, I see." She laughed lightly.

The sound was like the gentle feathering of fingertips along his spine. "I don't exactly consider myself a runt, but yes, I am the youngest and most favored by my mother."

"Oh?"

"Yes. She and I are very much alike. We are quiet and calm and prefer the peace of a moonless night to any activity. We're passionate about many things, and those we love are always our first priority."

Alexandra watched him intently. "If you don't mind me asking, how old are you?"

Marius felt his mouth curve into a grimace. "How old do I look?" He'd expected this question, only not so soon. It seemed that Ms. Barret was true to her profession.

"Well…" She inclined her head, causing the wealth of her hair to spill over her shoulders. "If I consider your gray hairs, hunched back and facial wrinkles, I'd say you were about thirty-five or thirty-six."

By the time she was done, he found that his grimace had mutated into a smile. He nodded.

"Which one? Thirty-five or thirty-six?" she asked.

"You pick."

She reclined in her chair and raised a sleek brow. "And who said only women were afraid to reveal their age? In case you're curious, I'm twenty-eight and quite proud of it," she announced.

"Yes, but will you be saying that in ten years?" he countered.

"Of course I will."

She began to laugh, but something beyond the glass window drew her attention and Marius watched the smile fade from her lips. He followed her gaze to the busy street.

"What is it?" he asked. When she didn't respond, he reached a hand across the table to touch her arm. "Alexandra…"

"He's there," she said softly.

Her attention snapped back to him, and for a moment she looked as if she didn't recognize him. He searched her face, noting the distant look in her eyes. It was as if she'd just seen a ghost.

"I have to leave," she announced breathlessly as her attention returned to what Marius now realized was a blue van parked across the street. "There's something I have to do."

The tremor in her voice didn't go unnoticed. A frown crossed his face. He could tell that something was severely amiss. From her hasty desire to leave, he guessed that, as before, she was going to walk carelessly into danger. And that he couldn't allow. He needed her alive. At least until he completed the final step of the ritual.

She snatched her purse from the foot of her chair and started to stand. "I'm really sorry about this, Marius, but I need to leave."

Making a quick decision, Marius placed a firm hand on her arm, stalling her. "Will you allow me to go with you?" he asked.

His offer was initially met by silence as hazel eyes searched his face. He could see the battle waging within those pools as she decided if he could be trusted or not. Her answer was irrelevant though. There was no way he was going to allow her to leave alone.

Alexandra pushed open the door to the book and antiques store that sat opposite the Greek restaurant. A small bell chimed and she paused to look around. It was a congested little space with tables of tattered books and vintage items spill-ing into the aisles. *He's here.* From the moment she'd seen the blue Mercury van parked on the curb, she'd felt that Mady's abductor had entered the store.

Behind her, Marius eased the door shut. She was glad that she'd accepted his offer. She wasn't sure why he'd made the proposition, but having a tall and sinewy man at her side did bolster her courage. Admittedly, she was still shaken from the ordeal in the alley a few nights ago and didn't expect to be rescued by the gargoyle a second time.

Marius moved to her side, his gaze combing the vacant room. He remained silent, but Alexandra had the odd feeling that he'd assessed every inch of the place within those few seconds. Something within her fluttered, but she dismissed it. This was definitely not the time for fanciful thoughts. Somewhere in the building was the man she was sure was the Penn State Serial Killer. She didn't have a plan of action in mind and could only hope that if she came face-to-face with him, she would be able to glean something that would assist her in finding Mady.

Her gaze fell on the small notebook in her

hands with the license plate number of the van scribbled on it. She stashed it in her handbag just as an old man appeared from a room behind the counter.

He greeted them with a smile. "Hello, I'm sorry for keeping you waiting. How may I help you?"

"Hi," Alexandra said as they approached the counter. "My husband and I are looking for a gift for his mother." She shot Marius a glance and was grateful that he didn't react to her announcement. In fact, he seemed to be playing along. She could feel his lean fingers moving to span the small of her back.

The cashier's smile brightened. "Ah, are you looking for anything in particular?"

"Not really. I thought we'd just have a look around," she replied.

"Go right ahead." He nodded. "Be sure to check aisle two. Everything's from a recent estate sale. Just let me know if I can help you with anything. I'll be right back there unpacking some boxes."

"Thank you. Oh, wait, there is something you can assist us with." She affected a look of concern when he turned to face them again. "There's a blue van parked out front. Do you, by any chance, know who it belongs to? I'm afraid I scratched it while parking."

The old man massaged the graying stubble on his face. "Can't say that I do. There were a few folks in here earlier, but they've all gone now. Maybe it's someone's from across the street."

"Perhaps." She nodded. "Thank you. We'll let you know if we find something we like."

She turned to Marius once they were alone again, pretending not to notice the contemplative look on his face. She could just imagine what he was thinking. His hand remained on the small of her back and she felt as if a hole was being burned through her clothing in that spot.

Unexpectedly, the hint of a smile tugged at one corner of his firm mouth. "You are quite the actress," he commented softly.

She turned away, breaking the intensity of his silver stare. "I become whatever my job requires," she told him before stepping away to look down one of the aisles.

The cashier had said that the store was empty, yet strangely she felt the presence of Mady's abductor. She couldn't determine if he was still there or if he'd simply passed through. A wooden door at the rear of the store drew her attention and she headed toward it. Marius was close behind.

"Will you tell me what your purpose is here?" he asked.

"I'm looking for someone," she replied. She wasn't exactly sure how or if she should mention her premonitions. The last thing she wanted to do was give Marius the impression that she was some psycho enthusiast who went around stalking people.

She gripped the handle of the door. "He has important information on a story that I'm following," she told him then slowly turned the handle.

The door eased open with a soft creak and Alexandra exhaled a shaky breath. A small 1940s-style bathroom with a flickering light and leaky faucet was revealed. It was also empty.

Marius raised a brow and a humorous glint registered in his eyes. "Did you expect to conduct your interview while he attended his personal needs?"

She sent him an exaggerated look of annoyance. "Hold this, please." She handed him her purse and entered the bathroom.

The feeling that overcame her was an odd one. She felt the killer's nearness, yet there seemed to be something that separated him from the establishment. Apart from the door, a small window near the ceiling was the only other portal. She shot Marius a look, feeling very much embarrassed about what she was about to do. She was sure that after today she was either going to gain his admiration or his disapproval.

Putting aside the thought, Alexandra slipped the plastic trash bag from the tall copper waste bin that sat next to the sink. She flipped the receptacle over and placed it beneath the window.

Surprisingly, Marius remained silent as he watched her step onto the trash can to peer through the window. She hoped he was soaking up the full view of her legs and backside in the fitted dress she wore instead of thinking she was crazy.

She gripped the metal bars and looked outside. She could see a back alley with a set of large Dumpsters and several fire escapes on an opposing building. It was vacant, yet her feeling that the killer's trail was near remained with her. She scanned the area again, looking for any possible places of concealment. Either the killer was in the Dumpster or he'd...

She realized it the moment she saw it. The

killer hadn't come through the store, but had gone around the back to the alley and had entered a manhole. The lid was slightly lifted and a steady stream of smoke wafted out.

Stepping down from the bin, Alexandra turned to Marius. He was leaning against the doorjamb with his arms folded across his broad chest. It was obvious that he was enjoying her display.

With a jerk, she righted her clothing. "How do you feel about narrow, wet places?" she asked.

He raised one dark brow. "I enjoy them thoroughly," he replied in a heavy voice.

Alexandra cleared her throat when she realized how lewd her inquiry sounded. "The sewer," she corrected quickly. "There's a manhole in the alley out back. I need to go down there."

He was silent for a moment then he pushed away from the doorjamb. "Am I wrong to assume that you are seeking far more than an interview?"

She closed the distance between them and slipped her purse from his fingers. "Does it really matter? You offered to come along, and you're free to leave if you feel uncomfortable. This is my job." She tried to appear indifferent, but the idea of scampering around alone in the sewers of New York City wasn't that appealing. Especially if a serial killer was lurking within those murky shadows.

To her relief, Marius stepped aside and motioned for her to lead the way. Together they left the store and circled the building. The alley was quiet with no signs of activity. As they moved toward the manhole, Alexandra could feel her premonition growing stronger. Mady's abductor had definitely passed through there.

She knelt and placed a palm against the metal lid. He'd been in a hurry, running perhaps. She could see his blurred image in her mind's eye, his frantic breathing and the sweat on his skin. There was something he had to do, something urgent.

Her heart began to race and Alexandra looked up at Marius. "Can you open it? I have to go down there." She could tell that he wasn't keen on the idea of entering the sewer, and his compliance was definitely a mystery. It was almost as if he felt compelled to remain with her.

She stood and stepped back as he rolled up the sleeves of his shirt, revealing the swarthy skin of his arms. Strong hands took hold of the lid and with very little effort, Marius rolled it aside. Below, the sound of running water could be heard and the scent of stale air poured out.

Marius turned to her. "Are you certain about this?"

Alexandra exhaled an anxious breath. "Yes," she replied.

He nodded with a grunt and when she moved to begin the descent down the rail ladder, he placed a hand on her arm. "I will go first," he said.

The look in his eyes told her that he'd guessed that the possibility of danger lay beneath the city's streets. A sense of security and warmth crept over her. No man had ever been willing to take risks for her.

With easy grace, Marius entered the man-hole and proceeded down the ladder. Alexandra peered after him until he disappeared into the darkness. She draped the strap of her purse over her shoulder then began climbing down. Her pumps weren't exactly made for such activity and she found that she had to steady herself a few times.

At the bottom she found Marius staring into the darkness. "Do you have a light?" he asked as he assisted her to the ground.

She thought quickly then reached into her purse and pulled out her cell phone. The small illumination revealed that they'd entered a fairly wide tunnel with stone walkways on either side of a flowing drain of muddy water. They moved forward. Alexandra ran her hands along the walls, hoping to connect with any energy left behind by either the killer or Mady Halman. She felt certain that he'd been hurrying to get to the girl. And she knew that Mady was still alive.

"This place is foul," Marius commented.

Alexandra shot him a glance, humor filling her thoughts. "It's a sewer. What did you expect? A perfume shop?"

Her eyes trailed over him in the dim lighting. He certainly looked out of place in his designer clothes. She'd bet anything that this was the most excitement he'd had in his entire life.

She laughed softly, drawing Marius's attention. "What amuses you?"

"Nothing," She sobered and drew to a halt. The tunnel had come to a split.

Alexandra closed her eyes, hoping to sense any lingering energy in the air. It was no use. The signals were too scattered, no doubt the result of the killer's frantic mood. For an instant, she considered suggesting that they split up, but realized that it wasn't feasible. Not only did Marius not have a light, but he also had no clue what he was looking for.

"We must go left," he said suddenly.

Alexandra looked at him. "What?"

He met her questioning stare. "The individual you are seeking went in that direction."

She sent him a curious look. "How can you be sure?"

"I can smell him," he replied.

Alexandra searched his face. Did he actually expect her to believe that he could smell the killer? His expression told her that he was being honest. Perhaps he'd picked up a trace of cologne, she told herself. Like women, men could probably identify a familiar fragrance.

She nodded, having no time to fuss with it in her head. "We're going to have to cross this trench. Do you think we can jump it?"

He took a moment to examine the drain and the concrete walkway on the other side. "Yes, it is a short distance." He backed up and leaped over the chasm.

Alexandra approached the edge and frowned at the raging water. A short distance indeed—for him maybe. She'd never been athletic and really doubted she could make it across in her pumps and fitted dress.

Marius extended a hand to her. "Come," he beckoned.

There was no other way. She had to put aside her apprehension. Failure was not an option. With renewed resolve, she jumped, reaching for him. She landed against his firm chest and strong arms encircled her, keeping her on her feet.

Pressed so tightly against him, Alexandra could feel the thick, corded muscles beneath his shirt. His body felt so hard and so solid, a mass of steel chiseled into perfection.

Slowly, she eased away from him. "We have to keep going," she breathed.

His arms lingered about her for a moment longer, then fell away. Alexandra reactivated the light on her phone and proceeded down the left passage. Marius followed silently.

They'd been walking for a few minutes when something in their path caught her attention. As the light spilled over the area, she knew that she was looking at the spot where Mady Halman had been kept since her disappearance.

A dirty blanket lay on the cold concrete and a length of rope was attached to the metal pipe that lined the concave wall. The rope looked as if it had been cut. Alexandra reached out and drew it into her hands. She was immediately assailed by an agonizing pain that radiated from her wrists up along her arms.

She gasped and fell to her knees. Mady's energy was so strong, so distressed. She'd been tied and left alone in the darkness for days, crying out with no one to hear her. She was gone now, moved to another place.

Marius appeared at Alexandra's side, his brows furrowed. "What is it? Are you hurt?" he asked.

Alexandra shook her head, grateful that the darkness concealed the tears forming in her eyes. "No, I'm fine."

Her eyes combed the area again. It was hard to believe that anyone would leave a child in such a state. If she'd had any doubts before, she was certain now that she was dealing with a cold and ruthless killer. She couldn't fathom why he'd deviated from targeting women to kidnapping a child. It didn't make sense. Unless his perversions came in a twisted assortment, perhaps he had other reasons for taking Mady Halman.

"Let's get out of here. I have to contact the police," she said quietly.

She was about to stand when she noticed a large pool of hardened wax near the base of the wall. A few inches from it sat a matchbook. She picked it up and held the light over it. An image of the killer appeared before her, his face partially concealed in shadow. He struck a match and brought it to the cigarette in his mouth. The flame danced in cold, dark eyes, and then he was gone.

Alexandra exhaled a shaky breath and read the name on the matchbook.

Zappo's Bar.

She slipped the matches into her purse, certain it could lead her to the killer. Feeling weak, she allowed Marius to assist her to her feet. Unexpectedly, he gripped her arms with a gentle but firm hold. She looked up at him, uncertain of what to expect.

"We are not leaving this place until you explain everything to me," he demanded.

She searched his eyes. He seemed angry—no, furious. "I told you already—" she began.

"No. I am no fool, Alexandra. What is this?" He motioned toward the bloodstained blanket. "What have we discovered? And why do you feel that you must risk your life to learn more about it?"

She swallowed, trying to clear the tightness in her throat. If she wasn't mistaken, Marius was concerned for her safety. So much so that it angered him to see her taking risks. She didn't understand where this emotion was coming from. Until now, he'd shown a moderate amount of interest in her, his eyes trailing over her as if he was trying to figure her out. She could only guess that his reserve had concealed his true feelings for her. The thought of this strong and beautiful man actually caring and wanting to protect her filled her with warmth. There was no turning back for her now—she'd fallen for him.

Chapter 9

It was obvious that Detective Tyrese Beckford was skeptical about Alexandra's report. She glanced at April then returned her attention to the man sitting across the table from them in the lunchroom at the *Daily Sun*.

For the last half hour, he'd thoroughly questioned them about the incident at the police ball. Of course, Alexandra hadn't been strictly truthful. She didn't think she would benefit from helping detectives find the gargoyle, especially ones who were all about shooting first and asking questions later. April was the only person who knew the complete truth and Alexandra was grateful that her friend had kept quiet. Detective Beckford wanted answers, though. Her actions that night had been far more than questionable, and her excuse was not the best.

He tapped his pen against the tabletop. "Let me get this straight. You went up on the roof to see if the creature really existed because you wanted a picture of it for the newspaper. Then, when you got up there and saw it, you tried to get an interview?" he asked with a measure of incredulity.

"Not exactly an interview. I was trying to find out where it came from and what it was," she corrected.

"So you asked it questions?"

"Yes." She nodded.

"I believe that's the same thing. Anyway, did it speak to you? Did you learn anything?"

"No, you guys interrupted before I could get my tape recorder out," she said sarcastically and pinned him with a serious look. "I wish you detectives would put so much effort into finding missing children." She tossed her Mady Halman file in front of him. "That little girl has been missing since last week. What's being done to recover her?"

After leaving the sewer with Marius, Alexandra had made an anonymous call to the South

Bronx precinct. That had been in vain, as there'd not been enough evidence to attract police attention. The area had been dismissed as a homeless camping site. She'd also given the authorities the description and license plate number of the van, but again, with no proof that it was connected to the Penn State Serial Killer, the tip had gone nowhere. She'd known better than to mention her psychic abilities on an anonymous tip, for she was sure that would have thrown any possible credibility right out the window.

Detective Beckford glanced at the file and took an exasperated breath as he leaned back in his chair. "I know there are detectives working on that case. Now, are you going to tell me why you tried to stop me from shooting that creature?"

Alexandra frowned at him. The detective had a way of dismissing anything she said, and she was steadily loosing her patience with him. "Detective Beckford, that creature is one of the most profound discoveries in the history of man. It amazes me that you even thought of harming it."

"That creature, Miss Barret," he said as he leaned forward, "is responsible for attacking three men and nearly killing one of them. It is dangerous and has to be contained before someone else gets hurt."

Her eyes narrowed. "Are you even listening to me? And how do you know those guys were telling the truth?" she countered. "How do you know they weren't the ones being stopped from committing a crime? Did you see them? They're degenerates!"

"An eyewitness's appearance doesn't discredit his recount," he told her.

"You're right," Alexandra agreed. "Just as that creature shouldn't be prosecuted before being proven guilty."

Detective Beckford laughed. "You make it sound like this thing is some law-abiding citizen and not a dangerous freak of nature. If you would remember, it was carrying a sword. I hardly think there will be a trial when it's caught."

Alexandra's face remained impassive, but beneath it she was furious. It was so like people to want to destroy anything they didn't understand. Yes, the gargoyle had been armed, but he hadn't attacked anyone. He'd chosen to depart instead of retaliating. And she was sure his departure hadn't been due to fear of being shot.

The detective's eyes darted from Alexandra to

April then back. "What aren't you telling me?" he asked suspiciously.

Alexandra exchanged looks with April. "I've told you everything."

He watched her for another moment. With a deep sigh, he stood. "Fine. Then I guess this concludes our interview. You'll be seeing me around, though. And that includes you, too, Miss Harry."

April smiled. "I'm looking forward to it."

Detective Beckford nodded. "Have a good day, ladies," he said before leaving the room.

April hurried toward the door and peered around the corner. "That's a whole lot of man." She shook her head. "He can arrest me and throw away the key any day."

Alexandra joined her. Detective Beckford had paused near a desk and was speaking to another reporter. The pretty Latina seemed quite eager to answer his questions. She was leaning over her desk as she watched him write her responses in a notepad. Her breasts were practically spilling out of her shirt.

April snorted. "Slut. Does she have to pour over him that way?" she grumbled.

Alexandra moved back to the table and pulled the phone book toward her. "He seems to evoke that response in most women I've observed," she said pointedly.

"Oh, like you haven't checked him out!"

"I looked, I'll admit. But unlike you, I'm not swooning over the guy. He's trouble and I'm sure he's going to attempt to pry more information out of you concerning the incident on the roof." She removed the blue matchbook from her pocket.

She'd told Marius everything about the Halman case, leaving out the part about her psychic abilities. He hadn't been pleased to hear of her dangerous endeavor, but had understood her motivation. In an unexpected gesture, he'd made her promise not to follow any leads alone, but to include him. She'd been shocked, yet grateful. She knew the kind of danger that she was exposing herself to, and having a companion would definitely make things easier.

She'd traced the license plate number on the van and come up with a name. She had a place to start looking.

April was still ranting. "So you think the only reason he's interested in me is so he can learn more about your gargoyle stalker?"

"I didn't say that." Alexandra sighed.

"If you would recall, he did attend the ball with me before the incident occurred."

"I know." She flipped through the pages of the phone book. "I'm only saying that I have a feeling he'll try to use his charm to get information from you, that's all."

"Oh, I'm certain he will." April turned to face her. "And I can't wait. He can bribe, blackmail or threaten me with incarceration over dinner anytime."

"Just try to remember that you did promise to keep quiet about everything. There's too much going on right now. I have to find out what that gargoyle wants from me, and the last thing I need is some secret government group following my every step."

April smiled. "I think what that gargoyle wanted was quite apparent. I might've been half out of my mind with fear, but I think I know an erection when I see one. And I do believe that if Tyrese and I hadn't intervened when we did, you would've found yourself ten inches fuller." She slid into a chair and pulled out a nail file. "I think you would've enjoyed it, too. Don't give me that look! Think about it—he had you spinning on his tongue. Just imagine what he can do with his—"

"Okay!" Alexandra gritted out. "I get your point. And let's try to remember that we're talking about a *nonhuman* creature with horns and a tail. For all we know, he could be a demon."

April crossed her legs and began filing a nail. "Demon or not, he seemed quite anatomically compatible to me. Okay, okay, I'll change the subject." She held up her hands when Alexandra tossed an empty plastic cup at her.

"You are unbelievable! Trust me, the last thing on my mind is mating with a horned man-beast." She dragged one finger down the page until she found the name of that bar.

If she wasn't going to get any assistance from the authorities, then she was simply going to continue investigating on her own.

Zappo's Bar was a small establishment in the Jamaica Bay area. It overlooked the water and provided a cozy hangout for the odd crowd. Marius assessed the tattooed and disreputable-looking bunch as he and Alexandra entered the double doors. He'd been both impressed and angered by her dedication to find the missing child. The risks she was willing to take were remarkable, but dangerous nonetheless. Strangely, her enthusiasm had become infectious, for he now found himself hoping that they were able to rescue the child before the new moon—before he was compelled to kill her.

They approached the bar, drawing the attention of the customers who were sober enough to keep their heads off the tables. He hadn't expected an inconspicuous entry. They were clearly out of place and would no doubt draw some negative attention. He wasn't concerned about that. He had other things to worry about. The sun would be setting in a few hours, and his transformation would follow. He could feel the familiar ache in his bones and taste the metallic bile that always accompanied damnation. He was taking a risk just being there. Alexandra would have to conduct her interviews and be quick about it.

She slid onto a bar stool and offered the bartender a friendly smile. One of the men at the lower tables watched as she crossed one slender, stocking-clad leg over the other, his attention trailing higher to the gray skirt molded to her thighs and hips. Marius fixed the man with a lethal look, forcing him to turn away.

"What can I get for you folks?" asked the bartender. He was a heavy man with a beard and ponytail.

"Do you have any diet soda?" Alexandra asked.

He nodded. "I have Coke and Sprite."

"I'll have a Coke, thank you," she said.

Marius seated himself on the stool next to her. "I'll have a brandy. Thank you."

The bartender moved to the other end of the counter to fill their orders.

Marius glanced around the room a second time then looked at Alexandra. "How do you intend to gain information from these people?" he asked.

She sighed. "I'll use the same story I gave the cashier in that store. Hopefully it'll work." When the bartender returned with their drinks, she proceeded. "Excuse me, but I'm at my wits' end here. My brother and I have been everywhere looking for a man whose vehicle I hit yesterday while pulling out of a parking spot. He was nowhere in sight during the accident, and when I returned to the scene I was only able to get a quick look at him before he drove away. I tried to find him and was directed here."

Marius watched as she affected a helpless expression. He restrained a smile. Alexandra was as helpless as she was unimaginative.

The bartender nodded. "I'll help you if I can."

She paused as if trying to remember. "I think his name's Tom. Tom Richardson."

He shook his head. "Sorry, I don't really know anyone by name here."

"Well, perhaps you would know him if I told you what he looked like. He's tall, about six foot, dark hair, and he has a tattoo of a large spider on his arm."

The bartender nodded slowly. "Yeah, there's a guy like that who comes in here. He's in a few times a week. They call him Spider," he supplied.

She traced a finger along the rim of her glass and smiled softly. "Spider? Now that's an unusual nickname. Do you know anything about him?"

"Wait now. We don't talk personal about our customers here."

"That's too bad. I really thought you'd be able to help me." She dipped a finger into the soda and she brought it to her lips.

Marius's attention moved to her mouth as her finger slipped in. The woman was definitely a seductress. He steeled himself to remember that he was playing the role of her brother. It wouldn't do either of them any good if he became obviously aroused.

The bartender's eyes were fixed to her mouth and dipped into her cleavage as she reached for a napkin. "Well, I guess I can make an exception this time." He leaned over the counter until his face was mere inches from her. "Last I heard, the Feds were after him. Not sure why, but there's been talk about murder. I think he killed some guy out of state or something."

"So he's on the run?" she whispered in return.

The bartender shrugged. "I can't say for sure. You know how rumors go."

"I see." Alexandra sighed. "I guess I can forget about finding him, then. Well, thanks for your help, anyway." She gave him a little pat on the arm.

"Sure." He grinned before moving to serve another customer.

Marius sipped his brandy. "Is there no other way for you to learn more about this man you seek?" he asked.

She sighed. "I don't know. I can't just sit by and wait for this guy to show up. I'll try to gain the assistance of the Criminal Records Department. If he's got a rap sheet there'll be an address on it."

Marius narrowed his eyes on her. Again he wondered why she seemed so driven. Did she know the child? Her mother, perhaps? She seemed obsessed. It was a sad thing to see the innocent fall prey to the wicked, but then that was life. He'd seen it happen so many times in his many years. Alexandra's relentless determination was definitely something to be admired.

She took one last sip of her soda and stood. "Come on, we're wasting time here."

Grateful to be leaving the objectionable establishment, Marius downed the last of his brandy and tossed a bill on the counter. They left the way they'd come then headed toward his black Mercedes. He was about to disable the alarm when he noticed a vehicle pulling into the lot a few spots from where he was parked. Apparently it didn't slip Alexandra's attention, either, for she halted abruptly. It was the blue van that had been parked outside the bookstore. She looked ashen as she waited for the driver to exit.

"That's not him," she murmured as a man wearing a biker's jacket and tattered jeans stepped out of the driver's side. Hazel eyes turned to him then, reflecting a sense of security. "Marius, I'm going to talk to him."

He nodded, his thoughts momentarily flooded by the irony of the situation. To think that he was a predator, waiting to end her life, and now on this night he served as her protector. She felt secure with him.

As the man approached, Alexandra moved to intercept him. "Excuse me, can I have a moment of your time, please?" She greeted the man with a smile.

He slowed his pace and a grin crept to his lips. "Sure. You can call me Dash, and what's your name, beautiful?" He trailed his gaze over her body in a slow perusal.

She seemed taken aback by his blatant assessment, but continued. "Jennifer. And I just wanted to know if that van belongs to you."

Beady eyes shot to Marius then back to her. "Why you wanna know?" he asked suspiciously.

"Well, it looks exactly like a van that a friend of mine owns."

He laughed. "Lots of vans look like this one. What, you think your friend has the only one in the world?"

Playing along, Alexandra laughed softly. "No, I didn't say that. I just wanted…"

"Who the hell is this guy?" Dash nodded toward Marius. "I hope you two ain't cops."

"He's my brother, and we're not cops," she reassured him.

His lustful stare trailed over her again. "Your brother, eh? Well, why don't you leave him to enjoy his evening and you can spend some time with me. I'll answer all your questions." He grinned.

Marius experienced a surge of rage. He told himself that it wasn't the lewd manner in which this sot regarded Alexandra that angered him, but the time that was being wasted. Each second brought him closer to his transformation, and he needed to see Alexandra home safely before that happened.

Without hesitation, he stepped around her, gripped the collar of Dash's jacket and drove him up against the outer wall of the bar. He ignored Alexandra's gasp and pinned the man with a venomous stare.

His opponent struggled uselessly. "What the hell is wrong with you? Take your goddamned hands off me!" he barked.

"You failed to answer the question," Marius gritted out. "How did you come to be in possession of that vehicle?"

"I ain't telling you nothin'! Now get your hands off me before I bash your head in!"

He swung a fist and Marius caught his hand before it made contact with his jaw. There was a snapping sound and Dash cried out in agony.

"Speak!" Marius demanded. "I'll not ask you a second time."

The man groaned loudly. "Okay, okay! The van belongs to my friend Spider. He called me yesterday and told me to pick it up from somewhere in the downtown area," he mumbled.

"And where is this friend?"

"How the hell should I…ahhh! Okay! He was leaving town, didn't say where he was going, but he was in a hurry."

Alexandra moved to Marius's side. "When was the last time you saw him?" she asked.

Dash's eyes remained squinted in pain as he spoke. "I don't know. Maybe two, three weeks ago."

"Do you know where he lives?" she asked.

He shook his head. "We ain't lovers. I just see him at the bar once in a while."

Alexandra looked up at Marius. "That's enough," she said softly. "Let's go."

He complied, releasing Dash to fall on the

ground. Without waiting for him, Alexandra turned and began walking toward the car. His long strides brought him to her side and he sent her a glance. She seemed frustrated, disappointed, upset even.

She met his stare. "That wasn't necessary. I think you broke his arm."

"It is not broken, merely dislocated."

"It doesn't matter. Did you even consider what will happen if Dash decides to call this guy and tell him that someone nearly broke his arm asking questions about him? No, obviously you didn't. That killer is going to panic, if he hasn't already, and he's going to get rid of any evidence, including Mady."

Marius's eyes narrowed on her. He couldn't believe what he was hearing. She was admonishing him for obtaining the information she needed. "How can you be certain that he would not have made such a call even if I had not wrenched the information from him?" he countered.

Her mouth opened to argue, but a scream emerged instead. "Marius!"

He followed her eyes and shot a quick look over his shoulder. Dash was racing toward him, one hand limp at his side and the other gripping a jagged-edged blade. Marius spun around and the knife missed his back, but plunged into his arm. The pain was minute compared to the anger that surged through him.

A dangerous growl escaped him and Marius slammed a fist into Dash's jaw, sending him sprawling to the ground. The hairs on his nape stood on edge and he thirsted for blood. It was too near to his transformation for this. The beast within him was already taking over, and had Alexandra not been present, he would've ripped the man limb from limb.

He pulled the blade from his arm and tossed it aside. The laceration was fairly deep, but he'd survive. When he looked up at Alexandra, he could see the fear and worry mingling over her face.

She moved toward him. "We have to get you to a hospital," she said with a shaky voice.

He glanced at his arm again. The wound was nothing. He would heal quickly. "Get in the car," he growled and stormed past her.

Chapter 10

Men. They were all alike—stubborn and hard-headed. And Marius Drakon was no exception, Alexandra fumed. With his hot temper, he'd nearly gotten himself killed. She felt guilty for being upset with him though. He'd only been trying to help her. Yet she wondered if his help had done more damage than good. One thing was for certain—there was far more to Marius Drakon than what met the eye. Behind his expensive clothing and sedate demeanor lay a creature of ill patience and aggression.

She sighed as she wiped the last bit of blood from his arm. The wound he'd sustained needed stitches, but he'd refused to be taken to the hospital. She couldn't tell if it was his stubborn male pride that prevented him from going, and she'd given up trying to convince him that he needed medical attention.

Since they'd arrived at his apartment some thirty minutes ago, he'd said very little to her. She wasn't sure what he was thinking, for his features were shrouded in obscurity, revealing nothing.

She scanned the elaborate display of antique pieces in his living room. She'd been amazed to see how vast his collection was.

"So, how did you become interested in antiques?" she asked, hoping to warm the atmosphere.

Marius took the bait. "Let's just say that I am intrigued by old things. Times have changed, and although it can be said that life is easier, the world has lost so much of its beauty."

As he spoke, Alexandra found that she couldn't keep her attention from straying surreptitiously over him. His beautiful head was bowed and that sensual mouth of his tempted her to lean in and taste it. His chest was bare, too, emanating strength and stamina. He was like a prized Arabian stallion, and she was in the mood for a long, hard ride. Her eyes flitted to his strong fingers, which were busy tracing the edges of a small lacquered box that sat on a table next to the couch.

An unwanted image flashed in her mind: those lean digits, moving down to the soft slit of her body in the same fashion, and then slipping in when they found her portal. A soft moan forced its way out of her throat.

Marius looked up suddenly. "Does something ail you?"

She shook her head. "I need something to secure this. There's no tape in this first-aid kit." She forced herself to focus on the length of gauze she was wrapping around his arm.

He reached behind his head and drew the leather thong from his hair. "You may use this."

She accepted it and wound it carefully about his arm. "All done," she announced once the dressing was held securely in place.

Marius stood suddenly and turned to face her, his face framed by a heavy curtain of dark gypsy hair. With her heels off, she suddenly realized just how large the man was. He towered at least a head above her and his body exuded an intense energy that was a combination of what seemed to be savage lust and something darker, the very thing that drew her to him.

Silver eyes turned to assess her handiwork. "Thank you," he said.

She nodded slowly. She didn't trust herself to speak. She was too overwhelmed by the desire she felt mounting within him. And as his gaze raked the length of her, she knew he was going to kiss her. She could sense it.

He advanced a step, eliminating the distance between them. A dangerous look crossed his face and an unspoken ultimatum registered in his eyes; she could leave now with every part of herself intact or she could stay and face the consequences. Her heart began to pound and she was sure he could see the pulse throbbing at the base of her throat.

Another moment slipped by and when she remained as she was, he reached out and Alexandra found herself thrust against him as his strong hands encircled her slender waist. His touch was like molten lava—it seared her skin and sapped her energy.

And as he leaned into her, she shuddered. When their lips touched the sparks of passion ignited into a feverous holocaust. She moaned, but the soft sound was masked by the savage growl that escaped him.

The kiss deepened, sending her soaring into oblivion. Only they existed, climbing the crescent of desire. Their lips mated hungrily. It was a battle that had been brewing since the day she'd first laid eyes on him.

The strength of his body forced her backward onto the couch. Alexandra knew she should protest. She tried to remind herself that they'd only just met, yet she was helpless. His scent was like a potent drug. It encompassed her, surging into her nostrils with each ragged breath. And the taste of him was like nothing she'd ever known, and she wanted more.

His mouth slipped to the soft curve of her throat and she gasped. Never in her life had she been touched this way, and never had she experienced such intense pleasure and such longing. Her body arched against him, fitting perfectly against his contours. His touch became bold. His hands roamed her body, cupping and kneading her breasts then straying lower to caress the soft skin of her thighs. Alexandra clung to him for dear life, her nails biting his flesh. His administrations were enough to scatter rational thought.

His fingers moved to the buttons of her blouse and deftly undid them. She wore a pretty lace bra, and she watched as his head dipped and he caught one nipple between his lips. Greedily, he suckled through the sheer material and her nipple tightened.

Alexandra gasped and arched toward him. She desperately needed to feel his naked flesh against her own. She reached for him, pulling as if she was drowning and he was her lifeline. His torso was magnificent, a tapestry of thick cords and ripples that hinted at his sheer strength. Alexandra ran her hands over him, relishing the heady sensation that enveloped her. She wanted him. Already her body throbbed and ached and begged for his attention.

Marius drew back to look at her. A growl escaped him, a deep and carnal sound.

Her breathing ragged, Alexandra met his dark stare. His brows furrowed and he watched her as if she'd just grown an extra head. The strength had been sapped from her limbs and the searing heat of his lips remained on her mouth.

"What's wrong?" she asked in a shaky breath.

Marius's jaw clenched. Savage lust burned within his eyes as he loomed above her, dangerously close to possessing her.

"Leave," he rasped.

Alexandra blinked in disbelief. Was he actually dismissing her? The strained expression on his face told her that he was, and with much effort. Why? He obviously wanted her—the bulge in his pants was proof enough.

She rose to her elbows. "Did I do something wrong? Was I too forward?"

Without saying a word, he stood and turned away. He moved toward an antique dresser that stood against the wall and braced his knuckles on the surface, hanging his head.

Alexandra sat up and began buttoning her blouse. "We don't have to do this, Marius. I was really having second thoughts about it myself. It's too soon. We can just forget this ever happened."

"I said leave, now!"

She froze. Was he serious? She wasn't sure how to interpret his sudden change in behavior. Anger surged within her. It wasn't as if she'd caused the situation single-handedly. He'd been more than a willing participant. In fact, he'd initiated the entire thing. And now he was throwing her out without even an explanation!

Saying nothing more, she snatched up her shoes and left, slamming the door behind her.

Marius remained as he was for some time, scolding himself for sending her away as he had.

He knew he'd hurt her, and he rationalized that it had been for her own good, because in a few minutes his transformation would be upon him. Yet there was another motive behind his actions, one that shocked him. There was no denying that he wanted her body, but the thought of making love to her with the deception and his impending duty looming over their heads didn't sit well with him. Instead, he found himself wanting more than a moment of pleasure.

He opened the top drawer of the dresser and pulled out the object that sat in one corner. It was the gold charm bracelet. After rescuing her from the thieves in the alley, he'd hunted down the man who'd taken it from her. Retrieving it had been no difficult task.

He wasn't certain why he'd gone to so much trouble. Perhaps it had been the way she'd begged the thief not to take it. He knew it was important and decided that it was time to return it to her.

Alexandra examined the small box she'd found on her threshold after returning from the Criminal Records Department the next day. It was lavender—her favorite color—and bound with a length of silver ribbon. She gave it a shake and something rattled inside—jewelry perhaps. A warm sensation crept over her. Marius certainly didn't waste any time. One would think that with only two weeks of knowing each other, the proper apology gift would be a bouquet of flowers.

With restrained excitement, she pulled one end of the ribbon and slipped it off. She held her breath as she opened the lid…and her anticipation became panic. What she'd expected to be a finely handcrafted gold or silver necklace turned out to be a bracelet—*Mady's bracelet!*

With trembling fingers, she removed it from the box and held it up. There was no doubt that it was the one that Mady's mother had given her. *How?* her mind screamed. It had been stolen, and the only person who could have returned it to her was the thief who'd snatched it from her wrist. The question was, why would he do such a thing? Better yet, how the hell had he found her?

Stay calm, she told herself. She closed her eyes and remembered the night of the attack. Her purse had contained nothing with an address on it and there was no way the men could have followed her. How then had the bracelet found its way back to her? Had someone else witnessed the attack and retrieved it? *Unlikely.* The only other person—or entity—that had been present was the gargoyle. And there was no way he could have simply waltzed into her apartment building and left the box at her door.

Perhaps it had been delivered. No, that was even more preposterous. She could hardly imagine the gargoyle making a payment at a UPS counter.

She slumped on the couch. There was one possible way she could find out who had brought the box. Every floor in her apartment building was equipped with security cameras. All she would have to do was view the tape for that morning, and the mystery would be revealed.

She picked up the phone and dialed the security desk in the front foyer. "Hi, Mr. Rollins, how are you? This is Alexandra Barret from apartment 13B."

Mr. Rollins was a retired pastry chef who worked a few days out of the week as a security guard. He was an honest and kind man. "What can I do for you, dear?" he asked.

"Well," Alexandra began hesitantly. "I need to view the security tape for my floor, just for this morning."

"Oh, no, can't do that," he refused. "It's against building policy."

"You don't understand. Someone left something at my door, and I desperately need to find out who it was. We can keep it between us. No one has to know," she pleaded.

"Something like what? Should we call the police?"

"No. At least, not yet. It's a box."

"A box? Did it have a bow on it?" he asked with a hint of amusement.

"Yes, but the item inside was stolen from me a few days ago. I'm afraid one of the thieves might have located me." She tried again. "A young woman can't be too careful these days, you know."

He was silent for a moment. "Hmm. That is odd. Okay, you can come down and view the tape, but you can't tell anyone about this."

"Thanks, Mr. Rollins."

Alexandra hung up and hurried down to the foyer. Mr. Rollins let her into a small security video room, and after showing her how to review the digital footage for her floor, returned to his post. She rewound through a few hours of empty hallway, expecting the door to the elevator to open and one of the thieves to walk out. Instead, the door to Marius's apartment opened. He was naked to the waist and his hair was wild from an apparently restless night.

She went still as the footage resumed real-time play. Even in the inferior quality of the recording, Marius looked beautiful. But his appearance was hardly the thing that rendered her immobile. It was what he held. He crossed the short distance of the hall and stood outside her door for a full minute. Then, bending slowly, he placed the box at her threshold.

Alexandra sank slowly back in the chair in front of the monitor as she tried to organize the many questions wreaking havoc in her mind. How had Marius come across the bracelet? How long had it been in his possession, and was he somehow connected to the thieves or to the gargoyle?

Chapter 11

Marius stood before the large brick fireplace, his eyes fixed to the lapping flames as he waited. It was late afternoon, and he'd spent the last several hours driving from Manhattan in order to arrive at his cousin Andrew's estate before his father did. Lord Victor Drakon had decided to travel to the States to conduct business and expected a complete update on the progress of the Lunar Ritual.

Marius wasn't too thrilled about his father's arrival as this was the third day of the waxing gibbous moon and he had not drawn a drop of Alexandra's blood. Time was running out, yet he couldn't bring himself to harm her in any way. Somehow Alexandra had wound herself about his conscience and the idea of killing her had descended into cruelty. One so selfless and pure of heart didn't deserve such an end. In sorcery, there were often multiple ways of approach and if there was another way to break the curse, he was determined to find it.

He knew that his father would frown upon such emotions. Over the centuries, Lord Drakon had taught his sons to be wise and watchful. He would no doubt deem Marius's reluctance the result of witchcraft. Yet no spells had been cast and no incantations performed. Alexandra was an innocent, but the fact that she had no knowledge of the curse or its nature wasn't enough to exempt her from the fate his family intended for her.

His attention was drawn to the artwork on the wall above the fireplace. It was a painting from the 1500s, of his uncle Demetri and his family. Demetri was the many-times-great grandfather of Marius's cousin Andrew. That branch of the family had been spared the curse, for at the time of the witch's death, Demetri and his wife had been living on one of the Drakon estates near a town called Moldova. Only those living at Victor's castle had been afflicted, Drakons and servants alike.

The secret had been passed down and kept

through each generation of Demetri's family, who continued to serve and protect the gargoyle clan.

The door to the study opened and he turned as his cousin Elsthbeth entered. She was tall, dark and beautiful—true to the Drakon bloodline—and wore riding attire. She paused when she saw him, and confusion moved across her face. She'd never seen him as a man.

"Marius?" At his nod she moved forward and embraced him, kissing him on each cheek. "I heard you'd arrived."

"Only an hour ago." He smiled and looked her over. "You certainly have grown since I last saw you."

She'd been twelve years old when her family had last visited the castle in Romania.

Elsthbeth's eyes twinkled. "It's been five years. And you, Marius, you haven't aged a bit."

He nodded solemnly. For him five years was like a day. His body aged slowly, but it was his mind that bore the heavy weight of lifetimes of misery.

She placed her riding crop on a nearby table and stripped off her coat. "Father tells me that Uncle Victor will be arriving shortly, as well. Do you think Simion and Nicholas are coming along?"

At the mention of his older brothers, Marius's jaw tightened. The last thing he needed right now was an audience. "I am not certain," he replied stiffly.

"It would be real fun to have all of you here. Nicholas promised to teach me a new fencing trick. Perhaps I may even challenge you to a duel."

A smile tugged at the corner of his mouth. "I gather you've become quite efficient with the rapier?"

She nodded proudly. "Yes, and quite arrogant where my skills are concerned."

Her statement forced a laugh from him. She was a lot like him when he was much younger— before five centuries stripped the joy from him.

The muffled sound of voices emerged from outside and Elsthbeth hurried to the window. A smile leaped to her face and she spun around.

"They're here! Aunt Amelia, too!" she announced excitedly.

Mother is here, as well.

Marius moved to the window that overlooked the large, gravel-covered courtyard. He peered down two stories to see a butler garbed in formal attire assisting his mother out of a sleek black

Rolls-Royce. His father was on the other side, straightening his coat. Another car pulled up behind them—a flashy silver Lamborghini with tinted windows.

His brothers.

Simion was the first to step out. He was garbed, as usual, in a well-tailored suit, his long hair falling over his shoulders. He removed his sunglasses and flexed his shoulders beneath his coat. Nicholas, the younger of the two, was dressed like a heavy-metal guitarist in black leather pants and a tight-fitting white pullover and his hair fell down his back in a long braid. He reached into the car and pulled out a long metal case—his weapons. He never traveled without them.

Upon seeing him, Elsthbeth emitted an excited squeak. Marius suspected that the girl had developed a crush on his older brother. He suppressed a smirk. He hoped she kept him well preoccupied. That way Nicholas would have no time to criticize his delay.

His cousin turned to him, her face glowing. "Let's go down and greet them."

Reluctantly, Marius nodded. He wasn't quite ready for a confrontation, but the sooner he got it over with, the sooner he could dedicate his time to finding another way to break the curse.

They headed down the winding staircase that led to the main foyer. Elsthbeth's father, Andrew, was exiting the dining hall when they reached the front entrance. The girl ran outside, but Marius chose to remain inside. He sighed and leaned against the doorjamb.

Andrew Drakon came to stand beside him. He was an inch or two shorter than Marius, but possessed all the Drakon characteristics.

Although not a gargoyle himself, Andrew was an integral part of their lives. He handled all business affairs that required attendance and organized travel for the members of their clan who were unable to journey independently because of the curse. Several of those who served the Drakon gargoyles had been trained to fly their family's private aircraft for this purpose alone.

"Have you decided what you're going to tell him yet?" he asked with a knowing look.

"No," Marius replied, offering nothing.

"Life will be very different for you once the curse has ended, you know this?" When Marius failed to respond, Andrew continued. "It's easy to understand why you all must crave humanity, but in exchange for it you will be surrendering your strength, your superiority…your immortality."

Marius searched his eyes. Andrew wasn't in the dark about the workings of the curse nor what was necessary to end it. He knew why Marius had come to the United States, and he knew that time was running out. But could he have possibly read the frustration and confusion plaguing him? And if so, had he misinterpreted it for reluctance to end the curse?

Before Andrew could say another word, Marius's parents entered the foyer.

Andrew greeted Lord Victor Drakon with open arms. "Welcome, cousin! I hope your journey here wasn't too tedious." He embraced him warmly.

His father looked at his watch. "No, it was fine. It seems we still have several hours before sunset."

Andrew turned to Amelia. "My lady, you're looking lovely as always. Welcome again." He brought one of her slender hands to his lips.

She smiled, her gray eyes flickering. "Thank you, Andrew. It is a pleasure to be in your home again. I see you've made some changes, and your little Elsthbeth has grown into such a beautiful young woman."

He laughed. "Yes, indeed. Quite a handful she is. Her mother is seeing to supper, which will be ready in an hour. So that gives you time to relax and freshen up." He motioned to the butler. "Robert, will you show our guests to their rooms, please."

The servant nodded. "Follow me, my lord."

Lord Drakon paused at the door. "Marius," he greeted.

"Hello, Father," Marius said, studying his sire. Victor was tall and broad shouldered and his face was creased with lines that did no justice to his true age.

"I trust that all is well with you?"

Marius inclined his head and offered a subtle smile.

"Good. We will speak at dinner, then." Lord Drakon motioned to the butler and the man led the way down the hall.

Simion and Nicholas—with a chattering Elsthbeth hanging on Nicholas's arm—followed, each nodding to Marius in passing.

Once they were alone, Lady Amelia moved forward and placed a kiss on Marius's cheek. "I have sorely missed your presence in Romania. You are well, yes?" she asked as she adjusted the collar of his shirt.

Marius nodded. "I am fine, Mother."

The sleek lines of her still very beautiful face were etched with concern. "Are you certain? It seems that something troubles you."

The warmth in her gray eyes stilled some of his anxiety. If anyone could understand his plight it would be his mother, but he wasn't ready to reveal the true nature of his dilemma to anyone.

All he would ask of his family was to grant him time—time to find a way to spare the life of a woman who didn't deserve death. There still remained seven days in the Spring Equinox.

Lady Amelia smoothed a tendril of silver-streaked hair back into place. "Will you not tell me what is on your mind?"

"Not yet, Mother," he responded quietly.

She sighed softly. "Very well, I shall see you at dinner." She lingered a moment longer, her eyes searching his face, and then she left.

Marius ran his fingers through his hair. It seemed that for now he'd been spared the dissatisfaction of his family. But that did nothing to appease his anxiety, for he knew that soon the subject of the ritual would be breached. He decided that he would spend what little time he had trying to concoct a viable excuse for his delay.

Dinner was hosted early that evening in the main dining hall. Its ceiling was two stories high, its brick walls draped with tapestries of knights and dragons and picturesque castle scenes, some of which dated back to the early 1700s. The massive wooden table was the centerpiece of the room, extending nearly twenty feet, and a crystal chandelier hanging above it lit the room and sparkled in the fading daylight that slanted in through the tall windows. Charlotte, Andrew's wife, had organized an elaborate meal. Marius didn't have much of an appetite, but he forced himself to eat to avoid offending the hostess.

They were all dressed in the formal attire of the ancient nobility, in rich velvets and exquisite brocades. Marius had decided to wear black, as it better suited his present mood. He sat in silence through most of the event, waiting impatiently for his father to inquire about his progress. Instead, Lord Drakon and Andrew steered the conversation in the direction of business. Finally, when Elsthbeth had been dismissed—she wasn't quite ready to be privy to such matters—Lord Drakon's attention turned to Marius.

"Marius, the waning crescent moon is nearly upon us. Have you completed the Lunar Ritual?" he asked.

Marius said nothing for a moment then shook his head. "No, Father, I have not. I have yet to draw her blood."

Lord Drakon fixed him with an inquiring look. "Please, enlighten us, what delays you?"

Silence filled the room and Marius was met with the many curious and impatient stares of his family members. He'd spent the entire day constructing an explanation that would justify his actions, but now words fled from him. There was nothing he could say to appease them, yet an explanation was expected.

He cleared his throat and met his father's gaze. His mother sat beside Lord Drakon and smiled encouragingly. "I have not completed the ritual because she is not what I was warned to expect," he stated firmly.

Confusion crossed his father's face. "She is the Descendant, is she not?"

"She is," he replied reluctantly.

"Then explain yourself. What more do you need?"

Again he cast a look around the table. His brothers wore deep scowls while Andrew and his wife looked on with curiosity. "I've met her personally and she is not at all like a witch. She is an innocent—kind and gentle and honest."

Simion slammed his fist against the table, rattling the china and silverware. "You waste your time conducting a character assessment while your family's future is at stake!" he growled.

Nicholas guffawed loudly, obviously finding humor in Marius's announcement. "Brother, listen to yourself! Kind and gentle? Honest? We are talking about the Descendant, remember. She is a *bloody* witch."

Lord Drakon raised a hand, indicating that he would lead the questioning. "Marius, you know that every Descendant does not take on the characteristics of Necesar, but she remains our enemy. She remains the obstruction between our family and freedom. And, most important, she remains a threat to the world. In seven days Vivian's spirit will possess her, and all those characteristics that you praise will be no more," he explained.

"I understand this, but she is guilty of no crime. She does not deserve death."

"Just as you have committed no crime, yet you suffer. Her sin, Marius, is being born. She is the curse. And as long as she continues to thrive, our family's affliction will never be raised. We have suffered long centuries of hiding and now it is time to end it. The loss of one life does not equal the pain we have shared."

Anger was slowly rising within Marius. He wasn't sure if he was angry at himself for being so weak or at his family for failing to understand his dilemma. Even his mother watched him with a measure of disbelief. Centuries ago, she'd been a gentle-spirited farm girl who'd cherished life even in the most insignificant of creatures, but the many years of her life had hardened her. Now she would do whatever was necessary to save herself and her family from eternal damnation.

"Is there another way to break the curse?" Marius asked. "Give me five days. That is all I ask."

His request was met with silence. His brothers exchanged annoyed glares with him and his mother lowered her eyes. It was as if he'd just committed blasphemy.

His father's gaze was assessing. "Why, my son? Why are you willing to go to such lengths for this woman?" He waited.

Marius had been prepared for this question. "I have never killed an innocent before," he said.

Lord Drakon leaned back in his chair. "Is that all?" His eyes narrowed with suspicion.

Apparently Simion grew tired of listening quietly to the exchange. He pulled the embroidered napkin from his lap and tossed it on the table. "Father, why are you trying to reason with this madness?" he shouted. "It is obvious that your son has grown weak! Assign me the task and the Descendant's blood will be drawn before the sun rises again!"

His brother's declaration sent a surge of rage through Marius and he rose from his seat so fast that he sent it toppling backward. "Her name is Alexandra!" he roared.

Simion rose as well, matching him in height and brawn. "She is the descendant of the witch Necesar! She is our affliction! She is the ruin of this world and she must die!"

Their father had heard enough. "Silence! Be seated, both of you!"

Marius held his tongue, but he continued to

watch his brother with restrained anger. He was beginning to wonder what extent he would go to in order to save Alexandra. Would he betray his family?

"I said, be seated!" Lord Drakon commanded again.

They complied, each eyeing the other distastefully. Marius turned to his father and regarded him with a determined look. "Five days, Father, that is all I ask."

The older man shook his head. "I am afraid I cannot grant you that, my son."

Andrew interjected then. "Victor, why not give him what he asks? We know where the Descendent is. If he hasn't found another way to end the curse after five days, then we'll be free to act."

Lord Victor's attention riveted to Andrew. "There is just too much at stake here. Our every move must be carefully calculated, and wasting five days attempting to find a solution to a problem that is nearly solved is futile. Marius, I will give you two days to either finish the ritual or bring the girl to me."

Andrew was persistent. "Two days? I doubt very much can be accomplished in that little time. If anything—"

"I have spoken!" Lord Victor said in a tone that would bide no further interference. "He has two days and no more."

Andrew, obviously displeased with the solution, inclined his head slowly. "As you wish, my lord."

Two days, Marius's mind screamed. That wasn't enough time, yet it was better than nothing at all. He sent Andrew an appreciative look. It seemed Andrew and his father were always at opposing ends of any argument. Lord Victor would always listen to Andrew's opinions, but as the leader of their clan, his own decisions always took precedence. This time, Marius was sure, would be no different.

Marius looked at his brothers. It seemed Andrew wasn't the only one who was unhappy with the outcome. Marius wondered if they'd respect their father's words and allow him that brief time to make his decision. He'd intended to leave in the morning, but decided it would be best to leave as soon as the sun set. He had to return to New York and get Alexandra to safety.

Lady Amelia, who'd remained silent throughout the exchange, spoke then. "Marius, do you have feelings for this girl?" she asked.

Marius looked at her then met the waiting gazes of his family. "Of course not." His expression was impassive. "She is our enemy."

Chapter 12

Alexandra pressed the doorbell for the fifth time and, as before, she received no response. That and the fact that the day's newspaper remained at the foot of the door gave her the impression that Marius had left the city once again. His absence didn't bother her, for she hadn't come to talk to him. She wanted only to be sure he wasn't there so that she could put her plan into action. It was time she learned more about the man before it was too late.

Her hand went to the bit of gold on her wrist. So far, the item hadn't sprung any more visions. She suspected that there was just too much on her mind to be receptive to any psychic transmissions. And the one question that tormented her most was—how had Marius managed to return

Mady's bracelet to her? She intended to find out before the night was over.

She returned to her apartment, grabbed the large, ancient ironing board that had been her mother's from the broom closet and glared at her reflection in the mirror. She'd already missed her 7:00 p.m. appointment with her psychiatrist, so she was going through with it. *I can do this!*

Behind her on the television the weatherman beamed. "Chances for a thunderstorm tonight are ninety-nine percent, so all you late evening commuters, don't forget your umbrellas!"

She dragged the ironing board out onto her balcony and looked up at the sky. He was right. Gray clouds hung low and not a star was visible. The wind had picked up, too. A storm was definitely coming. She drew in a shaky breath as she reassessed the distance between her apartment and Marius's. The board was just long enough to reach the nearest rail of his balcony and sturdy enough to support her weight. She slipped a hand into her pocket and touched the credit card she'd placed there earlier. Once across, she would jimmy the lock on the sliding door the way she'd practiced on her own. Then she'd search Marius's apartment. She knew that what she was plotting was wrong, but it seemed the only way she could get answers.

Hefting up the board, she slid it over the seven-story drop that separated their balconies and slipped off her shoes. *Don't look down,* she told herself as she placed one foot on the rail and pulled herself up, using the wall for support. She took a moment to regain her balance then carefully placed one foot on the board, then the other.

The night air was cool and somewhere in the distance lightning flashed behind the clouds. The breeze whipped about her, scattering her hair and flipping up the skirt of the sundress she wore. She closed her eyes tight and suppressed a scream. She'd never been afraid of heights before, but then she'd never balanced her way across a seven-story building, either.

Without looking down, she inched toward the other side as quickly as her fear would permit. It was a relief when her feet finally touched the cool tile that covered the floor of the other balcony. She left the ironing board in place, knowing she'd have to return the way she came when she was done.

Gripping the handle on the sliding door, she slipped the credit card along the space between the lock and the door jamb. There was a soft click and the door slid open.

Her slender fingers reached around the side of the doorway and found the light switch, illuminating his bedroom. She paused in the doorway, her eyes wide with disbelief. It was like looking into the past—a vision of hundreds of years ago.

A king-size canopy bed dominated the room. Its moss-colored velvet drapes were partially drawn, permitting her a view of a heavy animal pelt and a reckless twisting of bronze and gold jacquard bedding. All the other furniture in the room appeared to be antique as well, each piece exotic and beautiful, adding to the visual splendor.

She entered slowly, her feet sinking into the soft carpet. Silently, she padded toward the bed. She could almost see him lying naked beneath the tangled bedding. His muscled torso and sinewy legs would be bare, while only a draping of fabric would cover his groin. She'd be entwined with him, her head resting on his broad chest as they slept after a night of frenzied lovemaking. Alexandra trembled as an electrifying pulse shot through her. She felt as if she'd been taken by fever—a hot burst of desire assailed her and she gripped one of the bedposts for support and moaned.

When the wave of dizziness elapsed, she reached out and smoothed curious fingers over what appeared to be a quilt of wolf pelts. The soft hairs tickled, and she imagined what the pelts would feel like covering her naked body.

Shaking herself, she focused on her purpose for being there. Fantasizing about Marius would do her no good. The man was a mystery that needed to be solved, and she would only be setting herself up for disappointment if she allowed herself to be swayed by the intense attraction she felt toward him. And so, with renewed resolve, she began searching his apartment for any clue that would lift her confusion.

A tall wardrobe that looked to be a piece from the Victorian era held only clothing, some of which she paused to admire. Marius certainly had expensive and unusual taste. Among the labeled shirts and blazers hung coats and vests of rich brocade like those worn by the ancient monarchs of Europe.

Next she searched his dresser and bedside tables, but found nothing. His living room, kitchen and bathroom all procured the same result. The place was clean—not even a smut magazine!

She was about ready to toss in the towel when she thought to look under his bed. She knelt on the floor and raised the bed skirt.

Nothing save a few dust bunnies.

With an exasperated groan, she flopped onto the bed and stared up at the underside of the canopy. The man was just too perfect! She'd found nothing incriminating at all, yet the fact remained that he'd somehow retrieved the bracelet from the thief. Could he have set up the whole thing? Perhaps he'd intended to rescue her himself, but the gargoyle beat him to it. Would a man even go to such lengths to impress her? Or maybe he hadn't been trying to impress her. Maybe the whole thing had been an attempt to gain her trust or gratitude. Perhaps he was a con artist!

No. She stilled her thoughts with reasoning. There was no way he could have known that she would visit Mady's home that night, or turn down that alley. The circumstances of the attack were just too random.

There was something else she found unusual, though. Marius claimed to be in the antiques business, yet her search had produced no proof of this—no purchases made, bank statements or travel records. And as a matter of fact, she hadn't come across one personal document with his name on it.

She closed her eyes as she tried to formulate her next course of action. There seemed to be nothing she could do short of asking him directly how the hell he'd gotten the bracelet.

She turned onto her side and ran her fingers over the fur pelt again. The bed was huge. It seemed to engulf her. Marius's scent—that masculine odor that never failed to fill her mind with thoughts of sex—lingered on the bedding. *Why,* she thought, *why does he have to be so puzzling?* They seemed perfect for each other. She hoped to God that there was a logical explanation for everything.

Sighing, Alexandra decided it was time to leave. She was about to roll off the bed when something caught her attention. In his closet, tucked to the right, was a large chest. It was easy to see how she'd missed it before, because it was half-hidden by a collection of long coats hanging above it.

She got up and went to the closet. She gripped one of the metal handles of the chest and dragged the thing out into the open. It looked old—tattered leather and rusting cast-iron handles. The latch on it was missing. *An antique no doubt,* she surmised.

She lifted the heavy lid and looked in. Her heart seemed to stop for a full minute then resumed function in a tumultuous staccato. Her breathing came in quick gasps and she was crippled by disbelief and confusion. Inside the chest lay weapons—a sword, knife, dagger and crossbow, two of which she remembered. The knife and the sword had both been used by the gargoyle.

What is Marius doing with these? Is he aiding the creature? Controlling it?

She bent down, reaching shaking hands to remove the knife. The thing was heavier than it appeared. The hilt was a masterpiece of silver carvings while the steel blade curved upward in a sleek arc. It was the knife the gargoyle had brought to her bedroom. She frowned, realizing now the coincidence; the very day Marius had moved in, the creature had come to her.

Eager to learn more, she placed the knife on the carpet and pulled out the sword. She had to stand, for the thing must have weighed a ton. Her effort was evidence of the strength of the creature who'd swung it over his shoulder as if it had been a stalk of bamboo. The hilt was identical to that of the knife, only bigger, and the blade looked just as dangerous. She shuddered.

Beneath the last two weapons lay a stack of documents. She pulled out the topmost one and looked at it. A sudden mixing of fear, anxiety and anger racked her body. It was all about her. Her name, age, social security number, address— everything! Frantically, she flipped through the other pages. They contained information about her job, her therapist, where she'd gone to school and even her old address in Washington!

He was following her, but why?

The last few documents she held answered her questions. She erupted in a painful sob and the pages crumpled in her fists. Marius had known everything about her parents: the day they were scheduled to arrive in Romania, the license number of the SUV they'd rented and how they'd died. He'd been following them all along, mapping their activities. Had he killed her parents? Was he here to kill *her?*

She'd be damned if she let him! She tossed the pages aside and scrambled toward the phone. She would call the police and then call April and have her contact Detective Beckford. She'd see that Marius was held for suspicion of murder.

She only had time to grab the receiver when a loud *thump* reverberated from outside. With a startled gasp, she snapped her attention in the direction of the sliding door. In walked the gargoyle. He was gasping as if he'd been racing against time itself. The sleek muscles of his chest were glistening, and his long hair hung in dripping straggles over his shoulders and down his back. At the rear of her mind, past the intense fear and desperation that was jerking every nerve ending she possessed, Alexandra realized that it was raining outside and that he had probably flown through the thunderstorm.

His glare went straight to her then to the scattered items of the chest on the floor. "How did you get in here?" he growled.

She'd been right! Marius was harboring the creature. Without responding, she quickly pressed the button on the phone that connected to the security desk. It rang once, then the entire phone was yanked out of her grasp as the gargoyle ripped the wire from the wall. The phone fell to floor with a *ping* and she knew it was useless to her.

Slowly she stood, her eyes pinned to the creature. In her peripheral vision she could see the weapons lying as she'd left them. If she could just get her hands on the knife, she'd be able to protect herself.

He extended a hand. "I will not harm you. Please, you must come with me." He beckoned.

"Stay away from me!" Alexandra inched toward the closet. "You and your master killed my parents! What are you, his pet? His minion?"

The creature glared at her with fiery eyes as he advanced a step. His large wings flattened against his back and he grimaced slightly. With the sound of her heart drumming in her ears, Alexandra's attention drifted to the blood-stained bandage on his arm. And the leather tie that held it in place.

"Marius?" she whispered, and her face contorted in pain.

She stumbled backward until she hit the wall. Tears blurred her vision and a twisting agony in her stomach made her want to throw up.

Marius and the gargoyle are one and the same!

Shame and anger came to a rapid boil in her heart.

All this time she'd been lied to, deceived, made a fool of! Their courtship had been a farce—a game, no doubt. All this time he'd pretended to care about her, to respect her, and it was he who'd come into her bedroom and violated her body while she'd slept! All this time, he'd been a beast!

Marius moved forward a step. He'd flown all evening in an attempt to reach her and get her to safety before his brothers did something stupid. He'd decided that there was no time for explanations and so he would have entered her bedroom and taken her away, kicking and screaming if he had to. But as he'd neared the building, the light in his apartment had drawn his attention. She was the last person he'd expected to find in his bedroom. He could see that she'd been crying, and he could guess the cause of her distress. He also knew that there was nothing he could do or say to make her trust him or believe that he had nothing to do with her parents' deaths.

When the time came he would make her listen to him. He would tell her the truth—tell her everything and beg her forgiveness. He only hoped that she'd understand, but for now his main priority was to get her to safety.

Alexandra snatched the knife from the floor and pointed it at him. "You lying bastard!" she shouted. "I hate you, and if you come near me I'll kill you!"

Marius tried reasoning with her first. "Alexandra, I never harmed your family and I could never do anything to hurt you. I can explain everything later, but we must leave here at once. You are in danger."

She wasn't hearing any of it. "I'm not going anywhere with you!"

He tried again. "You must listen to me. You will be harmed if you stay here!"

She shook her head, tossing her wealth of black tendrils. "No, *you* listen to *me!* I'll report everything to the authorities and see to it that you pay for everything you've done!"

Marius was losing patience. Of course, she had every right to feel the way she did, but time was wasting. He had no alternative to breaking his family's curse and no idea where to start searching. His father had given him two days, but by the look Simion had fastened on him, he was sure that their father's decision would be disregarded. After more than five hundred years of enslavement, his brothers were thirsty for freedom and were willing to do anything to obtain it. He was the only one who could save her.

"Alexandra, I am not making a request. You *will* be coming with me. Whether you go willingly or by force is your choice," he told her firmly.

His demand seemed to scatter the bits of lucid thinking she'd been clinging to and she screamed, charging at him with the blade held high.

Without moving, Marius watched her desperate advance. Did she really think she could ward him off with his own weapon? He waited until she got close enough, then he snatched her wrists together and effortlessly slipped the knife from her hands. It was tossed to the floor, and he pushed her backward onto the bed. She jumped up and tried to scramble away, but he grabbed one slender ankle and rolled her onto her back.

Alexandra fought like a banshee out of hell, clawing and kicking—anything to be free of him. He placed one knee on the foot of the mattress and crawled over her, pinning her hands above her head. She heaved and strained against him, but it was to no avail. Her strength was nothing compared to his.

"Let me go!" she screamed.

Marius glared down at her. All her fighting had caused the skirt of the red sundress to ride up well past her thighs and he had a clear view of the lace panties she wore. Many nights he'd envisioned her in his bed, twisting and heaving beneath him, but not like this. Her screams should be cries of passion and her writhing should be from the pleasure he'd be administering. Yet despite their present circumstance, he felt the first stirring sensation of an arousal.

"Stop this," he warned her in an ominous tone.

She looked up at the dark expression on his face and her movements stilled. Her eyes were wide and she trembled.

"Why are you doing this to me?" She sniffed. "Why me? Why my family?" Tears streamed down her temples.

He hung his head, his expression solemn. "There is much to be explained, but it will have to be done later. Right now I need you to trust me. You are in danger and you cannot stay here," he said in a gentle voice.

Her tears tugged at his heart. He'd never wanted her to learn the truth this way, not by accident. He finally realized that the last thing he wanted to do was hurt her, especially after all that had transpired between them.

He met her frightened glare. "Please, trust me. I

will take you to safety and no harm will come to you by my hands."

He sat up but remained above her, his massive body straddling her thighs. Her chest heaved as she fought to catch her breath and she quickly shoved her dress down.

Just then, a scent, mingled with the fragrance of the rain, drifted in on the wind and Marius's head snapped toward the sliding door. His eyes narrowed and he went still, listening.

He returned his attention to Alexandra, his eyes imploring. "You must remain within my chambers. No matter what, do not leave. When I return I will take you to safety."

Her mouth opened, probably to protest again, but she was intercepted by a loud crashing noise, like glass breaking.

Marius jumped to his feet and stalked to the door. His keen gargoyle senses hadn't failed him. His brothers had come to finish the ritual themselves. They'd broken through her sliding door and were in her apartment. She'd be safe as long as she did as he'd instructed, for although his brothers knew her address, they didn't know that he'd rented an apartment in the same building. Ducking his head beneath the doorway, he glanced at her one last time before leaving.

Alexandra scrambled from the bed. If Marius thought for one minute that she was going to sit and wait for him to return to take her to only God knew where, then he was a fool. She still couldn't believe that creature with horns and fangs—that beast—was Marius! There was even the possibility that he'd killed her parents and intended the same fate for her.

She ran through the apartment and opened the door to the hall. She would need to contact the police, then April. April's phone number was programmed into her cell phone. She would retrieve it from her apartment and go down to the foyer to wait for the police before Marius returned for her.

With shaking hands, Alexandra pulled her apartment key from her pocket. She slipped it in and turned the knob. Frantically, she looked about the room for her phone and spotted it on the accent table next to the couch. She snatched it up and quickly went to the menu and engaged April's number. It rang once before her friend answered.

"Hello?" came April's voice.

"April, it's me. I—"

"Alexandra! Oh, thank God! Where are you?" April interrupted, sounding frantic.

"In my apartment."

"I've been trying to contact you forever," April continued. "Listen, you have to stay put, okay? And don't let anyone in. It seems you're being stalked. I know this sounds weird, but Tyrese did a background check on you and realized that a few months ago someone else had accessed that same information and more. They knew about your parents, too—before they got killed. Just stay where you are. We're on our way over right now."

Alexandra couldn't breathe. It was all true! Marius was trying to kill her! She began shaking anew and moved toward the hall that led to her bedroom. If April and Tyrese were on their way, then she had time to pack some clothing. She'd stay with April until Marius was apprehended.

"How long will it—" Alexandra turned the corner and froze.

"What?" April asked, sounding worried. "Hello? Hello?"

Alexandra's hand fell away as she absorbed the tall figure standing in the doorway at the end of the hall. There was a scuffling noise behind him as if some wild animal was contained within her bedroom and fighting to be released. She took a step backward and felt for the light switch on the wall.

The narrow passageway lit up and the gargoyle before her sneered. Only he wasn't Marius! He was an inch or two taller and wore leather straps crisscrossing his bare chest. Behind him, she caught sight of Marius and another gargoyle locked in mortal combat. The one in the doorway took a threatening step forward, his dark eyes flashing as he raised his arms and aimed a crossbow at her. She screamed just as he pulled the trigger.

Chapter 13

The arrow flew through the air and Alexandra dropped to her knees. The moment she hit the floor she heard the splinting *thud* of the wall being penetrated. The gargoyle glowered at her and drew another arrow from a quiver strapped to his back.

She jumped up and ran by her dining room. An arrow whizzed past her and shattered the bulb of a contemporary floor lamp that stood in the corner. She screamed and headed for the door. This couldn't be happening! It was like a scene from a horror movie—or a nightmare. She hoped to God that she'd wake and find herself safe in her bed, shaken but relieved.

Another arrow splintered the door as she swung it open. Either the creature had poor aim or he was deliberately missing her, for she was certain she should have been hit by now. She ducked and raced down the hall toward the elevator. Once there, she began frantically pressing the button.

"Come on, come on." Her voice trembled.

The gargoyle appeared in the hall and aimed his crossbow again. The doors to the elevator slid open, and she was momentarily shocked to see April and Detective Beckford staring out at her. She dived in, and the arrow smashed against the door just as it closed. They all got a glimpse of the huge creature racing toward them.

April's face was contorted with fear. "Alexandra, what is going on? Is that thing shooting at you?"

Detective Beckford pulled a walkie-talkie from the holster on his hip. "Officer in need of assistance at the Petersburg Building on 102nd Street. Shots fired—well, arrows fired. I don't know what the hell's going on, but send everyone you got!" He removed his gun and took off the safety.

Alexandra was pressing the button marked *F* for foyer. She was in a state of shock. She'd already surmised that this was no dream, and she couldn't believe that there was more than one gargoyle in the city. And that Marius was one of them! And they all seemed to be after *her*.

April grabbed her hand. "Stop that before we get stuck in here! Now tell us what's going on!" She gave Alexandra a brain-rattling shake.

Alexandra took deep breaths and tried to still her racing pulse. "That creature, the gargoyle… it's Marius! But not the one that shot at me. There's more than one, and I think they killed my parents and now they're after me! I should've never trusted him!"

"Slow down!" April gave her another good shake. "Now, start—"

Her statement was cut short when a loud *boom* resounded above them and the entire elevator shook, sending them collapsing against the walls. They looked up to see a huge dent in the roof. The lights flickered, threatening to quit.

Detective Beckford aimed his gun above them. "Stay down! That thing's on the roof!"

Alexandra grabbed April's hand and pulled her to the corner near the controls. She looked up at the dial above the door: *Six, five…*

She exchanged looks with April and knew that they shared the same agonizing concern: how would the elevator hold up against an apparent three-hundred-pound Goliath? A moment later, and their unspoken question was answered when the thick blade of a broadsword lacerated the metal above them.

Detective Beckford dived to the side, the blade just missing his shoulder. "Damn! This thing means business." He aimed his gun and fired off a round, putting out a light in the process.

The loud *bang* bounced off the four walls that surrounded them and Alexandra and April were forced to cover their ears. They huddled together as two more shots were fired, each preceding the scraping sound of metal tearing through metal.

Half-shrouded in darkness now, Alexandra glanced up at the dial again. The number four was illuminated. She knew that they'd never make it to the ground floor in time. The roof of the elevator was already riddled with bullet holes and wide, jagged lacerations. If they stayed there, they'd be facing the gargoyle and their deaths.

She knelt and pressed the button to open the door. "We have to get out of here!" she screamed.

Above them, a shower of silver sparks rained down and the elevator came to a screeching halt. The door had partially opened and the fourth floor met them at eye level. The wires had been cut!

A middle-aged couple who'd obviously been waiting for the elevator looked in at them. "What happened? Did the power fail?" The woman's friendly smile faded into terror and she screamed when her eyes fixed on the huge claws that were peeling back the roof like the lid of a sardine can.

Detective Beckford fired two more rounds, momentarily stalling the creature. "Get out of here!" he shouted.

Alexandra didn't have to be told twice. She heaved herself up while the man outside extended a shaking hand to April.

Her friend scrambled out and turned back to Detective Beckford, who was busy reloading his gun. "Tyrese!"

He fired off two more shots then backed up, ran and leaped onto the fourth floor. "Run!"

They raced down the hallway, which was lined with glass windows on one side and apartment doors on the other. The only escape would be down the stairway. Alexandra glanced over her shoulder to see the gargoyle with both arms braced on the metal doors as he pushed them open. The man and woman who'd helped them were huddled in the corner behind a potted palm. The gargoyle spared them only a brief glance before he charged through the hall. Another couple was at their door preparing to enter when they spotted the creature. The man tossed up his keys and, grabbing his screaming wife's arm, dived behind a soda machine.

Detective Beckford slammed through the door of the stairway and held it open for April and Alexandra. "You ladies get out of here! I'll hold this bastard off." He raised his gun and was about to shoot when a large figure crashed through one of the glass windows, ramming into the advancing gargoyle. They smashed through the wall, shaking the entire floor.

Detective Beckford cast Alexandra and April a look over his shoulder. "There are two of them! Go, get out of here!"

They took the stairs two at a time. Alexandra knew that it was Marius who'd taken the other gargoyle down. She wasn't sure what to think about him. He'd warned her of this danger and now he fought to protect her, but for what reason? Perhaps while the others sought to harm her, he wanted her to fulfill another purpose. What still puzzled her was, why? Why was she so important, dead or alive?

They were nearing the door of the third floor when the sound of screams echoed up the stairwell.

April paused, her hands gripping the iron railing. "Do you think we should go back?" she squeaked.

Before Alexandra could respond, the door burst open and three tenants ran through, their eyes wide in terror. They headed down the stairs, stumbling over each other in the process. She eased toward the door and took hold of the handle, pulling it open just enough to peer through. The hall was trashed; doors had been kicked in, and items possibly dropped by frightened occupants littered the floor.

April was already on the third descending step and was poised to run. "What do you see?" she asked in a nervous whisper.

"Nothing yet, but something's there. I can feel it."

As the words spilled from her mouth, a tall figure emerged from one of the doors that had been left ajar and began stalking up the hallway. It was the third gargoyle!

His long hair fell to his waist in a thick braid and in his right hand he held what looked like a Japanese machete. He'd only taken a few steps when he turned his head slowly and looked toward the stairwell. She was acutely reminded of the day she'd spied on Marius through the peephole in her door. He'd turned and looked at her in the same way, as if he could sense her presence, which this gargoyle seemed to have the ability to do, as well.

She pulled the door shut and ran toward April. "Let's go, we have to keep going down! There's another one up there!"

"How many of those things are there?" April asked hysterically.

"I don't know," Alexandra replied in a shaky voice. "So far I've seen three."

"Three!" April screamed and picked up her pace. "I don't know if I heard you correctly, but did you say that *Marius* is one of them?"

"Yes," Alexandra replied. "I went into his apartment and found weapons and information about me and my family in an old trunk. And then he— the gargoyle—came in." Her vision began to blur and her heart constricted with pain.

"What the hell do they want with you? What have you ever done?"

"I don't know!" She stopped and leaned against the wall as she tried to banish the agony that was tearing through her. "He knew everything, April." She sniffed. "Even the day my parents were arriving in Romania and their SUV rental car tag number."

April's mouth fell open. "You don't think he's responsible for..." She trailed off.

Alexandra shook her head. "I don't know. He told me that he had nothing to do with their deaths. I want to believe him."

April gripped her by the arms and gave her a shake. "Listen to me. This is the same guy who deceived you. He made you believe he was human and he played with your emotions. There's absolutely no reason for you to believe him."

"I don't know." Alexandra shook her head in frustration. "It seems like he's trying to protect me from the others. He had all the time in the world to harm me, but never tried." Tears were running down her face as she fought for control. Now wasn't the time to have a nervous breakdown.

April pulled her into a hug. "We have to keep

moving. We *are* going to get through this and we'll find all the answers, but right now we have to get out of here."

Alexandra nodded and brushed the tears from her cheeks. April was right. The only way she was going to find out the truth about her family and Marius was if she got out of there alive. She had to survive to avenge her parents, and to save a little girl who needed her.

They continued down the stairs. The muffled sounds of gunshots could be heard and they realized that Detective Beckford was still fending off the first creature.

The sound of the door to the third floor slamming open echoed in the stairwell. Alexandra glanced over her shoulder and saw nothing, but she knew without a doubt that they were being followed. The hairs on the back of her neck were raised and there was a churning in the pit of her stomach. The gargoyle was approaching!

There was a smashing sound and the lights flickered out, flooding the passage in darkness.

April screamed and Alexandra reached for her and clamped a hand over her mouth. She tried to still her own labored breathing as she listened intently for any sound that would verify the feeling she had.

When her efforts were met by the scraping of heavy boots, she took a step down. "Let's go, we have to be quick. It's up there," she whispered breathlessly.

She realized that she was still holding her cell phone and quickly activated the light to guide them. They moved as fast as they could. The gargoyle was taking his time as a lion would while stalking his prey. A tremor coursed up her spine, for she knew that when the creature did attack it would be sudden and violent. Guilt washed over her—she would never forgive herself if anything happened to her friend. She was the one they were after, for what reason she couldn't begin to imagine, and she'd inadvertantly put April in danger.

They reached the second floor. Alexandra swung the door open and the darkness retreated down the stairwell.

April fixed her with a look of confusion. "What are you doing?" She grabbed her arm.

"April, I have to go on alone now. Those things are after me, not you."

"They want to kill you!" April said in a distressed whisper. "I can't let you do this!" Her full brown eyes shimmered with the first misting of tears.

Alexandra knew that her friend cared for her dearly, but she also cared for April, and dragging her into impending danger was hardly the way to show it.

The gargoyle's steps were moving closer and he'd picked up his pace. Alexandra grabbed April's hands and held them tightly. She looked into her eyes, imploring.

"Please. I need you alive. And not just because you're my best friend. There's a house, 115 Berkley Avenue. You have to get the police to search it. It's the Penn State Serial Killer's residence." She peered into the darkness. The gargoyle would be upon them at any moment.

"What are you talking about?" April asked, following her gaze.

"I found an address, in criminal records, of the guy I think committed those murders in the Penn State area. I'm also sure he kidnapped that little girl from the Bronx, Mady Halman." At April's confused look she groaned. "Look, I don't have time to explain. I just need you to do this for me. Now go!"

Without waiting for April's response, she spun around and ran down the hall of the second floor. Behind her she could hear April's heels racing down the stairs. Her friend would be safe. That knowledge eased some of her worries. Now all she had to think about was how she was going to get away with her own life.

The entire floor seemed empty—doors had been left open and only silence could be heard. She guessed that the building had been evacuated. Slipping into one of the open apartments, she shut the door and locked it securely. All the lights were off except for a small lamp on an accent table. Careful fingers turned the switch off. She had to be as quiet as possible. With her ear pressed against the door, she waited. As the gargoyle advanced up the hallway, each heavy footfall could be heard. He paused a few times and she imagined he was listening. She held her breath, not wanting to make a sound.

Then a loud noise nearly made her cry out, but she clamped her hands over her mouth. She didn't have to be psychic to know what had just happened—the gargoyle had kicked in a door and by the sound of it, it was the apartment adjacent to the one she was in.

As quietly as possible, she backed away from the door, feeling her way through the darkened, unfamiliar room. When she reached the hallway, she turned and headed toward the bedroom. She was only on the second floor and was certain she could get help from the balcony.

A popping noise that reminded her of firecrackers on the Fourth of July emerged from somewhere outside. But no fireworks were being displayed tonight. It was gunfire. A surge of relief filled her—the police had arrived!

She was just about to turn the bedroom doorknob when the sound of the door to the apartment being kicked in gave her a start. Fear coursed through her entire body. She spun around. The light pouring into the living room and the huge shadow moving on the wall was enough to tell her that she was in danger.

She inhaled two deep breaths and steadied her thinking. This was no time to lose her wits. Her survival depended on how well she kept it together. Without taking her eyes from the image on the wall, she reached back and took hold of the doorknob. Slowly, she turned it and eased it open wide enough for her to disappear into the enveloping darkness. Once inside the bedroom, she shot a desperate glance at the sliding door. It was closed. She would have no time to open it and escape. She had to hide and hope that the gargoyle didn't pinpoint her exact location.

The sound of footsteps in the hall made her entire body shake. Quickly she dived beneath the bed. There was no bed skirt, so she could see the exact moment when the door was pushed open and two large boots stomped in. In the dim light she could make out small silver spikes that wrapped around the ankles, and she was reminded of heavy-metal music.

She remained perfectly still and kept a hand clamped over her lips, in case her body should betray her and utter a squeak.

A spiked tail whipped back and forth and the creature inhaled deeply. "I know you are here, Descendant." He spoke in a guttural voice that was accent rich. "Show yourself."

Alexandra's gaze followed as he moved toward the closet and threw the door open. Why was he calling her *Descendant?* Had they all mistaken her for someone else?

Her heart was pounding so loudly that she wondered if he could hear it. She squeezed her eyes shut and tried to will herself to remain calm, but it was useless. It seemed that with each passing second, it was getting harder to breathe, to think.

The bathroom door creaked and her eyes flew open. There was a shuffling noise and she guessed that he'd yanked the shower curtain aside. Her eyes bolted toward the door and she wondered if she could make a run for it. The thought was dashed just as fast as it had come to mind. There was no way she could outrun the gargoyle. She wouldn't even get as far as the hallway. She had no weapon, nothing to protect herself. The most she could do was to wait and hope that he gave up or that the police came to rescue her. April should be on the ground floor by now, and she was sure her friend would instruct the officers where she had last seen her.

"Why don't you make this easy for both of us?" he continued. "Do you think I have anything against you? No, it is nothing personal. Show yourself, Descendant, and I may even give you the opportunity to bid your lover farewell."

Alexandra inched toward the other end of the bed as he approached. He stopped when his knees touched the mattress and he inhaled again. "Hmm, thank you for giving me the honor of drawing your blood," he said with what sounded like sincere gratitude.

Without warning he gripped the mattress and toppled it off the bed frame, uncovering her hiding place. Alexandra screamed and rolled out of reach as he lunged for her.

With tremors traveling through her body, she backed herself into a corner. He stepped over the iron bars and moved toward her. She was trapped! There was no way out, no way around him.

She began to hyperventilate and a thin film of perspiration formed on her skin. Shaking her head, she attempted to clear her blurring vision, but it was no use. She felt as if she would pass out.

The hazy image of the gargoyle hovered above her. "It is easy to see why my brother is so taken with you. You are very beautiful. It is a pity that you have to die, but I assure you, had your meeting been under different circumstances, our family would have gladly welcomed you."

His words echoed in her mind as if she was in a dream. Her head was spinning. An emotion far greater than fear was rising within her. It was a sensation she'd never experienced before, one she couldn't name.

Her body jerked into an arch and her mouth opened. Words that she hadn't conjured spilled forth. *"Sînge şi death ashes şi decay. Un plin moon ridicare şi al tău days de drum liber eşti număr! I vară art hot. Mare puternic de abadron, conducător de la a umbri!"* she hissed.

He paused and his face twisted into an incredulous scowl. It was obvious that he understood every word she said, even though she didn't. She did know that the language pouring from her mouth was similar to Romanian. She'd listened to her mother's music enough times to recognize it, but what she spoke was far from the modern language.

What is happening to me?

She slid to her knees. *"Mai art hot. Foc de un thousand iad erupţie cu tu."*

"Silence, witch!" he shouted and lifted his blade high for the attack.

Alexandra raised her hands in front of her and a surge of energy shot through her body. Before she knew what was happening, a bright blaze erupted before her. The gargoyle's yell rang in her ears and he stumbled back, twitching as if he'd been assailed by a great pain.

Drained of all energy, she collapsed on the

floor. She tried to drag herself back to the surface of consciousness. She lay there for a moment, watching the unbelievable scene before her. Bright red flames surged through the gargoyle's mouth and slowly engulfed him, yet he didn't burn! There was no doubt in her mind that she'd just done that to him, but *how*?

Strength seeped back into her limbs and she sat up.

"Witch!" the gargoyle screamed. "I will make you regret the day you ever heard the Drakon name!"

The fire that had been consuming him only moments ago was dying slowly. Alexandra decided that it was time to leave. She would figure out what had just happened later, when she was safe. She stood and stumbled toward the sliding door. When she shoved it open the rain greeted her, falling in heavy slanting pellets.

Unfortunately, the balcony overlooked the side of the building. She could see the flashing lights of the squad cars that were no doubt posted in front of the complex. All she had to do to live was make it there.

She swung one leg over the rail and then the other. She was contemplating the best way to jump from a second-story balcony when the gargoyle she'd left inside smashed through the glass door. A small flame still flickered at his throat, dipping in and out of his nostrils, but he seemed to be back to normal—and quite ready to return the favor.

He charged at her and swung his blade madly. Alexandra screamed and leaped to the ground below, landing on a strip of manicured grass. The wind got knocked from her lungs and she gasped in pain. She crawled to her feet and looked up to see him shaking off the last of the fire. That gave her just enough time to race around the side of the building. She could see about a dozen squad cars, two Special Forces armored trucks and a bevy of armed guards.

With renewed energy, she raced toward them, her bare feet hitting the wet stone pavement. A throng of onlookers with umbrellas and raincoats and some with no protection at all had gathered behind the yellow tape. The street had been barricaded and there were a number of abandoned cars parked down the middle. As she neared, a series of screams erupted and several hands lifted to point at the sky behind her. She shot a look over her shoulder in time to see the gargoyle advancing, his large wings spread to their full length and slapping against the heavy rainfall.

With a scream, she dropped to her knees just as he swooped down, missing her by a few feet. The onlookers began to scatter, yelling in terror, and the police aimed their weapons, firing when the creature got near enough. He disappeared into the heavy rain clouds above.

Alexandra stood and backed up a step, ignoring the burning pain in her knees where the skin had been scraped away. The gargoyle would attack again, she was sure. An officer holding a large assault rifle was heading her way, wildly motioning for her to leave the perimeter. She spared him a glance, then her attention was drawn again to the sky. Lightning flashed and what she thought she'd seen was confirmed. The gargoyle was returning, only this time he was hefting something large—something that resembled a broadcasting satellite. And he was heading directly toward the officers. They abandoned their vehicles and began to scatter, some firing off a few rounds in an attempt to stop the creature.

Alexandra turned on her heel and fled the other way. She'd only taken a few steps when there was a loud crashing noise closely followed by a deafening explosion that shook the earth and sent cracks snaking up the sidewalk. She fell forward and covered her ears. Gunshots rang out behind her and she braved a look back. Three squad cars were engulfed in flames and a large, circular satellite lay in the middle of the street, smoking from the attack.

The creature hovered in the air, far out of shooting range as he admired his handiwork. Then he turned his attention to her. He dived gracefully then surged forward, only to be stopped by another gargoyle that appeared out of nowhere.

Marius, Alexandra thought with mixed emotions. She wasn't quite ready to accept any of what was happening, but something within told her that Marius had spoken the truth to her. With that comforting thought at the back of her mind, she turned and fled up the street.

Marius slammed a fist into Nicholas's abdomen. "I warned you, brother!" he growled.

The other gargoyle recovered quickly and leaped over him, gripping his neck from behind in a deadly lock. "You are a disgrace to our family!" Nicholas shouted.

Marius spun in circles as he tried desperately

to dislodge his brother, and together they went smashing into the side of the building, raining brick and glass down on the onlookers.

He pinned Nicholas to the wall. "Harm her and you will forfeit your life!" he told his brother in a lethal voice.

After leaving Alexandra in his apartment, he'd gone to confront his brothers. They'd demanded to know where he'd taken her, and he'd warned them to leave before he lost his temper. Only a few minutes had lapsed before they all heard the door to her apartment open. That was when Nicholas had attacked him. Marius had fought his brother as if he'd been fighting for his own life. He realized now that he was willing to betray his family for Alexandra, yet his motive eluded him.

"So this is how it is, then?" Nicholas gritted out. "You choose to betray your family to protect our enemy—that witch?"

Marius's grip tightened on his brother. "She is no more a witch than you or I," he countered.

Nicholas heaved his arms up, shoving him off. "So quick to defend her, I see," he scoffed. "Do you honestly think she would do the same for you? Look at yourself—or have you forgotten what we are? And do not forget—after the equinox is done, she will be possessed by the spirit of Lady Vivian. What words of defense will you utter then?"

Marius didn't respond. They remained as they were in silence, their breathing heavy as they hovered high above the ground. *Nicholas is right,* Marius thought. Soon he would be drawn again into the fierce cycle of existing as a gargoyle during the night and being trapped in stone during the day. And Alexandra would be a mere vessel. But he would concern himself with that when the time came. For now he would do everything in his power to prevent his brothers from completing the Lunar Ritual.

Nicholas rose a few feet above him. "It is obvious that you have allowed yourself to be bewitched, brother. You have fallen prey to her evil and now look at yourself. Pathetic! I am sure our father will not be pleased to hear of your defection."

With that he swooped upward and faded into the dark storm clouds. Thunder rumbled and Marius gazed down at the crowded streets some ten stories below. Inwardly, he knew that what had taken place this night could never be undone. There would be no turning back, no redemption.

* * *

Alexandra was huddled in the shadows beneath an overpass. The rain continued to pour down and lightning flashed. Sirens could be heard in the distance, but the gunfire had ceased. She sniffed. She'd been crying for the last hour. All she could think was that her parents should be alive today. The car crash had been no accident—they'd been murdered. She couldn't understand why their lives had been taken or why her own was in jeopardy. They were normal people with no great amount of wealth or status. Or were they? Her mind kept drifting to what had happened in the apartment. Something had taken her over, dousing her with an ability that far surpassed her gift.

She glanced at her watch. The small face was illuminated. It was 11:45 p.m. She reached into the pocket of her dress and pulled out her cell phone. Apparently, the rain had damaged it, for it refused to turn on. It seemed she would have to leave her hiding place to seek help after all.

Carefully, she crawled over the small pools of water that had settled beneath the overpass. She stood and tried to see past the heavy curtain of rain. The bright headlights of cars zooming by and the orange glow of streetlights were visible.

All the stores would be closed now, but she was sure she could find a restaurant where she'd be allowed to use a telephone.

Hugging her arms around herself, she stepped into the rain. Her thin, spaghetti-strapped sundress didn't provide much protection from the elements. And to top it off, she was barefoot. Quickly she walked across the small stretch of grass that would take her to a main street.

Midway she stopped suddenly. The low rumble of thunder wasn't enough to disguise the noise she heard. It sounded like a forceful wind—a brief gust—but she knew better.

Tossing her head back, she searched the sky and a scream formed in the pit of her stomach but never surfaced. The dark shadow lunged toward her, scooping her up with one swift effort. The air left her body and Alexandra found herself dangling over the broad shoulder of one of the gargoyles. He soared higher, his powerful wings propelling them forward.

She quickly overcame the shock and began pounding against his broad back with her fists. She kicked and screamed, yet he maintained a steady pace. The streets below grew smaller and smaller, and soon she couldn't see them at all.

Her vision was obscured by the thick haze of a low-altitude storm cloud. Her chest became tight and she gasped for breath.

I am going to die!

Her vision faded and blackness engulfed her.

Chapter 14

She had a dull headache. Alexandra moaned and turned her head to the other side. Her neck was sore, too. Her eyes opened a measure and she squinted against the soft lighting. Through the blur of her vision, she could see the pale fingers of dawn, filtering in through cracks in boarded-up windows. Outside, the rain continued; the soft sound was lulling, tempting her to fall back into her dreams.

Then the memory of all that had taken place came flooding back to her and her eyes widened. She tried to sit up and a sharp pain tore through her back and ribs. Biting down on her lips, she eased backward until she lay flat again. She moved to cradle a sore spot on her chest and realized that her hands and feet were bound. She began to struggle madly, but it was useless. The thick lengths of frayed rope had been tied with an expertise that would make a veteran sailor proud. She gave up and made an attempt to sit again.

Carefully, she rotated her body, trying to ignore the pain that moving caused her. Finally, she came to a seated position and assessed her surroundings. She'd been placed on a step covered in worn carpet and before her, rows of dust-laden pews sat in silence. A large wooden cross was mounted high up on the wall behind her and four tall wooden beams supported the arched ceiling. She was in a church, abandoned by the look of it.

Her clothing and hair were still damp and a chill ran over her. She was also alone. She looked at her watch and realized that she'd been out for hours. She wasn't certain which gargoyle had brought her here or what he intended to do with her, but if the tight binds chafing her skin were any indication, she needed to find a way out and fast.

Her fingers began to work at the firm knot at her ankles, pulling and tugging at the frayed ends. It didn't yield. Whoever had taken the time to bind her had no intention of letting her leave.

She was still working at the knot when a dark

figure leaped down from the wooden balcony, coming to land in the shadows near the rear door. She froze. She was helpless. If this creature had returned to kill her there was nothing she could do to save herself!

He emerged from the darkness and drew a knife from his boot. Alexandra realized that her captor was Marius. And he was human again. Naked from the waist up, he was still garbed in tight-fitting black pants and heavy boots, and his wet hair fell about his shoulders. He stalked toward her.

Alexandra's breathing quickened and her eyes focused on the long blade in his hand. Had he had a change of heart? Did he intend to harm her after all?

"No, please! Stay away from me!" she cried.

He said nothing. He looked exhausted, as if some great and invisible burden was strapped to his shoulders. He bent before her, ignoring her screams, and took hold of her wrists.

Alexandra tried to pull away and failed. She screamed again just as he brought the knife be-tween her hands, severing the rope. She fell back onto her elbows and watched as he did the same for her ankles. Then he scooped her up in his arms and headed toward the left rear corner of the church.

She didn't fight him—didn't have the strength to. The heat from his body seeped into her, sapping any resistance that may have lingered.

"Where are you taking me?" she asked.

Without responding, Marius used a foot to thrust the door open then proceeded up a narrow flight of stairs. The old wood creaked beneath their weight and the smell of aged dust was heavy in the air.

Alexandra tried to banish the fear that was still creeping over her like spiny tentacles. She told herself that if he'd wanted to kill her, she'd be dead by now. Yet she couldn't shake the realization that he wasn't the man she'd come to know. He was a stranger. She had no knowledge of who he was, where he'd come from or even *what* he was. Nor did she understand her connection to him or the strange power she seemed to possess.

At the top of the stairway, they entered a room that was aglow with candlelight. It looked to be an old office that had been fashioned into a temporary bedroom. There was a desk on which two tall candles were lit, an oval mirror hanging above it. Against the rear wall, a bed sat beneath another boarded-up window. The bedding was identical to what she'd seen in Marius's apartment. Even the fur pelt that lay near the pillows looked familiar.

He stopped at the foot of the bed and lowered her feet to the wooden floor. She noted that the room seemed devoid of any dust. It was obvious that it had been cleaned—had he done so for her?

"Remove your clothing," he said as he went to the door and eased it shut.

"What?" Alexandra quickly adjusted one of the thin straps of her dress that had slipped from her shoulder.

Marius turned to face her.

"I said, remove your clothing. It is wet." When she continued to stare at him, he pointed toward the wolf pelt. "You may drape that over yourself until your clothes have dried."

She hesitated for a moment then pulled it from the bed. "Thank you," she said quietly.

He was polite enough to turn his back. She moved toward the mirror and looked at her reflection. She was a mess. Her long hair was nearly dry and had twisted into a tangle of curls that hung around her in disarray. The soft, damp material of her dress clung to her curves, displaying the very suggestive outline of her underwear beneath it.

She stripped off the dress and draped it over the desk, removing her phone from the pocket. She briefly considered taking her underwear off as well, but decided that she needed more than just the length of fur between her naked body and Marius. She wrapped the heavy pelt around her, covering her red lace bra and matching panties.

Marius must have guessed that she was done for he turned around. "Are you hungry?" he asked, his tone solemn.

Her brows puckered. Food was hardly at the forefront of her mind. In the last six hours she'd discovered that the man she was growing to trust was capable of sprouting wings and a tail, she'd been attacked with medieval weapons and practically thrown from a second-story balcony and she'd realized that she could speak fluent Romanian while casting fire spells. She wanted answers, dammit!

"Marius, what happened out there?" She pinned him with a determined look.

He sighed and motioned toward the bed. "Sit."

"I don't want to sit! I want you to tell me who

or what you are, why I'm being hunted and what happened to my parents!" she demanded.

His head fell a measure. "First of all, I had no part in your parents' deaths. Everything else I told you about my name and origin are true. I am the third and last son of Lord Victor Drakon. Five hundred years ago, a witch cursed my family to avenge her cousin's death. It was the curse of the gargoyle. Five years passed before it manifested. But when it did, all the members of my clan who had been living at our castle when the spell was cast and anyone born to them after was afflicted. I was but an infant at that time. Since then we have been condemned to an eternity of suffering. The other gargoyles you saw tonight are my brothers, Simion and Nicholas. We were born in the early 1500s."

Alexandra had to take a moment to absorb what she'd been told. It sounded insane, like some elaborate gothic script, but after all she'd seen, there was no doubt in her mind that his spoken word was indeed the truth. And if so, he was hundreds of years old and should be stone as it was early morning. She looked at him more intensely then.

"I read that gargoyles are stone during the day.

How is it that you have the ability to become human?" she managed.

"The Spring Equinox," he said simply. "It occurs annually when the sun crosses the celestial equator. For centuries this season has been deemed sacred by all witches and the use of sorcery of any form is prohibited before sunset. So, the spell has no effect on us during the day."

She thought about what he was saying—he wasn't permanently a man! He had only a limited time to be human—a season. "How long does this last?" she asked.

Marius looked away. "Twenty-nine days," he replied in a sad voice.

Her head spun. *Twenty-nine days!* She counted the days since their meeting and realized that his human existence was nearly done. "What will happen when this time is over?" Her voice trembled.

"We will become stone during the day and will remain gargoyles at night. The way it has always been. The way it will be for the next year."

Her legs weakened and she sank to the edge of the mattress. A frown pinned her brows together and she blinked back the mist of tears. She fought the disappointment that raged within her, then the anger that quickly joined the torrent to rival for precedence and won.

She locked a livid gaze upon him. "If you knew all this, how could you start a relationship with me? You knew you had only twenty-nine days to be human! What, did you think I would simply accept everything you're telling me now when the month ended?"

He approached to tower above her. "I never expected any of this, Alexandra. My only purpose for coming to New York was to end my family's curse."

Some of her anger seeped away and her eyes widened with hope. "There is a way to break this curse?"

"Yes," he replied solemnly. "But I am searching for another."

"What's wrong with the option you have now? I can help you. What do you need, potions? I know where a few Wiccan stores are in the city."

He shook his head and his beautiful eyes were somber. "To break this curse, more than simple potions are required. Blood has to be spilled." He inhaled a deep breath and continued. "And for this reason we sought you out."

"So your brothers were going to sacrifice me, like some kind of cult?"

He shook his head and sank onto the bed next to her. "Alexandra, the only reason I came to New York was to find you."

She was assailed by confusion. He was talking in circles and dragging her into it. "What do I have to do with all of this?" In her mind she wondered if her ever-developing gift was somehow linked to witchcraft. When Marius looked away, she knew that it was far more than that.

"The witch that cursed my family was called Necesar," he told her reluctantly. "Necesar Dancescu. And the only way to end the curse is to end her bloodline."

At the mention of her mother's maiden name, Alexandra's stomach clenched and understanding flooded her mind. She was the descendant of the witch! The last descendant! That explained the spell she'd cast in the apartment. It also explained why her parents had been killed. And why Marius's brothers were trying to kill her.

Tears welled in her eyes and she suppressed the urge to scream. "Who killed my parents?" she gritted out.

Marius didn't look at her—it seemed he

couldn't. "My family caused the accident," he spoke softly.

She blinked, dislodging a stream of tears, and she stood suddenly. "Your family! All this time you knew that your very own family was responsible for killing my parents, for taking everything away from me and yet you pretended to listen to me when I talked about them! You pretended to care!"

He was on his feet, too. "I never pretended with you, Alexandra."

She continued as if he hadn't interjected. "Why should I even believe that you're innocent? You obviously conspired with them to come and find me!"

Her tears were flowing freely now. Rage and disbelief flashed through her body. She was angry at herself for trusting him so fast, allowing him to make a fool of her. How could she have not seen through his facade? How could she have been so blind? She was a journalist, for God's sake!

Marius tried again, his eyes beseeching. "Please, listen to me, Alexandra. I came here with the intent to kill you, but after meeting you I found I could not. My family, however, refused to listen to reason and I knew I had to get you to safety, but I was too late. My brothers followed me to your apartment with the intent of taking up the task themselves."

She didn't want to hear any more of his excuses. Nothing he said could bring her family back. *Nothing!* She wondered if she would have met the same fate if he hadn't found himself desiring her body. The memory of what he'd done to her in her bedroom was still etched clearly in her mind. She remembered the large knife he'd brought with him. Perhaps he'd intended to end her life that very night.

Marius's jaw tightened. "Alexandra, I know this is hard for you and I do not expect you to trust me. All I ask is that you believe me. I will never lift a hand to harm you and I will try everything in my power to find another way to solve this problem." He reached a hand toward her as if to brush away the trail of tears that lingered on her face.

She'd heard enough and slapped his hand before it made contact with her skin. "Don't touch me!" she spat. She marched around him and headed toward the door. She had to get out of there, away from him.

Marius leaped over the bed and barred the way. "I cannot allow you to leave."

She fastened a scowl on him. "Get out of my way!" she demanded. She wondered if she could summon the powers she possessed once again.

He folded his arms over the thick muscles of his chest. "It is not safe, and I intend to keep you here until it is. Once my father hears news of what happened during the night, he will attempt to find you himself and bring a conclusion to this insanity."

She marched toward him. "I don't care about all that! I'm going to the police, the FBI, the military—whoever will listen and *I'll* put a stop this insanity!"

"You are going nowhere."

She narrowed her eyes. "I'm not your prisoner and I refuse to be held here!"

"Alexandra, I am thinking only of your safety—"

"I don't need your help!" she interrupted. "I think you've done enough damage. I can handle things from here, thank you. Now move out of my way."

He sighed. "You are many miles from the city,

deep within the woods. How do you intend to get back?"

"I don't care. I just need to get away from you. I would sooner brave the elements than spend another moment here waiting to be killed." She moved to step around him and immediately found herself snatched off her feet. "Put me down!" she screamed as loud as her lungs would allow.

He cradled her in his arms, moving his head to avoid her flailing limbs. "No one can hear you, Alexandra. We are alone for miles and miles."

She twisted in his arms, prying at his fingers and pushing at his chest. "Get your hands off me, you murdering bastard!" Her tears returned.

She continued fighting and the wolf pelt slipped to the floor. Garbed now only in her very revealing underwear, Alexandra pushed away from him as she frantically tried to separate her body from the searing heat of his. She struck him twice in the face before she noticed he was moving toward the bed, his face taut with checked impatience. She screamed again as he landed her on the mattress and then she struggled wildly, but he pinned her in place.

"Leave me alone!" she cried. "I hate you! I

hate…" Her voice trailed off as a sob rose within her throat.

Images of her parents flashed in her mind—her mother's soft smile as she would sing sweetly, and the way her father's eyes would crinkle at the corners when he laughed. Their lives had been stolen from them, snatched away before they even had a chance to say goodbye to the ones they loved. She turned her head away from him. She didn't want him to see her cry.

He lifted her shaking body from the bed and cradled her in his arms, rocking her gently. Surprisingly, she didn't resist. Instead, she found herself drawn to the warmth his body offered and curled into him and wept.

Alexandra found the strength of his arms and his tender whispers comforting. She cried until her energy all but left her and a numb feeling replaced her sadness. Only then, when the shaking of her body ceased, did he release her. He lowered her onto the bed, and when she would have reached for the comforter to cover herself, he stilled her hands.

She watched as his gaze combed her tight body and anger seemed to overtake him. "Did my brothers do this to you?" he asked as he examined the bruises that marred her skin.

The dark look in his eyes sent a shiver over her—he seemed sincerely infuriated by the knowledge that someone might have harmed her. "I fell," she told him.

He took a moment to look her over again then stood and left the room. Alexandra used what little strength she could muster to drag the bedding over her. Something at the back of her mind told her to run while she had the chance, but now she didn't want to leave. She wasn't sure she could fend off the dangers that awaited her beyond this sanctuary alone. She also didn't know if she could trust Marius, but sensed she would be safe with him, if only for the night. He had yet to lay a wounding hand upon her, and he'd comforted her when she'd needed it. Such weren't the actions of a man who intended to cause injury. She would stay with him, but tomorrow she had to head back to the city.

Lifting her wrist, she looked at Mady's bracelet. Coupled with her anxieties, she could feel a pang of desperation rising within her. Mady's time was running out. She had faith in April though. Her friend would do whatever it took to lead the authorities to the killer's address.

When Marius returned, he held a bowl of water and a strip of cloth. He sat on the bed and placed the items on the floor. "Let me tend to your wounds." Slowly he pulled the comforter away, revealing her near-naked body.

Alexandra lay still as he carefully cleaned the blood from the scrapes on her knees then moved to brush at the purple bruise that had formed on her rib cage. She watched him silently. His touch was gentle, like the feathery kiss of the first spring rain, and when he looked at her, a promise reflected in his silver eyes—a promise to protect her at all costs. Her heart clenched with a new emotion, a compilation of feelings and wishes, and she desperately wanted to trust him.

Yet one question remained unanswered. "Why?" she whispered. "Why couldn't you bring yourself to harm me?"

Marius's hand paused over her rib cage and he met her questioning stare. "You are an innocent," he admitted simply. "I could never lift a hand against you."

Alexandra experienced a sudden flush of sentiment. The intensity of his stare drew her in and before she could stop herself, she was reaching for him. His large body covered her, lending warmth and strength, and their lips met in a soft, brushing kiss.

Her grip tightened on his neck. "Hold me," she breathed.

Too much had happened too soon already. Yet, in this moment, she yearned to be near him, to be embraced by his warmth. She needed that comfort.

Marius watched her for a few seconds before he placed the washcloth aside. Then, silently, he drew her into his arms. Seeing her in so much pain was tearing at him. Sadly, his plan to reveal everything to her in slow and careful degrees had been dashed and now he suffered the guilt of having her learn the truth in such a crude manner.

Alexandra wound her fingers through his hair and pulled him closer. He tried to read her expression. Her eyes were half-shrouded by her lids, her thick lashes casting shadows on her face. Her full lips were slightly pouted as if begging for another kiss.

Slowly, his mouth descended upon hers. Alexandra's lips parted eagerly, welcoming the heated invasion. Her hands wandered over his muscled back in a gentle caress, and his powerful muscles flexed beneath her administrations.

One large hand reached behind her to unfasten her bra. It was quickly peeled from her body and discarded on the floor. His mouth lowered on one hard nipple, his tongue teasing it, teeth gently nibbling. He moved to the other, worshiping it in the same manner. His fingers slipped along her flat abdomen, tracing the smooth lines until they brushed the frilled edges of her panty.

He withdrew suddenly, his eyes alight with a dark flame. "I want you," he told her in a roughened voice. "I need you."

Alexandra gazed up at him. He knew that all it would take was one gentle caress within the nucleus of her desire, and she would be his. She would open willingly for him and grant him the pleasure her body promised.

She said nothing, but the look in her eyes was encouragement enough and he claimed her with another feral kiss. His fingers slipped between her shapely thighs and over the bit of red lace that covered her womanhood. With a growl, he wound it in his fist and ripped it from her body.

Alexandra gasped and opened her legs in anticipation of his touch. Like a separate entity, his fingers slipped into her hot, moist core, parting the folds as they sought out the source of her nectar. Her hips thrust upward in a slow sensual rhythm. Marius felt his desire peaking, sending a wave of hunger over him, and his shaft hardened. He wanted to feel himself inside her, wanted to take her with savage abandon.

Fighting for control, he stood and stripped away his clothing. Their eyes met as he settled between her thighs and positioned his thick and pulsating erection at her soft opening. If he could stop time, he would do it. Nothing else mattered right then except the driving need that made him ache.

Battling for patience, he eased into her warm center and as their bodies became one, she cried out in pain.

Marius froze and pinned Alexandra with a dark look. "You are a virgin?" he asked incredulously.

Hooded eyes met his query and she shook her head. "Not anymore."

Self-disgust and disbelief mounted within him and his head fell. Silently, he cursed himself. How could he have not known? In his carelessness he'd just unwittingly completed the final step in the

Lunar Ritual. By severing her maidenhead, he'd drawn her blood.

With a soft moan, Alexandra shifted her weight beneath him, and that small action forced his offering deeper into her trembling core.

Marius growled. His hands moved to grip her backside and he held her still. He was trying to think amid the driving lust and self-loathing that clouded his mind. The ritual was complete now, but his brothers had no knowledge of where he'd taken her. If he could keep her safe until the new moon passed, then his purpose would still be served.

"Marius," Alexandra spoke quietly. "What's wrong?"

He looked at her. So beautiful she was. Her eyes were imploring, beckoning him to finish what he'd begun. He drew out of her slightly and was rewarded with a tiny gasp. Beneath him, Alexandra arched off the bed and her fingers trailed across his back.

Pacing himself, Marius began a steady thrusting, his hands still clenching her firm backside. He closed his eyes, trying desperately to control himself. She felt so tight and soft around him, her smooth thighs splayed beneath him, her round, full breasts rising and falling against his chest.

His control fled then and like a man starved, he thrust into her. Her hips began to move, synchronizing his actions.

Harder and faster and deeper he ground himself into her, driving them both toward desperation. Slender fingers clawed at his back and her body began to tremble. A moment later she cried out in ecstasy as she shuddered with an intense climax.

Marius followed suit. He plunged into her one last time before flooding her with his hot seed. He collapsed onto her and in one swift movement, rolled onto his back, bringing her with him.

One large hand caressed the silken skin along her spine. In the dim light from the candles, he looked at her. Her head lay peacefully near his heart and her long, inky mane splayed over them. Her lips were swollen and her gentle breathing stirred the hairs on his chest. She was so perfect. He would not stop until he found another way to break the curse, and until then he would be damned if he allowed harm to befall her.

Chapter 15

Some time later Alexandra stirred. A comforting warmth hung over her and her entire body ached, but, oh, such a sweet pain it was. It had been raining. She could hear the gentle rumble of thunder outside, and the air was cool and scented. She inhaled deeply, drawing its fragrance into her lungs. Another scent was mingled with it, too, the heady scent of masculinity.

Her head lifted as she was brought abruptly to the present. As her eyes adjusted to the dimness, she gazed at the man beneath her. *Marius*. She'd slept by his side, and even now he held her close. His breathing was silent and even in sleep.

With cautious movements, she sat up and her body mourned as his heat left it. She looked at the window and could see slivers of light peeking in around the edges of the board. She decided she should try texting April. She needed to let everyone know that she was okay.

She crawled away from him and on her hands and knees, bent over the side of the bed in an effort to reach her phone on the desk. She grabbed it and was about to sit up, but a firm hand on her backside held her in place.

"It's generous of you to offer yourself to me this way." Marius's fingers slipped along the folds of her exposed womanhood. "Had I known you were so insatiable I would have paid more attention to you during the night." His mouth fell to her softness and he pressed a gentle kiss there.

Alexandra bit her lip to suppress a moan as a large finger eased into her, testing her and she trembled.

"Do you know how many nights I have dreamed of this?" he asked in a husky whisper. "Long have I entertained thoughts of holding you in my arms, kissing you and loving you."

Her eyes fluttered closed. Nothing had ever felt so good. And as he positioned himself behind her and their bodies joined to become one again, exhilaration overtook her and the pleasure that ensued was limitless.

When Alexandra awoke a second time, it was to the sound of birds singing. She looked for Marius, but found herself alone. Lying next to her in his place was a sheet of paper. She picked it up. It was a brief message, saying that Marius had gone to the city to consult a reputable witch and that he would return to Alexandra before sunset.

She sat up and looked for her phone. She didn't intend to be there when he got back. Now that she was thinking with her brain again and not the very tender place between her legs, she was questioning whether Marius could be trusted or not. She wasn't just going to sit and wait for him to decide where his loyalties lay. She also needed to know if the authorities had checked out the lead she'd given to April to pass along. Every moment wasted brought a little girl closer to death. Alexandra had made a promise to Mady's family and she intended to keep it.

She spotted her phone lying on the floor where it had been dropped haphazardly when Marius had pulled her back into bed with him. She picked it up and pressed the power button. She nearly squealed when the lavender light chimed on. It seemed the water damage hadn't been bad enough to break the phone. Accessing the menu, she tried to call April. There was a beep, and a *no service* message flashed on the screen.

"Shoot." She frowned. She needed reception.

She slid out of bed and slipped on her bra then her dress. Her panty was of no use to her anymore as it had been torn from her body. With a flush of embarrassment, she stuffed the bit of red lace into her pocket and looked around the room.

She found a box on the desk, filled with food and water—enough for several days. How long did he intend to keep her here?

Alexandra left the room and headed down the stairs. The church looked even older now than before. Dust and spiderwebs covered everything, and a flock of pigeons watched her from the rafters, cooing and fluttering among themselves.

The large wooden door at the rear was the only exit. She tried one of the rusting handles and the door squeaked open, flooding the room with bright sunlight and a much needed gust of fresh air. Five wide concrete steps led down into a muddy clearing that was surrounded by tall pines and thick bushes. To the left she noted a bramble-infested path. It wasn't wide enough to allow passage to a vehicle, but she was certain she could scramble through it without becoming entangled. And even if she did, it was certainly worth the effort, for the path might very well lead to civilization.

She was sure that by this time last night's mayhem was plastered on the front page of every newspaper in the country. That, and her mysterious disappearance.

She pulled out her phone as she headed up the path and attempted the number again—still no reception. Clearly Marius had been telling the truth—she was miles and miles from anywhere.

She was at the end of the trail and of her rope when she came to an abandoned gas station that sat on the side of a dirt road. She looked in both directions and could see nothing. Cautiously, she approached. There was a sign swinging from a pole.

Bob's Service Station.

There was a phone number at the bottom, too. That was an indication that there was possibly reception there. She pulled out her phone again and accessed April's number. When it began ringing, she squeaked.

"Hello?" April answered.

"April, it's me! It's Alexandra! I'm alive and I'm okay. How are you?"

"I'm fine. Where are you?" she asked.

Alexandra looked around. "At some old service station on a dirt road. I really don't know. I walked here from an abandoned church."

"How did you get there?"

"Marius. He brought me to some abandoned church near here, but he hasn't hurt me. I just need to get away from this place."

Her friend was silent for a moment. "Where is he now?"

Alexandra spotted a street sign lying near the side of the road and she walked toward it. "He went back to the city. Hey, I think I'm on Route 67 North. I'm reading a road sign I just found."

"Near an old service station, you said?"

"Yes. Bob's Service Station. Please find a way to get me out of here."

"I think I know where you are," April said. "Listen, go back to the church for now and I'll meet you at the service station tomorrow at this time, okay?"

"Tomorrow! April, I can't spend another night out here. I need to get back to the city," she complained.

"Listen, please, just do what I say," April told her. "Stay put and you'll be fine. I'll take care of everything on this end." The line went dead.

Alexandra frowned. "Hello? Hello?" She sighed. "I can't believe she hung up on me."

She looked at her watch with a groan. Tomorrow was hours away. And so was Marius, she remembered. She crossed the vacant road and hurried back down the bushy trail.

Thunder rumbled and the rain fell hard. Marius looked up at the sky—it was going to be an all-nighter again.

He stood at the rear of the church under a dilapidated porch that overlooked a yard thick with hedges. He'd returned from the city a few minutes ago and had been surprised to find Alexandra missing. A search had revealed that she was actually taking a shower in the rain out back. He'd watched as she'd stripped off her clothes, pulled her watch from her wrist and maneuvered her way over the small patches of grass.

During the course of the day, he'd replayed the events of the night over and over in his mind. Amid all the chaos and aggression, the look that she'd bestowed upon him after he'd told her the truth tormented him the most. The pain in her eyes had been palpable.

The rain continued to fall and he remembered the items he was carrying. He moved along the long porch until he had a clear view of Alexandra as she washed herself. Her attention snapped toward him and she looked as if she would scream. Instead, she raced behind a tall hedge and fixed him with a perplexed look.

"You're back! What are you doing here so early? It's not even near sunset!"

He moved forward until he stood at the rail. "It's only moments from sunset," he informed her.

"It's only about three-thirty," she countered.

He looked at her watch. "Your watched has stopped. It's 6:10."

He watched as she squirmed uncomfortably behind the bush. To think that after a night of lovemaking she would be so shy with him. A smile tugged at the corner of his mouth—that was all a part of her charm.

"Continue your bath. I brought you some things." He lifted a plastic bag for her to see.

"What are they?" She was starting to shiver from standing in the rain so long.

"Toiletries. I know these accommodations are not the best, but it was the only place I could think of at the time. I've rented a small cabin for us a few miles from here. After you're done, we'll go there."

"No!" she said quickly. "I don't want to leave. I want to stay here."

His eyes narrowed a measure. "You want to stay here? Are you certain? The place I rented has running water, a stove—"

"I feel safer here," she interrupted.

He was silent for a moment then shrugged. "As you wish." He moved down the stairs with the plastic bag of items.

Her eyes widened. "What are you doing?"

He paused and regarded her with amusement. "I am bringing you your toiletries."

She reached a hand over the hedge. "Throw them."

Marius ignored her request. He'd already seen and tasted every silken inch of her. He felt safe to assume that there remained no secrets. The rain soaked his hair and his clothing as he approached and he laughed when she pinned him with a disapproving scowl. Stopping right in front of her with only the sparse vegetation between them, he reached into the bag and handed her the shower gel.

"Thank you." She accepted it.

Next he handed her a fluffy green loofah with a little stuffed animal attached. She laughed and looked closer at the spotted frog.

"Uh, this is interesting," she commented with a teasing smile.

Marius inclined his head in a slight nod. "It was the last one they had." He backed away under a nearby tree to provide her some semblance of privacy.

Alexandra squirted a glob of gel onto the loofah and began washing herself. "What did the witch tell you?" she asked.

His humor faded and he shook his head. "Let's just say she was of no help. Today's witch-craft is not the same as the practiced sorcery of Necesar's time. Tomorrow I will go to my mother. Hundreds of years ago, when my family was first afflicted, she went to every reputable sorceress and wizard in an attempt to find a cure. She must have learned something from them."

A look of guilt crept over her face. "Why did my ancestor curse your family?" she asked.

Marius sighed. "It was before my time so I only

know what my parents have told me. My father was betrothed to Necesar's cousin, but he broke off the engagement to marry my mother. My mother was only the daughter of a poor farmer, yet my father loved her with all his heart, as he does even to this day. In a fit of rage, the woman burned her castle to the ground and her entire family perished inside with her."

Alexandra was in the process of washing her hair and she paused, her face ashen. Marius noted her expression and he pushed away from the tree, a look of concern on his face. "What is it?"

"Is your father's name Victor?" She met his stare.

He nodded slowly. "It is. How do you know?"

"I dreamt it," she told him. "All my life I've had the same dream, always with the castle and the flames. I was always looking on, always trying to stop her from killing herself."

"Your dreams are memories, Alexandra." He was trying to read her expression when he experienced a sudden searing ache in his joints and his muscles began to tense.

It was time. He didn't want Alexandra to see him release the dark creature that lurked within him, but it was too late. The transformation had already begun. He had just enough time to strip off his coat before his knees weakened and he collapsed to the ground.

Alexandra raced to his side. "Marius, what's wrong?" She looked him over frantically.

The thick muscles of his back expanded and tore at the shoulder blades. Marius gritted his teeth as he felt his skull splitting and two horns pushed through. Still on his knees, he fell forward and clenched his fists in the earth as his muscles bulged and thickened. His jaw bone was aflame with an excruciating pain and his teeth lengthened into jagged fangs. A roughened tongue snaked out, hindering the scream that lingered in his throat and he arched his back upward as his flesh was ripped open and two colossal wings spread out.

When the pounding in his head stopped, Marius looked up and fought to catch his breath. His long hair had grown at least five inches and fell forward in a thick, dark curtain. Slowly, he drank up the lovely vision of nakedness before him. The rain continued to pour over her, plastering her hair to her body like a shawl of shimmering silk. The cool rain must have given her a chill for her nipples were taut, standing erect, beckoning his mouth nearer. His lustful gaze dipped and raked over her flat abdomen, the soft place between her thighs and her long, slender legs. A growl escaped him.

Alexandra looked as if she would run if she could, but his eyes held her in place. She swallowed as he stood. Marius flexed the thick muscles of his neck. He could read the desire in her eyes and hear the throbbing of her heart. She wanted him. This surprised him as he'd thought that she would fear his gargoyle form more than anything. The knowledge that she was aroused by him heightened his craving for her and he advanced.

Alexandra started to retreat, but didn't get very far. One large arm encircled her waist and seized her. She didn't struggle, but gazed up at him and waited for his next move.

Marius emitted another growl as his lips descended on her mouth in a crushing kiss. She wrapped her arms tightly around his neck and welcomed it. His large hands moved down to her backside and he pressed her suggestively against him. His conscience screamed at him— she was forbidden! He'd already gone too far with her, but he wanted her fiercely and there was no denying it. He swept her off her feet and marched toward the door.

They didn't even make it to the bed. Once inside, Marius pinned her to the wall, lifted her high and buried his face between her legs. His tongue found her tight opening and surged into her.

Alexandra gasped and arched her back away from the wall. Her legs encircled his neck and she began to writhe with the violence of desperate yearning. Her fingers gripped his hair and she pressed his face even deeper into her.

When he'd drunk his fill, Marius slid her down in front of him and freed his pulsing member from his breeches. Alexandra's eyes widened. With his transformation, his erection had increased in both length and width and now pressed firmly against her abdomen. She had only a moment to gaze upon it before he gripped her thighs, splaying them, and then surged up into her with one powerful thrust.

She screamed as he filled her tight passage and her body clenched around him. His mouth had weaved a path down to the curve of her neck and had locked into place. His fangs bit gently into her flesh as he held her still. Impaled on him now, she could do nothing, but succumb to his fierce thrusting.

He pressed deeper into her with each hungry penetration. His grip tightened on her thighs.

A delightful pressure was building within him, preparing for an explosion. The sting of her nails biting into the thick muscles of his back as she trembled with her orgasm drove him even closer. When it came he erupted in a feral growl and pressed deep into her, filling her body, completing them both.

It was dark by the time they found their way to the bed. Marius laid an exhausted Alexandra onto the thick folds of the comforter. Her eyes drifted closed and he drew the covers over her. He sat there watching her in the flickering light of a single candle, reflecting on the weeks that had preceded this moment. It was hard to comprehend the odd feeling that overcame him whenever he was near her. It lingered long after his lust had been sated, and he craved something more, something he couldn't identify.

Standing, he flexed his wings. The night was young and his tortured mind was sure to find no peace. He needed the air. It never failed to clear his head. He would find a way to save her and his family. Leaden strides took him out of the room and onto a rear balcony that overlooked the yard. He gazed up at the waning moon. Majestic it was on this night, casting its silver rays over the tree-tops. He only wished it was a beacon to guide his tortured soul. Great wings spread to their full length and he took flight, beating against the night as if he were trying to extract solutions from its shadow.

Chapter 16

Anger pulsed through her. The three horse-men advanced. Amid the orange haze of the torchlight flashes of a great twisting dragon circled her. A crest. There was danger here. Still, she'd come to fulfill a task and would depart only when it was done—either on foot to descend back into the darkness of the forest from whence she'd come or in spirit, leaving her earthly body to those who despised her.

One of the men dismounted. He was speaking, his teeth bared in a livid snarl. He approached, yet her eyes remained fixed as she spoke. Her words were inaudible, a scared breath escaping her, lifting to the ears of the man who watched her from above. It was he that she loathed. He'd done a great wrong to her, taken away those she loved. And now she'd come to exact vengeance.

The horseman advanced still, his weapon drawn. The steel flashed wickedly beneath the torchlight. And she looked at him. She knew him, could read into his soul. She saw the day of his birth and the day when he would breathe his last. And she knew he was a threat to her. He would be the one to take her life. She wasn't afraid. Her life would go on, her soul would be eternal.

She continued speaking words that would serve justice—that would avenge her loved ones. Then it came. The pain she'd anticipated when she set out to face her enemy. It was piercing, unbearable and she gasped, her eyes riveting to the length of steel that passed through her slender frame. She fell to her knees, fighting for breath, and a calming sensation came over her. Her task was complete— her enemies would suffer a fate far worse than the death they'd so freely administered to her. They'd be damned for all eternity.

The steady beat of her pulse began to slow, thumping in her ears. A figure appeared above her, his face initially obscured by shadow. As he neared, she realized that it was Lord Victor Drakon himself, his face grim and in awe as if he, for one moment, regretted the deeds done. He draped a cloak around her, but it was in vain, for already the chill of death was seeping into her.

He reached for something that hung around her neck; her amulet, she knew. Mustering what little strength remained within her, she snatched his arm, stalling his intent. Within that moment, with her nails biting so deep that they drew blood, she was assailed by a vision.

Vivian stood before Lord Drakon, her face contorted in rage as she spoke. The light from a large fireplace danced over them.

"How dare you disgrace me this way?" Vivian spoke. "What can a poor peasant give you that I cannot?"

In her vision Lord Drakon shook his head. "It is not about social status, Vivian," he told her. "I have said all I need to say and my offer still stands. You will have the money and the land you desire, but I cannot wed you."

"Is it her body?" Vivian screamed, tears gliding down her cheeks now. With angry jerks she began separating the ties of her bodice. "You need not sully yourself with inferior flesh." She yanked her dress open, revealing ample breasts.

Lord Drakon cast his eyes aside. "Cover yourself, woman." He moved to pull her sleeves up, but she thrust him away.

"Get out!" She snatched up a lute that had been leaning against the wall and swung it at him. "Go to your peasant whore, then! Get out!"

Lord Drakon moved back, his brows furrowed in disbelief.

"I said get out!" Vivian screamed again, this time hurling the instrument at him just as he slipped out of the room.

It smashed against the wall, and she sank to her knees, sobbing as she shouted after him. "I will make you rue the day you ever laid eyes upon her!"

As the vision faded, she knew that she had been deceived. Nothing was as it had seemed. The man she'd just cursed was completely without fault.

The world around her began to spin and amid the encroaching darkness, she could see his face. A new anguish assailed her even as her consciousness faded and she joined her kin in the stillness of death.

"What have I done?"

Alexandra awoke with a pained gasp as if she were being born into the world anew. Despite the cool of the darkened room, she was covered in a light film of perspiration. She lay unmoving for a long moment as she dissected her dream. It had been as clear as the summer sky and she understood everything now. Necesar had possessed no evil. She was a healer and her powers had always been used for good. Her only deviation had been to avenge her family. Necesar had also been deceived. Her cousin, in a froth to gain Necesar's compliance, had spun a tale of lies, declaring that Lord Victor Drakon had tricked her into riding with him to inspect his lands. That once they were alone, he'd forced himself upon her. She'd also asserted that the union had brought an unwanted pregnancy upon her. These untruths and the idea that Lord Drakon had sought to marry another woman even after knowing of the child had fueled Necesar's passion for revenge.

It was all clear now. The curse, the burning of

Elburich Castle, the deaths, they'd all been the result of one woman's ruthless jealousy. Lady Vivian Dancescu had been unable to cope with the shame of Lord Drakon's rejection and the fact that he'd chosen a peasant girl. She'd driven herself into insanity.

Alexandra sat up slowly and reached over the mattress next to her. The sheet was cool and had obviously been vacant for some time.

"Marius," she called softly.

The room remained silent. She climbed from the bed and felt in the darkness for something to drape over herself. Her fingers clutched the soft material of Marius's shirt and she pulled it over her head. The garment fell to midthigh and filled her senses with the scent of him.

She opened the door and walked into the dark passage. She started down the stairs, but a dull glow in another doorway caught her attention. She changed direction and walked toward it. She hadn't noticed the room before.

The room was empty except for a few dusty boxes stacked to one side. A set of white paint-chipped French doors opened onto a veranda and the light she'd seen had been from the moon pouring in.

Crossing the vacant expanse, she stepped out onto the balcony and looked around. The trees stood tall and majestic beneath their crowns of silver moonbeams, and the sky was clear and speckled with glinting stars. Not even a trace of a rain cloud remained. In the distance she could see the shimmering stretch of lake. The reflection of the moon danced upon it, making it look as if it had been drizzled with liquid silver.

"Beautiful, isn't it?"

The voice startled her and she spun around. Marius was perched above her on the roof. His wings were folded and he looked as if he'd been enjoying the view himself.

She nodded slowly. "Yes," she breathed and experienced a flush of embarrassment.

The memory of his fierce lovemaking and her shameless abandon was still burned fresh in her mind. Something about him in this form made her blood boil and her body ache. Something lethal and demanding, and when he looked at her the way he did, she felt as if she'd been dipped in hot lava.

Marius eased off the roof, coming to stand before her. "Did you rest well?" he asked.

Her gaze traveled up the length of his large

form. "I had another dream," she told him. "I saw everything, and I know that your family should've never suffered through this."

"What have you seen?"

"The truth." She turned to look out over the forest. "Lady Vivian Dancescu lied to Necesar. She told her that your father had raped her and that she was pregnant. Necesar reacted only according to what she'd been told. Lady Vivian was a jealous woman and she would've gone to any lengths to get revenge, but in the process she wound up going mad. And that's how she killed her family. She burned the entire castle down." When she was finished she looked at him. "You see, none of this should've ever happened."

Marius hung his head as he absorbed this revelation. Guilt and pity enveloped Alexandra. Just the knowledge that Marius would never lead a normal life as long as she lived or multiplied was enough to tear at her heart. His family had been wrongly punished and she had the source of their injustice within her. The blood of both Necesar and Lady Vivian Dancescu ran thick in her veins.

She reached up and placed gentle fingers at the base of a protruding horn. "Does it hurt?"

He looked at her, searching her face. For a

moment she thought he would pull away, but he didn't. "Every time," he responded.

Her fingertips moved down his firm jawline, past the thick muscles of his neck to his broad shoulders. Curious hands stroked the knots of muscle where his wings were attached and she trembled. He was so beautiful and powerful and she was fascinated by him. She could also feel the desperation that plagued him.

"I must tell you something," she said, following a sudden urge to reveal more of herself to him. "I have a gift. I can sometimes perceive the emotions of others by tapping into their energy." She waited for his response, but when he said nothing she continued.

"I can also see things that have occurred, but that talent has been pretty vague until a few weeks ago. It's how I've been tracking Mady," she finished.

She decided to keep the incident of the fire spell she'd cast on his brother to herself. If he thought she possessed Necesar's power, then he might believe she was more than just an innocent descendant of the witch. He might even blame her entirely for all that had happened to his family. That was the last thing she needed, especially considering that she was alone with him in the middle of nowhere.

A look of understanding crossed his face. "I see. And what have you gathered from the matter of this curse?"

Alexandra met his dark eyes. "Oddly, I sense nothing. It's as much a mystery to me as it is to you."

They gazed at each other in silence as if an unspoken understanding was being exchanged. These were perhaps their final moments together. Tomorrow was the last day of the Equinox and neither of them knew what lay beyond it.

With both sadness and desire mingling within her belly, Alexandra closed the distance between them. And on the tips of her toes, she leaned into him, securing her arms around his neck. She pressed her lips against his in a feathery kiss. Marius's arms wrapped around her slim waist, drawing her into him. Their kiss deepened a measure, but retained its tenderness.

When he withdrew to look at her again, a fire blazed in his eyes, deep and consuming. And as he stripped his shirt from her shoulders, she gladly surrendered herself to him.

* * *

Marius stood opposite the desk where his mother sat. He'd managed an audience with her without the knowledge of his father or brothers. At the moment she was the only one he felt he could trust and he was desperate, willing to do anything it took to save Alexandra *and* free his family. He only hoped that his mother would see past his wrongs and help him.

Lady Amelia had been staring out the front window as he'd made his plea. Now she turned to face him. She looked radiant in an elegant, pearl-colored skirt suit and diamond accessories.

She watched him intently. "So you say you are protecting this girl? Have you completed the ritual?"

His head fell a measure. "I have."

"And do you believe that she is worth betraying your family for?"

His jaw tensed. "I did not betray you, Mother, just as Father did not betray Lady Vivian centuries ago. Such feelings cannot be measured or controlled. The way I feel was not conspired."

"And what are these feelings that have brought you to this state? How do you know that she has not bewitched you?" Her brows rose as she waited for his response.

He shook his head vehemently. "No, Mother. Alexandra is not like that. She is pure and kind. I wish you would understand that. She is the Descendant, but she is not the witch that cursed our family and she should not suffer for crimes she did not commit."

Lady Amelia moved toward the sofa and picked up a book she'd been reading. "Is that so? Do you know that your brother Nicholas was wounded by her? She cast a spell in his presence, one that only a powerful and well-practiced witch could be expected to conjure." She walked toward the tall bookcase that lined the entire left wall and slipped the text onto a middle shelf.

Marius's heavy brows drew together in confusion. Alexandra had not mentioned anything about casting a spell to him, nor had he witnessed her practicing any sorcery.

"He lies, Mother!" he accused. "She has the gift of sight and nothing more."

She turned to face him, her look admonishing. "You know your brother. Has he ever lied to you or to any of us?" When he didn't respond, she continued. "I beseech you, think this over,

Marius. When the sun rises again it will be too late to remedy this. And the woman you're trying so desperately to save will be no more."

"There is nothing to think about. I came here seeking your help in finding another way to break the curse and that is all. If you cannot help me then I will leave."

Their gazes locked and a silence lapsed between them. Marius had expected her to understand if no one else did. He'd always been able to rely upon her for advice or aid in solving problems. It seemed things had changed. Through the window behind her, he could see the soft streaks of evening color manifesting in the sky. There was no hope and time had all but run out. He would return to the church and reveal the entire truth to Alexandra. He only hoped that she had the strength to resist the evil that would consume her when the sun rose again.

With a deep sigh, Marius picked up his coat and headed toward the door.

Quickly, his mother stepped forward, her eyes hesitant. "Wait," she called out to him.

His hand was already on the doorknob. He looked at her.

Lady Amelia sank slowly to the edge of the

couch. "There is another way," she breathed softly.

Marius turned toward her, yet remained silent. His expression was impassive, but his heart was racing. He waited for her to continue.

She inhaled, her gaze lifting to the painting above the mantelpiece. "A few years before you were born, your father and I tried everything in our power to find a spell to counter the one Necesar placed upon us. We went to every sorcerer and witch and discovered that there was one other option. An old witch in the Netherlands told us that any curse can be broken by reversing the initiating factors."

"What does that mean?" he asked in confusion.

She looked at him. "Our family's curse is one crafted from passion, love and shame. There has to be a union between the two parties, and this shall dissipate the spell."

Marius took a step closer, his mind racing. It all sounded simple enough. "What kind of union?" he asked.

She shrugged. "I do not know. Your father and I never considered this as an option and so we never explored it. I would never release him to another woman, most especially not a Dancescu.

And it was hardly expected that any of you would take an enemy for a bride."

"So we must be wed?" he asked with some reservation.

Marriage was something he'd never considered, but if he ever decided to bind himself into a relationship, he would prefer to share a love that resembled that of his parents. He cared for Alexandra's safety and there was no denying that he desired her body, but he didn't love her. Yet he was willing to make the sacrifice to save them all from damnation. Especially if the only other alternative was killing her.

"It could be likely," his mother replied. "Marriage in that time was considered holy and pure, the foremost method of joining any two houses." Hooded eyes narrowed on him. "But, let me ask you this—have you taken her to your bed?"

He didn't answer at first. Sex was hardly the topic any man, regardless of his age, wanted to discuss with his mother. Yet there was no time for uneasiness. If there was a way to break the curse then he was willing to reveal whatever was necessary.

He nodded. "I have."

"Hmm. Then I suppose marriage is the joining

that is necessary." She stood and approached him, taking his hands within her own. "My son, is this something you are willing to go through with? Are you prepared to wed this girl, our enemy, just to spare her life?"

He squeezed her hands. "Yes. If Alexandra agrees, then I will. There is no other choice."

"Do not make me regret revealing this to you," she said with shimmering eyes.

Marius shook his head. "I promise you will not."

She nodded and smiled, a soft and sentimental expression that never failed to calm him. "Tell me more about her," she requested with an air of acquiescence.

Marius delved into his thoughts to find the words to describe Alexandra. He went to the window and peered out. "Her name, as you know, is Alexandra. She is smart and brave. She is also very kindhearted and selfless." He turned to her then. "You would love her, Mother. She is so gentle and caring. She could never hurt a soul."

Lady Amelia smiled wanly. "She must be very special if she drives my son to such lengths to see her unharmed." Her eyes narrowed on him again. "Marius, do you love this girl?"

His brows drew together in a slow frown. Again he told himself that it was his ravenous craving for her body and his appreciation of her gentle personality that had forced him to such a state. Yet, deep within himself, he knew that more reason lay behind his decisions. Only, he didn't know what to call it.

"I am concerned for her. That is all," he said at last.

She accepted his response with a curious expression. "I only wish you had come to me sooner. There is so little time now, but if we hurry we can try to make things right." She went behind the desk and took a seat.

"I have a few loyal friends within the country that I can call upon in such a time of need." And she picked up the receiver of the brass Victorian phone that sat on the desk.

Chapter 17

Patience wasn't one of Alexandra's best virtues. She paced around the service station, checking her watch every few minutes. Marius had been right, the thing had stopped working, but she checked it anyway. She'd tried calling April several times already and had gotten only a busy signal. She was getting anxious now.

Ever since Marius had left her that morning, she'd been plagued by an unsettling feeling. Something, and she wasn't sure what, was deadly wrong. The speculation was driving her insane. Could Marius have changed his mind about sparing her life? Would he return with his brothers? Or had something happened to Mady?

Her fingers strayed to the charm bracelet on her wrist and she thought of Mady. Was the girl still alive? Suddenly a blinding light seemed to flash before her eyes. She froze, uncertain of what to expect but knowing that her abilities were in gear. She watched as an image of Mady formed before her. Huddled on a dirty mattress on the floor, the child appeared to be sleeping. A tall shadow loomed above her, the menacing figure partially obscured by darkness.

The phone rang, jarring Alexandra out of her trancelike state. She gasped and leaned against a wall for support. She'd never been able to summon a vision before. It seemed her gift was getting stronger.

He phone continued ringing and with a shaking hand, she answered it. "Hello?"

"It's April."

She exhaled a deep sigh of relief. "Thank goodness. I need to get out of here right now."

"I'll be there in a few minutes. Is Marius with you?"

"No."

"Okay. Wait for me."

April hung up and Alexandra continued pacing. Soon a black Jaguar slid to a stop a few feet away. A rear door opened, and April stepped out.

Alexandra hurried toward her. "I'm so happy

to see you," she said with relief. "We need to get back to the city."

April paused, a strange look on her face.

Alexandra embraced her tightly. "I knew I could count on you. How long will it take to get back to the city?" She looked at April and her smile faded. "What's wrong?"

It was obvious that April had been crying. Her pretty face was streaked with tears and she was wearing no makeup. Not even lip gloss, and that was highly unusual.

"I'm so sorry," she whispered.

Alexandra frowned in confusion. "Sorry? What for? What's wrong, April? Talk to me."

April's eyes fixed on the sleek black Jaguar. The engine was running, but the windows were tinted, obscuring her view inside.

Alexandra peered at the car. "Who's with you? Whose car is that?"

"I'm sorry," April said again.

At that moment, the two front doors opened and two men stepped out. They were both tall and beautiful—dark hair and swarthy skin. They wore sunglasses that shielded their eyes, yet they seemed familiar to her.

"Who are they?" She didn't need a response when her eyes dropped to the heavy black boots one of them wore. The spikes that encircled the ankles flashed wickedly in the sunlight and she knew that the men were Marius's brothers—the gargoyles who'd tried to kill her and who were probably going to kill them both right now.

Panic surged through her. She wasn't about to die, not now and definitely not by their hands. If they wanted her they were going to have to catch her!

"Run!" she screamed as she grabbed April's hand and headed toward the back of the gas station.

She heard the car engine shut off and the doors slam, then the heavy thud of approaching footfalls. She and April plunged into the woods, ducking to avoid the low-hanging limbs that barred their way. Alexandra's heart was racing and she could hear April's frantic breathing behind her. The smells of moist earth and vegetation were thick in the air and filled her lungs with each inhalation. Leafless arms snaked out to scrape at their exposed flesh, but they continued running.

It wasn't long before the ground began to angle downward and the thick mud at their feet caused them to slip. They screamed as they went toppling down the slope, snapping extended branches and slamming into tree trunks. Their rapid free fall came to an end when they landed in a narrow stream at the base of the slanting hill.

Alexandra was on her feet immediately and urging April to do the same. "C'mon, get up! We have to keep going!" she said in an urgent whisper and cast a look behind them.

There was no sign of the two men, but Alexandra knew they couldn't be far behind. The memory of the chase through her apartment building was still fresh and she didn't think the absence of wings diminished their strength or speed by any significant measure.

April scrambled to her feet and they picked their way across the stream. On the other side the ground was level and the area was covered with a thin scattering of tall pines. Alexandra knew that they would surely be spotted if they didn't find a place to conceal themselves. Then again, she wasn't so sure hiding was in their best interest, either. The gargoyles had exhibited a frightening ability to sense her, and it was possible that it remained with them even while they were human. They had to keep moving no matter what.

The trees thickened again and they still found themselves alone in the woods. April collapsed against a tree, using it to hold herself upright as she gasped for breath.

"Alexandra, I can't go on," she panted.

Alexandra, who was also tipping over from exhaustion, stopped and leaned against a tree. She bent over as she tried to steady her breathing. "How did they find you?"

"They must've followed me that night. When I got home one of them had broken into my apartment and was waiting for me," she said. "I'm so sorry. I didn't have a choice. He said he was going to kill me."

"It's all right. Anyone would've done the same thing in that situation. The important thing is that we got away. Do you know Detective Beckford's number? We need help." She pulled out her cell phone.

April nodded. "I have it memorized." She smiled briefly, looking like her usual self in that instant.

Alexandra passed the phone to her. "Call him and tell him where we are. He should be able to initiate a search for us."

Her friend accepted the phone and began dialing the number. Alexandra took a moment to scope the area for any signs of the brothers. She exhaled a shuddering breath when she was met only by the chirping of birds and the buzzing of insects. The men had definitely been left far behind, but she wasn't taking any chances. They had to get out of there.

Behind her, April was relaying the events of her kidnapping and the unceremonious chase through the woods. When Alexandra turned around, her friend was motioning for her to join her. As she hurried toward April, she realized that the woods ended and a paved highway was visible from where they stood.

They began weaving their way through the woods until they wound up at the edge of the road in waist-high grass.

April repeated the number of the highway over the phone then hung up. "He's sending help."

"Did he say how long it might take?"

"No, but he said to stay put and he'll be here. I also gave him the license plate on that car." She returned the phone to Alexandra. "By the way, I convinced him to check out that address you gave me. Tyrese got a warrant and searched the apartment. The rent was paid up until the end of the month, but the place was completely cleaned out."

Alexandra frowned at her. "They found nothing at all?"

April didn't have a chance to respond. She spotted a vehicle moving quickly along the highway and she grabbed Alexandra's arm, stalling her. "Look!"

Alexandra could see a car approaching in the distance. Her heart began to thump in her chest. "Get down." They crouched in the grass.

"What if it's not them?"

"What if it is?" She peeked over the top of the grass.

As the vehicle got closer, it slowed and came to a stop. Alexandra ducked low, her heart racing. She looked at April and nodded. Had they been spotted?

The sound of a door slamming made her jerk. She and April were near enough to smell the exhaust from the engine and she spied through the grass to see one brother gazing around. He inhaled and said something to the other, who grinned and pulled a gun from his waistband.

The first brother took a step forward. "Show yourself, Descendant!" he shouted. "I can smell your fear!"

Alexandra lowered her head and met April's

terrified gaze. Together they remained perfectly still and listened as the sound of approaching steps grew louder.

He continued speaking. "You did not think you could get away from us, did you? We have a special evening planned for you."

There was a clicking noise, followed by the soft tunes of cell phone buttons being pressed. April's brows snapped together and she frantically patted her pockets. She met Alexandra's questioning look and mouthed the words *Turn off your phone.* Alexandra quickly dug into her pocket and pulled out the item, but it was too late. The popular R & B song she'd set as her ring tone began to play.

Heavy steps moved toward them and in the next moment they were staring into the barrel of a revolver. Marius's brother smiled and jerked his head toward the road.

"Move it!"

With their hands up, the women stood slowly. Although he looked nothing like the gargoyles that had attacked her, Alexandra knew he was the one whom she'd cast the fire spell on. It was the intensity of his stare and the cautious way he watched her for any deviant actions. She wondered if he had just reason to be wary of her. Could she perform another spell?

He nodded toward the highway again. "I said, move it!" He snatched Alexandra's phone from her hand and stuffed it into his pocket. "I'll take that."

They stumbled through the tall grass toward the second brother, who was waiting calmly near the Jaguar holding April's phone. When they got near enough he tossed the phone to his brother.

"Secure that, Nicholas. We may have use for it again," he said as he looked Alexandra over for the first time. So this was Simion.

Nicholas complied, stuffing it into his jacket. Then, with the gun still pointed at their heads, he motioned for Alexandra and April to get into the car. April slipped into the backseat and Alexandra was about to follow, but Nicholas gripped her arm, stalling her effort.

He lowered his head so that his lips brushed the soft place behind her ear. "Do you think that it was your fragrance that lured me to you?" He inhaled softly. "No, it was the scent of my brother. I can smell him all over you. Where is he?"

She wrenched her arm from his grasp and sent him a defiant glare. "I'd rather be burned at the stake before I tell you," she gritted out before climbing into the car.

The door shut behind her, muffling his laugh.

They drove for nearly an hour, racing along the winding highway. The sleek Jaguar purred; it ran smooth as the wind, conforming to every bend in the road. Alexandra remained silent. She was busy trying to harness the power that she guessed lurked somewhere within her. The only problem was, she didn't know how.

When she was about to go out of her mind, the car began to slow and she realized that they were pulling into a long driveway. A mansion sat at the other end, bathed in the saffron glow of the twilight. They circled the driveway and the car skidded to a stop. Simion stepped out and was greeted by an old butler. He whispered something to the man, who glanced at the car before hurrying back inside.

Nicholas joined his brother and they began talking. Alexandra turned to April, who was trying to pull up the lock on her door.

She slammed a shoulder against it, but it didn't budge. "We have to get out of here! They're planning to kill us!"

Alexandra gripped her shoulders and gave her a

shake. "That won't do us any good! We're locked in. Just try to stay calm."

The door on Alexandra's side swung open then and Nicholas looked in. "There is someone who is dying to meet you. It is not wise to keep him waiting." He stepped aside.

They climbed out of the backseat and Alexandra realized that they were alone with Marius's brother in the driveway. She exchanged a look with April. Was there a chance for an escape?

As if reading their thoughts, the tall man pulled out his revolver. "Think carefully before you act. It would be a pity if I had to kill you before everyone arrived. Move, now!"

They were ushered into an elegant foyer that reminded Alexandra of one of the five-star hotels she'd stayed in with her parents. The stairway was no less grand. With its mahogany banister and polished marble steps, it could have been taken right out of the Mandarin Hotel.

Simion appeared again and whispered something to Nicholas. Nicholas's eyes narrowed, and he looked at Alexandra.

"Come with me," he said, and he took her by the arm.

April reached for her. "No!"

Simion pulled April in the other direction. Alexandra looked back to see her friend being dragged into a room at the end of the hall. Her trepidation rose a few notches and she wondered what would become of her friend. The gargoyles didn't want April. They wanted her.

She looked at her captor. "Please, you have to let her go. She hasn't done anything," she pleaded.

Nicholas continued to lead her up the stairway silently. When they finally mounted the last stair, he dragged her toward a set of tall wooden doors and swung one side open.

"His lordship awaits," he said with a mocking bow.

She swallowed. She assumed he was referring to his father, Lord Victor Drakon. And if Victor Drakon was anything like his two eldest sons, then she had everything to worry about. She tried to maintain her calm. She had to convince him that there was another way to break the curse—she would try to use Necesar's power to reverse the wrong that was done.

Slowly, she entered and the door closed behind her. The room was a large office with tall windows and a fireplace. A heavy desk faced her and a floor lamp glowed in one corner.

The chair behind the desk moved slightly. It was turned away facing one of the windows, showing only the top of what must be a large man's head silhouetted in the light.

"Five hundred years ago a young man found love," came a deep male voice. "It was rare in those days to wed a woman because she held your heart. Instead, an heir to a title was expected to fulfill his duty to his family and to his people. The consequence of neglecting this duty was often being disinherited by one's family. A fair enough punishment, for sometimes a man is expected to make choices. But, should a man and his entire house be expected to suffer for centuries for such a simple folly?"

The chair swiveled around and a man who appeared to be in his mid-fifties looked at her. Alexandra knew better. If he was indeed Marius's father, he'd be well over five hundred years old. He stood and ambled around the desk. He was tall, perhaps an inch or so shorter than Marius. His hair was heavily streaked with gray and he was dressed in a beautiful brocade coat that fell a little past his knees. The dark emerald made him look regal, like a king from a time long ago. A layer of white ruffles was visible near his neck-line and at his wrists.

"My family has lived long and hard, and now it is finally time for retribution," he continued. He looked her over as he approached. "Your ancestor's dark sorcery has plagued my family for too long. It is time to put an end to it."

Alexandra didn't think it fair that she was being blamed for a crime she hadn't committed—a crime that had occurred five hundred years before her own birth. Her fists curled at her sides and her shoulders squared with determination. "I'm not Necesar, and I'm not a witch," she told him firmly.

He continued toward her. "You would not understand, child. Her magic lurks within you."

When he stood a few feet away, he paused, his eyes appraising. Alexandra did some assessing of her own. He was handsome, much like all the Drakon men she'd had the misfortune of meeting, except Marius, of course. His features were stern, yet his spirit lacked the fire and brimstone that Simion and Nicholas had displayed without reserve. He looked like a grandfather who was ready for retirement, done with the hassles of the world. Alexandra wondered if she could use this apparent weakness to her advantage, if only to reason with him.

"You're right," she admitted. "I don't understand, and yes, her magic is within me. It has manifested before."

"So my son tells me." His gaze narrowed on her.

She took a step closer. "I believe I can harness her power again and break the curse she cast on your family. If you'd only give me some time, I believe I can end all of this."

He focused on her face. "Somehow you have managed to soften the heart of my youngest. He has never loved before you, did you know? I suspected as much the day he came here with no logical excuse for wanting to spare your life. He had been given four weeks, and all he could say was that you were an innocent. But then, weren't we all." He sighed.

Alexandra blinked in surprise. Love? Was his father kidding? Could Marius actually hold such feelings for her?

"Nevertheless," Lord Drakon continued. "I think that now I am free to assume that his feelings are not due to witchcraft. The tenderness in your eyes cannot be feigned. Sadly though, time is something we do not have." He turned his head to look through a window.

The sky was overcast with the colors of sunset. Alexandra knew that he was only moments from becoming a gargoyle. They all were. She also knew that these were their last moments as humans for the next one hundred years—unless she was killed. Trying to reason with him was hopeless. Her only option was to try to harness her powers to escape, but she wasn't going to beg for her life. If she was to die then she would have it said that the last of the Dancescu bloodline was brave and died with honor.

Her chin went up a notch and she restrained the tears that were threatening to spill. "And what about my friend? What will happen to her?"

His attention left the window. "You need not concern yourself about her. We are not bad people, only long-suffering."

"You consider killing innocent people a good deed, then?" she asked with contained anger.

Lord Drakon's head lifted and a dangerous glint that hadn't been there before sparked in his emerald pools. "There is something you must understand. We are all innocent in this game. Your ancestor placed a curse upon me and my entire house because of her jealous and deceitful cousin.

I am an honest and just man, and I put my family before even myself. Everything I have done and will do is for them. Marius does not understand this yet, but he will. Something has to be sacrificed, and I do believe that my family has filled that role for far too long."

He moved to tower above her. "Ah, so defiant. I see now that my son failed to enlighten you of your own fate. This equinox marks the final season for Necesar's soul to dwell within you. At its end your body will become the vessel for another entity—her wicked cousin, Lady Vivian, whose spirit I am sure will not rest until she rains destruction upon us all. You should be grateful to die with both your consciousness and sanity intact."

Without another word, he walked around her and left the room. There was a clicking sound once the door was shut. Alexandra remained as she was, trying to absorb all she'd been told. As if learning that she was an ancient witch incarnate hadn't been enough, now she had to digest the fact that within a few hours she'd either be dead or in dire need of an exorcist. An unsteady weakness came over her and she sagged to her knees. With her head hanging low, she tried to search the magic within her for a solution.

Chapter 18

Marius watched impatiently as his mother hung up the phone. She'd been speaking with the arch-diocese of the Wessex Parish, a devoted acquaintance who'd agreed to assist her without question. Marius had until morning to propose the idea of marriage to Alexandra and should she agree, take her to the priest who would perform a ceremony to bind them as husband and wife. It was his last hope to save Alexandra and erase his family's curse.

Lady Amelia stood and moved toward him. "Marius, the sun will be setting soon. Go quickly and take my blessings with you. Father Paul will be waiting for you in the steeple of the parish. I explained everything to him and he knows that I urgently need his help." She slipped a ring from her finger and placed it in his palm. "Give this to your bride."

Accepting the ring, Marius ran his fingers over the intricate carving in gold. It was her wedding ring, he knew. He looked at her, his eyes reflecting his appreciation. "And what of Father? How will you explain what you have done for me?" he asked, sounding weary.

She smiled up at him, a gesture that he guessed took more effort than it should. "You leave your father to me. I will speak to him of our plans and try to make him understand," she promised.

"And if he does not?"

"Then it will be too late for him to intervene and he will have to accept it. Now go, my son. Your lady is waiting."

Marius nodded. As he turned to leave, the door swung open and his brothers sauntered in.

Simion regarded him with resentment. "Well, well. It seems the traitor has returned to the fold," he said coldly.

Marius slipped the ring into the pocket of his coat. "I am leaving now. Get out of my way." He moved to walk around them, but Nicholas sidestepped to block his way.

"Not so fast, brother. Are you rushing off to

see your little witch? Well, you will be pleased to know that Simion and I have taken the liberty of bringing her here for you."

Marius's jaw clenched. Surely his brother was lying. Alexandra couldn't be at the mansion. There was no way they could have found her at the church!

At his dubious expression, Nicholas pulled out a small lavender, rhinestone-encrusted cell phone. "We got her cute little friend, too. I think I might just keep that one for myself when this is all over. I cannot allow you to have all the fun."

His brother was referring to April. In that instant, Marius knew that Nicholas spoke the truth. Somehow he and Simion had discovered the sanctuary and taken Alexandra and April prisoner. A deep, seething rage quickly filtered through every fiber of his being and a growl erupted from the pit of his belly like boiling lava from a volcano that had been dormant too long.

He gripped Nicholas by the collar of his jacket and slammed him into the wall. Several books fell off the shelves and a framed picture hanging near the door smashed to the ground.

"For your own sake, brother, she had better be unharmed," Marius snarled.

Simion didn't hesitate to join the scuffle. He gripped Marius from the back, wrenching him off the other man.

It was then that their mother slammed a fist on the desk. "Stop this!" she demanded.

Simion turned to face her with a struggling Marius in his grip. "Ah, Mother. I do apologize. We did not see you there."

Lady Amelia stood slowly, her silver eyes flaring. "Release him," she said sternly.

Simion held Marius for a moment longer before shoving him aside. Marius turned and plunged a fist into his midsection. Simion doubled over and his jaw met Marius's knee as he brought it up in an angry thrust.

"Marius!" Lady Amelia shouted.

He was on his knees, preparing to administer another punch, when Nicholas's steel grip clamped onto his wrist.

"That is enough!" Nicholas growled.

Marius experienced a moment of shame and hung his head. Ever since they were children, he and his brothers had forged their own methods of managing situations, and that usually resulted in violence. Their mother had tried relentlessly to mold their temperaments, to tame the savage nature of the beasts that were a part of them. She'd failed terribly.

Lady Amelia circled the desk and regarded them with dissatisfaction. "What is wrong with you? You are of the same flesh and blood and yet you fight among yourselves like animals!"

Simion stood and wiped a trickle of blood from his mouth with his sleeve. "We have been raised to protect our family at all costs! That strength is what binds us and makes our fortress impenetrable. And when one of us falters, he weakens us all." He looked pointedly to Marius.

She stepped forward. "I also taught you to support your brothers, to stand beside them. They are your blood and your family," she stated. "If there ever was a time that your brother needs you, it is now."

Nicholas laughed in disbelief. "Mother, how can you condone this? We are speaking about the same thing, are we not? Your son has allowed himself to be bewitched by our enemy. And yet you stand before us preaching about supporting our brother! Do you wish to live another one hundred years, dreaming of the day when it will be safe for us to return to civilization again? That is, if there is anything left to this world once this little witch has her way with it. The time is now, Mother. This must be done."

She looked sympathetic. "You are right, my son, the time is now. But there is another way to achieve this without spilling the blood of an innocent."

"Oh?" Simion said suspiciously. "And why have we never been told of this 'other way'?"

"It has never been relevant until now," she stated simply. "When you two were little, I went to a witch named Hecate and sought her help. I was told that a joining of the two bloodlines would sever a curse such as this one."

"A joining you say?" Simion snorted. "I assure you, Mother, Marius has taken care of that already, and you see we are still damned."

She raised a hand quickly, halting Marius's attack. "I speak of marriage. Even now he is anticipated at the parish in Wessex where Father Paul will perform the ceremony."

Again Simion snorted. "I hardly believe that the blessings of some old man will alleviate our curse. We have the Descendant here and there is no time for dallying over possibilities. Tonight she must die, and when the sun rises life will begin anew for all of us."

Marius was trying everything in his power to contain his anger. His brothers were as stubborn as they were arrogant. He knew that there would be no reasoning with them. And time was wasting. Alexandra was somewhere on the estate and no doubt frightened half to death. She needed him.

"Where is she?" he managed to say in a low and lethal tone.

Simion looked at him. "She is being held for a ceremony that will take place tonight." He looked at his watch. "As a matter of fact, many of our relatives should have arrived by now."

Lady Amelia looked from Simion to Nicholas. "Does your father know of this?" she asked with a frown.

Nicholas laughed softly. "He has authorized it."

Marius had heard enough. He was going to find Alexandra and get her out of here. He turned and stalked angrily toward the door. There was a subsequent click behind him and he stopped.

"I cannot allow you to leave, brother," Simion said.

Marius looked over his shoulder and noted the semiautomatic handgun pointing at his back.

His brother waved the weapon. "I am sorry, but

you are not going to ruin this for us, especially not over some woman. If you try, I will shoot you."

Marius turned slowly to face him. Simion wasn't one to be taken lightly. He was determined to see the curse end and would do away with anything that stood in his way. As much as he was tempted to, Marius refrained from challenging him. He, as well as Simion, knew that a strategically placed bullet wound would serve to incapacitate him. If Marius intended to save Alexandra, he needed his complete strength. Tonight marked the eve of the new moon and with his entire family wanting Alexandra dead, he was her only chance of seeing the sunrise again.

Simion motioned to Nicholas. "Bind him."

Nicholas moved to comply, his expression suddenly solemn. "I am sorry it had to come to this, Marius. But what must be done can no longer be left to you." He produced one of the plastic cuffs he'd used to restrain April. "You have been weakened by your sorceress."

Lady Amelia shook her head in resigned disappointment. "Where is your father? I wish to speak with him." She began walking to the door.

Nicholas placed a gentle yet firm hand on her

arm. "We are sorry, Mother, but Father has ordered that you be kept out of this."

She spun on him. "He has *what?*"

Nicholas shrugged. "He knows your heart. It is better that you leave this to us," he told her apologetically.

She was fuming now. "He has no right!"

Marius's jaw tightened. He knew that his father could do whatever he wanted. Lord Drakon commanded an empire of gargoyles and humans alike. His word was law. And during such times, not even Lady Amelia's coaxing could sway him. With his wrists tightly strapped together now, he glanced outside the window. Sunset was nearly upon them. His joints were aching and he knew his transformation would begin soon. If they lingered a bit longer he would have an opportunity to escape and perhaps locate Alexandra before his brothers could stop him.

Simion followed his gaze and swung the door open. "Take them to the cellar."

Chapter 19

The driveway below was well lit and lined with more luxury cars then Alexandra had ever seen outside a car dealership. For the past two hours she'd observed the odd mix of affluently clad guests arriving at the mansion. There was some sort of celebration in progress, and she didn't have to use witchcraft to guess what all the festivity was about. She'd searched the room from top to bottom and had discovered only one possible route of escape—the huge fireplace. Old ashes lay in a heap over the remains of charred wood, and she imagined the soot that was waiting for her on the way up.

She was frantically tying together strips of lining that she'd torn from the heavy drapes. In the event that she did make it to the roof, she'd need some way of getting down. Even if it meant lowering herself down to a balcony and breaking inside. She would look for a telephone and contact the police, then locate April and get the hell out of here.

It was dark now and her thoughts strayed to Marius. She wondered where he was and what he was thinking. He would be looking for her, no doubt.

She stood, testing her links, then wound the entire thing up. She slipped one shoulder into it and draped the loop over her neck.

"Here goes," she murmured to herself.

Gingerly, she stepped over the silver screen that sat in front of the fireplace. She'd leave everything intact to buy herself some time. If the Drakons had no idea how she'd escaped then they wouldn't know where to start looking. She was actually hoping that they'd assume her disappearance was due to witchcraft.

Squinting, she looked up the narrow passage. Having a flashlight would have certainly helped. Cautiously, she began her ascent as she'd seen it done in the movies. She braced her back against one wall and her feet on the opposing side. She also used her arms for support as she sidled her way up. The air was surprisingly cool and she could smell the light hint of a fragrant plant beneath the smoky odor. She slipped a few times, falling a foot or two.

She was halfway up when she heard the door to the study open. She went completely still.

"Where is she?" The voice sounded like Lord Drakon's.

There was a mumbled response followed by what sounded like the window slamming shut.

"She has to be in here! There is no way she could have gotten away without being noticed. Find her!" he continued.

Alexandra imagined he was no longer the passive man who'd greeted her initially. He was a gargoyle. Her heart raced, for she feared that he would capture her scent as his sons had. She watched the shadows at the bottom of the fireplace and fought the urge to scramble upward. Sweat trickled down her temples, plastering stray tendrils of hair to her face and neck. She wondered if she might still escape should he discover her. There was no way such a large creature could fit into the chimney, but if she made it to the roof, he'd be waiting for her there. He had wings; they all did.

When the door to the study finally slammed shut, Alexandra exhaled a shaky sigh of relief. She wondered if the heavy scent of ashes that was nearly choking the hell out of her had saved her from being detected. Not wasting time to ponder her good fortune, she continued upward. She knew she was nearing the top when the breeze began to dry her perspiration, cooling her body and sending a chill over her. She looked up and had a clear view of a starry sky.

When she finally emerged, gasping from the climb, she found that the roof was covered in gray shingles that didn't make her task of standing upright any easier. Instead, she straddled one of the triangular peaks and began crawling her way across. She decided to fasten her makeshift rope to the base of a chimney near the rear of the mansion. If she was going down, then she wanted to do so as far away as possible from anyone. She tied the other end of the rope to her waist and tugged on it as hard as she could. Once satisfied that it would be able to support at least most of her weight, she crawled to the edge of the roof and peered down. Her eyes squeezed shut and she took a moment to pray to every deity known to man.

There was a third-story balcony directly below her and she decided that it was her best option. Clinging to the rope for dear life, she lowered one leg over the edge of the roof then the other. She waited for the ripping sound, the terrifying fall, the spine-twisting crash onto the balcony, but it never came. Again, a shuddering sigh escaped her lungs. *So far so good.*

Slowly, she slipped down the rope, releasing her weight one inch at a time. It seemed to take forever before she felt the hard stone beneath her. She stood on shaking limbs and glared up. She'd forgotten one thing—the rope! There was no way for her to retrieve it!

She uttered a curse under her breath then looked down. She was still three stories high. Jumping was entirely out of the question. The French doors behind her were shrouded in darkness and covered with heavy drapes. She placed a shaking hand on the door handle and tried it. The door creaked open and she was abruptly reminded of the night she'd stolen her way into Marius's apartment. That hadn't produced anything pleasant. She just hoped she had better luck this time.

The room was completely dark. She felt the adjacent walls for a light switch, but found none.

As her eyes adjusted, she saw the outline of a large bed and a circular mirror that sat atop a tall dresser. It appeared that she'd entered a very elaborate bedroom. She could also see a door. With careful steps, she crossed the wooden floor and pressed an ear against it. Silence.

She opened it and peered down a dimly lit hall before making her way cautiously past three more doors that appeared to be bedrooms. The hall ended in a set of tall, arching doors. On either side, two wall sconces glowed with candlelight. She braced a hand against the heavy, elaborately carved wood and pushed.

The room on the other side was unlike anything she could have imagined. It was a huge chamber with a high, arching ceiling supported by four thick pillars that reminded her of the Roman Colosseum. As she neared the polished mahogany banister that went around the entire third level of the room, she could see the intricate mosaic tiling of the floor far below. It depicted a horned dragon being slain by a mighty angel. A series of tall candelabras positioned at intervals around the room cast light on the image, granting it an ethereal appearance. Mounted on the walls of this great chamber were weapons, many of which looked to be hundreds of years old. To her right, high above everything, was a large oval stained-glass window.

Alexandra glanced back down the hall from which she'd emerged. Passing through the room seemed to be her only option. She pushed the door to its original position and looked around the third level for a doorway of some sort. At one end there seemed to be light flickering from a stairwell, and she headed in that direction.

She had taken only two steps when a loud creaking noise echoed in the chamber. Her attention was drawn to the ground level where a door swung open. At the first sound of voices, she dived to the floor.

"It is nearly 3:00 a.m. I do not understand how you allowed her to slip away from you. It was your duty to guard the door!"

"She is a witch, my lord," came a weaker voice.

"She is the Descendant. She may possess some remnants of ability, but her powers are not so profound that she can perform such a spell. I want her found—search this entire estate if you must. And when you find her, bring her to me." Lord Drakon sounded outraged.

Alexandra chanced a look below and could see

two figures. One was a massive gargoyle, a Goliath. His hair was streaked gray and he wore a long emerald cape that trailed the ground behind him. The other was a short, thin man.

Another entered then. Nicholas, she knew. She recognized the long braid in his hair.

"Father, our guests grow impatient. When will we conclude this? Have they not found her yet?" he asked with annoyance.

Lord Drakon stalked toward one side of the room. "Not yet, but we will prepare for the sacrifice nonetheless." With one powerful sweep of his hand, he cleared a stone slab of all the weapons that had been displayed there.

Sacrifice!

Alexandra knew they weren't talking about a lamb. They were talking about *her!* She was the sacrifice! She was going to be placed on that stone slab and…what? Stabbed? Beheaded? Disemboweled?

She took several deep breaths and tried to remain calm. Lord Drakon had said it was nearing 3:00 a.m., which meant they all had several hours before they became stone. If she could just avoid getting captured until dawn then she would be free. She would deal with whatever transformations were waiting for her when they manifested.

Nicholas was ranting. "Imbeciles! How does a woman simply disappear from a locked room three stories above the ground?" He was pacing the floor. "Such incompetence! I will simply have to find her myself."

He turned to leave, but his father stopped him. "Nicholas, I want her alive. You must remember, her only crime is having Necesar's blood in her veins. She will be treated humanely."

Nicholas nodded then stalked out of the room.

Alexandra eased her head away from the rail and pressed it to the cool marble floor. She was pretty sure that it was only a matter of time before Nicholas realized that she'd escaped up to the roof. And when he found her makeshift rope, it would lead him directly to her. She couldn't wait around to be discovered.

The sound of Lord Drakon leaving echoed in the room and she refocused her attention on the light around the bend. *That has to be a stairway!* She stood and made her way toward the light.

It was a stairway, all right, with wide and beautifully fashioned steps covered in bronze-colored marble. Despite her circumstances, she couldn't help but admire the splendor of the entire place. When Marius had told her that his family was wealthy, he hadn't been kidding.

She began her descent slowly, pausing every few steps to listen for any noises that would indicate a threat. A huge tapestry on the wall in front of her portrayed a tall and majestic castle cresting a green hillside.

At the bottom of the stairway was a room with three tall peaked doors on one wall. She swallowed. The consequence of opening the wrong one could very well be fatal. Deciding not to waste time choosing, she moved toward the one nearest her and pressed her ear against it. She could hear only silence beneath the rapid thumping of her heart. When she turned the handle, a breath that she hadn't been aware she was holding escaped her lungs. She was back in the oval chamber, but this time she was on the second level. She looked up and could see the spot where she'd been hiding. She was peering at the ground floor and contemplating the possibility of jumping when the double doors at the top slammed open. The vibrations shot throughout the entire room, rattling the huge metal chandelier and surging along the wooden banister. The tremors shot through Alexandra's fingers and she leaped backward.

From where she stood pressed against the wall, she could see a very disgruntled-looking Nicholas with a uniformed butler in his company.

"Check the second level!" he told the elderly man. "I'll check this room. She could not have gotten far."

Alexandra's stomach clenched. She had to get out of here! She had no chance eluding Nicholas, but if she moved fast, there was a chance she could outrun the old geezer.

The man nodded and moved to do Nicholas's bidding while the gargoyle spread his wings in preparation for flight. Alexandra eased back into the hall. She could hear the old butler's crippled steps as he limped down the stairs.

She took only a moment to listen at the second door before rushing inside and pushing it shut. She found herself at the top of another stairway and she quickly ran down. At the bottom, she entered a familiar hallway and she realized that she must be near the main entry foyer, but she wasn't going to leave April behind. In their fury over losing her, the gargoyles might very well decide to sacrifice her friend instead.

Adrenaline raced through her and she hurried toward the first door across from the stairway. She was about to open the door when a shuffling noise behind her forced her to turn around. The old butler's eyes widened and a toothy grin leaped to his face when he saw her.

"There you are!" he exclaimed and began hobbling toward her.

Alexandra gasped and raced down the hall toward a set of double doors. She was certain that the old man wouldn't be able to catch her, but he was quite capable of raising an alarm. And raise the alarm he did. His crackly voice reverberated through the hall as he screamed after her.

Alexandra burst into the room and went crashing into a solid wall. When she hit the floor a sharp pain shot up the back of her skull and blackness filled her vision. It was short-lived, however, and when her eyes opened she had a clear view of a beautiful arched ceiling. Looking to one side, she saw that she had returned to the oval chamber. She groaned painfully as a shadow fell over her. In that instant she realized that the wall she'd crashed into wasn't really a wall. It was Nicholas!

Chapter 20

Marius ignored the pain in his wrists as he wrenched at the chains that bound him to the wall. He could tell that they were made from a very strong alloy, perhaps titanium. Had they been of a more inferior metal he was certain he would have broken free by this time. In the dim lighting of the cellar, he could just make out his mother, sitting quietly a few feet from him. For the past several hours she'd remained silent. He understood that she must feel helpless and ashamed—helpless because there was nothing she could do to aid him and ashamed to witness her family's deterioration to such a state. And so, in silence she'd remained, no doubt contemplating the lasting result of the entire ordeal.

He hadn't resigned himself so easily. He was

determined to save Alexandra. It was nearing midnight and he was certain she was still alive, for had she been killed the curse would have been lifted. He couldn't understand the desperation that was overtaking him. It was as if a part of him was in jeopardy and he was willing to risk everything to alleviate it.

With renewed determination, he yanked away from the wall again and yielded the same results. His deafening roar shook the entire room, rattling the floorboards overhead. The chains were just too strong. They'd been placed in the cellar in the early 1900s to bind members of his family who would have used their abilities to create mayhem in the city. If one gargoyle was being hunted, then they were all in danger. Certain measures had been a necessity to assure the survival of their clan. During the last one hundred years such punishments had become unnecessary, as the many wayward youth of his family had achieved maturity. Nevertheless, the shackles had remained.

Marius fell to his knees and smashed the floor with his fists in frustration, causing a miniature quake in the stone beneath him. Each passing hour had brought him closer to insanity and he was quite ready to chew off his own hands—anything to be free. As his gaze searched the darkness, he had a thought. The wall behind him was made of stone. If he could shatter the foundation he would be able to free himself.

Without wasting another moment, he was on his feet and charging forward as far as the chains permitted. Then, with all his strength, he slammed into the wall behind him. The room shook and he could hear the sound of the wall cracking.

The noise drew his mother's attention and she stood. "Marius, stop this before you bring the ceiling down upon our heads!" she demanded.

He flexed his shoulder. "If that is what it takes to get me out of here, then so be it." He charged into the wall a second time. The force of the impact sent him sprawling to the floor.

Lady Amelia moved to his side and knelt beside him. "It is nearly dawn, my son. It is too late," she said sadly.

"It is *not* too late!" Marius forced himself to stand. "She is still alive, and I am going to save her from this madness. I *need* her."

His declaration shocked him and he met his mother's knowing gaze. He realized that he couldn't deny it any longer. Yes, he needed Alexandra. She'd opened his eyes and brought joy into his life. He couldn't imagine returning to the bland existence he'd been maintaining before. The mere thought of losing her filled him with desperation. He loved her.

Chips of solid rock crumbled away after his third assault, and Marius turned to assess his handiwork. He could feel a filtering of cool air and knew that he'd penetrated the exterior wall. Victory began to stir within him, fueling his next assault. When he rammed the wall again, stone went flying and a gaping hole appeared. He peered through and could see the stables in the dim moonlight. He brought one heavy boot up and kicked away the stubborn remnants.

He looped the chains around his fists and yanked his arms forward. The huge bolts that had secured them in place tore from the wall with such force that they flew across the room and struck the opposing surface, leaving dents.

"You are free!" his mother exclaimed.

Marius looked at the lengths of chain that remained attached to his wrists. There was no way to remove them now, but that was the least of his concerns. He needed to find Alexandra and halt whatever ceremony was taking place.

He took a moment to kick in the wall that held

his mother's chains. Turning to her, he memorized her image in the dim light. Defying his family was going to be no task easily accomplished. In fact, it could very well result in his death. He was prepared for that.

"Do not regret this night, Mother, or the choices you made within it. Your love has given me more strength than you know," he said solemnly.

She frowned. "Do not speak like this, my son—"

He raised a hand, silencing her. "I must go. Time is running out." With that, he ducked through the gaping hole he'd created and disappeared into the night.

Chapter 21

Alexandra twisted her head away from the flask as the old woman tried to force the contents into her mouth. She was strapped to the stone table in the oval chamber with her hands bound above her head. She struggled uselessly, heaving and straining against the steel binds.

After being knocked to the ground, she'd put up quite a fight with Nicholas, who'd been in no mood for games and had subdued her quickly. Then he'd told her that Marius had been captured and was being held in the cellar. That news had crushed her. The knowledge that Marius had been imprisoned by his own family because of her was unbearable.

The woman placed a wrinkled hand over Alexandra's mouth and pinched her cheeks together so that her lips were forced open. "You must drink this. It will cloud your mind and you will feel no pain."

The flask tilted and Alexandra felt the warm concoction trickling over her lips. She pressed the tip of her tongue behind her teeth to prevent the liquid from entering her mouth. She wasn't about to lie still and let this old hag poison her!

As she continued to struggle she could see Lord Drakon moving around the table to face the throng that filled the room. He stood above her, a great and hulking creature whose horns rose high above his head, curling like those of a ram's. At the apex of his wings, two sharp talons glinted in the light from the candles and a mane of silver hair fell over his shoulders. The long cloak he wore was pushed back and fastened with a golden clasp. Bracers of the same material encased his wrists, and she noted the long silver scabbard he balanced between his clawlike hands.

For a moment their eyes met, his reflecting victory. Then he looked to the old woman who was still busy trying to drug her. "That is enough, Gertrude," he ordered. "Her will is strong. Allow her to die with that honor."

The woman retreated immediately, bowing low. "As you wish, my lord," she croaked.

Alexandra turned her head to the side and spat the putrid brew from her mouth. His words rang in her head, one word clamoring the loudest— *die!* Her eyes bolted to the long knife he held again. This was really happening. She couldn't believe it. In modern-day America, the land of the free and the home of the brave, she was going to be sacrificed on a stone slab. They might as well have had a witch hunt and burned her at the stake in Times Square.

"You're insane! Let me go!" she screamed. She turned her attention to the mix of gargoyles and humans who were waiting anxiously for her death. "Do you think you can get away with this? This is murder. I hope you all rot in hell."

When the doors to the great chamber had opened and all the guests had poured in, Alexandra had been astonished to see just how many gargoyles were present. There had to be at least twenty. They were all different in appearance— not all of the Drakon bloodline. Perhaps many of them had been servants in the castle who'd had the misfortune of being present when the curse was laid. They were all in various states of undress and she imagined it would be difficult to accommodate their wings comfortably into any manner of clothing. The women wore mostly loin cloths and severed tops, while the men wore pants and some cloaks. The humans among them looked like old money. They wore furs and diamonds and had that stiff-lipped demeanor that only aristocrats were capable of pulling off.

Her outburst stirred the room into a chorus of angry grumbling. The word *witch* was uttered several times, passing through the crowd like a foul odor.

Lord Drakon raised a hand to silence them and spoke for her ears alone. "Watch your tongue, girl, if you do not wish for a tortured death. There are those among us who would not hesitate to tear you limb from limb."

She scowled up at him. "As if having a knife plunged into my abdomen is not torture enough," she spat and continued struggling.

He focused on his impatient guests. "My people, our lives have been torn for centuries, wasted in hiding, in waiting." His voice echoed into the ceiling. "On this night it shall end. We have gathered here to at last sever the curse of the witch Necesar. Before you lies the final descendant—last in her bloodline! Her death will free us!"

There was a loud cheer as he pulled the knife from the scabbard. Alexandra struggled harder, turning onto her side as she tried to squeeze her hands through the shackles.

Lord Drakon would have continued speaking, but the two huge double doors that served as the entrance to the oval chamber swung open, slamming against the walls behind them. Everyone turned to see the slender female silhouetted there.

Alexandra looked at the female gargoyle who seemed to have captured everyone's attention. With her back straight and her head high, she advanced through the throng that was quickly parting for her, lowering their heads respectfully. She wore a long silver garment with splits running up both sides, exposing her slender thighs. Her long gray hair fell about her in a wild and enchanting cascade and her wings were folded against her back like a cloak.

She paused a few feet away from the stone table with her attention fixed on Lord Drakon. A flash of anger reflected in her silver-gray eyes and Alexandra recognized her instantly. She was Marius's mother!

"I suppose you are pleased with yourself," she said to Lord Drakon. "Ordering your wife and son locked away in the cellar."

"This is not the time for this, Amelia. There are only a few more minutes left to the equinox and this task must be completed."

Lady Amelia's eyes dropped to Alexandra, who met her gaze with an imploring stare. She experienced a fluttering of hope. Could Marius's mother save her? And if Lady Amelia had managed to escape the cellar, then where was Marius?

"Release her," Lady Amelia said, and her eyes snapped back up to her husband. "There is another way to break our curse, a way that will not shatter our son's heart."

Outbursts of disbelief fanned through the audience.

Lord Drakon shook his head slowly, regrettably. "I am sorry, my love. In this I cannot oblige you. In time, both you and Marius will come to forgive me."

Lady Amelia's eyes widened and her lips separated in a desperate gasp as he lifted the knife high.

Alexandra's scream echoed throughout the chamber and she squeezed her eyes shut in anticipation of the pain. The loud smashing of glass didn't register in her mind, nor did the outraged cries and the ensuing commotion. Her head was spinning and she could see her parents' faces. Were they calling to her? Were they waiting for her to join them? Tears streamed down her temples. She'd failed them.

It wasn't until she felt the chains on her wrists being yanked off that she realized something was amiss. Her eyes flew open and she was surprised to see an outraged Marius tearing away at her shackles. He was streaked with blood, and bits of colorful glass reflected in his hair. She gasped as she looked beyond him to see the shattered stained-glass window near the ceiling. Had he actually flown through it?

He took a second to look her over before turning his attention to the huge dent in the wall behind them. Alexandra followed his gaze and realized that his father had been thrust away from the stone table and now lay beneath a pile of rubble.

Around them, the occupants of the room, including Marius's brothers, weren't very pleased with the proceedings. His mother was trying to calm them, to explain, but Alexandra could tell that her words of a new solution were falling on deaf ears. Why bother to try something different when the Descendant lay before them, ready for the slaughter?

Marius scooped her up and lowered her to the ground. "I'll hold them off," he said. "I want you to run out that door and keep going. No matter what happens, do not turn back." He pointed to a passage that she hadn't noticed before, perhaps because it was half-hidden behind one of the large posts.

Her fingers tightened on his wrist. Strangely, she didn't want to leave him. She wasn't sure what the repercussions of his actions would be, but from the angry throng approaching them, she knew he wouldn't be able to face them alone. Lord Drakon growled, and she cast a look over her shoulder. His massive form was rising from the pile of stone and dust and he was reaching for the knife!

Marius shoved her toward the doorway. "Go!"

Alexandra hesitated for the slightest fragment of a second and their eyes locked. The intensity within his silver stare told her that he accepted his fate regardless of its nature. It was in that instant that she realized just how far he was willing to go to protect her, just how sincere he'd been. So much so that he was willing to challenge the will of his own father. She knew then that she wanted him, needed him—this powerful and beautiful male, her mate, her partner, her guardian. She loved him.

With those thoughts consuming her, she raced toward the doorway. She chanced a glance behind her and saw Marius atop the stone table dueling with another gargoyle. Several of them had taken to the air and were swarming toward her. Surprisingly, his mother was heading toward her, as well. She'd taken flight and was fending off the other gargoyles, giving Alexandra ample time to make it through the doorway.

The grandfather clock posted in the hall just outside the main double doors began to chime. It was striking six! Alexandra was nearly at the doorway when a series of gunshots rang out and she heard her name bellowed over the chaos. She spun around, knowing the voice.

April stood behind one of the tall pillars, motioning to her. Detective Beckford had his gun aimed and was firing at anything that came within a five-foot radius of them. Her heart leaped with joy. April was all right!

Lady Amelia flew above her then, keeping the other gargoyles away from her. They seemed torn between the desire to kill Alexandra and to respect the wishes of their mistress.

Lady Amelia looked at her. "Linger no more, child. You must go!"

The clock chimed.

Alexandra looked at April. She knew that there was no way she'd be able to make it across the room to her friend and the detective. There were just too many gargoyles. Her only hope was to follow the passage that Marius had directed her to.

She was about to exit when she heard Marius cry out. She spun around, afraid that something had happened to him. She was shocked to see him moving swiftly toward her and fear gripped her when she saw Nicholas just a few feet away. Marius's brother had ripped a medieval spear from the wall and was aiming it at her. With a ferocious growl, Marius dived in front of her just as the slender object zipped through the air. It lodged within his chest and he cried out, stalling in the air before plummeting to the floor.

Stillness filled the room and Alexandra looked on in horror as Marius pushed to his feet, gripped the long spear and wrenched it from his chest. Blood streamed down his body in a heavy flow as he stumbled a few paces toward her, his hand reaching out. Then he collapsed.

She screamed. Forgetting her own danger, she raced to his side and dropped to her knees, rolling him onto his back and cradling his head in her lap.

"Marius!" she cried. "Marius, talk to me!" Shaking hands pressed on the wound in a vain attempt to stop the bleeding.

She could feel his heart thumping wildly beneath her palms, trying desperately to adjust to the extreme blood loss. "Someone get help!" she shouted to the throng of onlookers.

Lady Amelia was at her side immediately, her gaze frantically combing her youngest born. Tears welled in her eyes and her lips trembled as if she wanted to speak but couldn't find the words.

The clock chimed.

Marius's eyes opened to slits and he looked up at Alexandra.

Alexandra was sobbing now. "Marius…" was all she managed.

"I love you, Alexandra," he declared faintly, his

breathing coming in short gasps now. Then his hand fell away.

His words struck her like a bolt of bittersweet lightning. To think that after all they'd been through and only now just realizing their love for each other, it was too late.

She watched his eyes drift closed and knew the moment when his last breath slipped from his body. He went perfectly still in her arms, his face a vision of peace rendered within a most exquisite and beautiful portrait. A burning agony consumed her and she cried out. She looked to the occupants of the room who'd stood by and allowed this to happen. Her gaze paused on the one who'd wielded the spear—his own brother.

The clock chimed.

Nicholas had fallen to his knees and now watched his brother's lifeless body with anguish.

Alexandra fought to find words, wishing she could damn them all to hell, but nothing could slip past her lips as she struggled to breathe. Dizziness washed over her and she fell over Marius's still body. From the ache deep within the pit of her stomach came a mournful cry with the echo of a voice that wasn't her own, riding on its tail.

"Cerc de viată şi cerc de death, lumină şi dark-

ness..." The voice grew louder. *"Rival nu mai mult şi consulat this vas. I chemare upon art.hot. puternic de bun şi beseech art.hot. puternic de evil la spre reignite this a umbla soul."*

All present looked in disbelief at Marius's body and at Alexandra, who was spewing the ancient language. The grandfather clock chimed its last tune, marking the morning hour.

Solemnly, many of the gargoyles lowered their heads or bent at their knees, bracing themselves for the inevitable change. Their time was done, they knew, yet none raised a hand to harm Alexandra. The love she and Marius shared was apparent now—an emotion that was self-sacrificing and unbiased.

A chill infiltrated the room and thickened the air. It prickled over Alexandra's skin and frosted her breath so that each exhalation came as a cloud of white smoke.

The gasps of disbelief and the touch of cool fingers on her arm drew Alexandra's attention and she mustered enough strength to look up. A beautiful middle-aged woman knelt before her, her hair softly wreathed by the pale light of dawn that shone down from the shattered window above. Saddened eyes met Alexandra's own and she

knew immediately that this was Lady Amelia...
but she couldn't understand how she'd come to be
human.

Alexandra cast a look around her. The other
gargoyles were gazing down at themselves in awe
as they, too, were changing. *The curse has been
lifted.* But...how? Had Marius's sacrifice for her
broken the incantation? Had he forfeited his life
to spare hers and to free his family? Or had it
been Necesar's intervention?

Nicholas, who remained on his knees, swiftly
drew the sword from the sling across his back and
the rasp of steel echoed within the chamber. Wondering if she was still in danger, Alexandra shot a
glance at Lady Amelia, who was rising slowly to
her feet. With his head bowed in remorse, Nicholas brought the blade down into the mosaic tiling
and began carving a large circle about himself.

His mother took a step forward. "What are you
doing?" she asked with some measure of disbelief. "Do you wish for your brother's death to be
in vain?"

Without looking up, Nicholas brought the steel
against his palm and lacerated his flesh. And as
his blood trailed down his fingertips, he began to
trace a symbol within the confinement. Regard-

less of her lack of knowledge of the arts, Alexandra knew immediately that he was drawing a Triquetra about himself. A symbol of the white craft, this protective spell was simple yet powerful enough to ward off most magic. So many times had Necesar performed that very spell and others like it.

Simion quietly crossed the room and entered the boundaries of the circle. He wound his fist in the leather strapping across his chest that held his quiver in place and stripped it away. The steel arrows clamored to the floor and he met his mother's gaze.

"We are not worthy of this gift," he said solemnly. "Had we listened, our brother would still be alive." His attention fell to Alexandra. "Please, forgive us," he beseeched.

Alexandra looked away. No amount of apology would bring Marius back to her. They'd chosen to forfeit their right to humanity as penance, but it solved nothing. In her arms still lay the lifeless form of the only man she'd ever love. Their sacrifice was as useless to her as her death now would be to them.

Just then there was a mild stirring in her arms and her attention snapped to Marius as he gasped.

Her breathing stopped. He was alive! And he was changing—thick horns sank back into his skull, the heavily chiseled features smoothed into the masculine face she recognized, and his wings were incinerated by a burst of blue flame.

Her heart raced as his eyes opened. She was oblivious to the gasps of disbelief that filled the room. *He is alive!* And the wound in his chest seemed to be closing! He looked lost, as if he'd been on a long journey and returned to an unfamiliar place.

With a mix of emotions filling her heart, she smiled down at him. "Marius, you're going to be okay," she reassured him.

Her tears continued to flow, but these were tears of joy. She'd seen the spear penetrate his chest, had seen him fall and had watched him die. How it was that he breathed again and was a man, she didn't know and decided not to question this good fortune. For now, it was enough for her to hold him in her arms, to feel his warm breath against her skin and the racing of his heart.

He was alive! Marius had come back to her!

"Get down, all of you! On the floor!" Detective Beckford was moving through the crowd with his gun braced in his hands. "I've had enough of this freak show. I'm taking all of you in for conspiracy to commit murder!"

Everyone began complying. They were human now and would die just as easily from a gunshot wound as the next person. Only Simion and Nicholas hadn't been released from the curse, and they looked on in disbelief as Marius stirred in Alexandra's arms.

April crossed the room to Alexandra, her eyes fixed hesitantly on the man whose death she'd witnessed and who now breathed with new life. "Are you okay, Alexandra?" she asked.

Alexandra nodded. "Somehow we broke the curse," she told her. "We have to get Marius to a hospital. I don't want to lose him again."

April knelt beside her. "Don't worry. Tyrese called for backup. An ambulance is on its way, too." She placed a reassuring arm over her shoulder. "He traced the license plate of the car. That's how he found us."

Alexandra looked past April to see Detective Beckford slowly circling the two gargoyles with his gun aimed as he read them their rights loudly enough for everyone to hear. Her gaze swept to Lady Amelia, who'd moved to stand next to her husband. She had a resigned look in her eyes, as if she was prepared to face incarceration.

"No!" Alexandra cried, then looked to Detective Beckford. "Leave them," she said.

April frowned at her. "What are you saying? These people kidnapped us and tried to kill you!"

Detective Beckford sent her a wary look, but said nothing. Alexandra knew he must think her insane, but she wasn't. She wanted the suffering to stop. Enough had transpired and she wanted it all to end. Marius was alive, and that was what mattered to her. She looked down at him, resting quietly in her arms. She didn't want him to awaken to find his entire family facing another life sentence.

She shook her head. "It's over, April." Then to Detective Beckford, "Please, let them go. I won't press charges. I just want to leave this place."

Detective Beckford looked from Alexandra to April then back again. Slowly, he lowered his gun and replaced it in his holster. "An ambulance will be here in about fifteen minutes. Is he well enough to be moved?" He nodded toward Marius.

Alexandra looked Marius over again. The wound had closed considerably over the last few minutes and the color had returned to his face. "Yes, but we have to be careful." She brushed a stray hair from his face.

Lord Drakon moved to tower above them, his face laden with regret and anguish as he looked Marius over. "You may leave if you wish. I will see to my son's care," he said without meeting her eyes.

Alexandra frowned up at him. "I'm not leaving Marius," she told him.

Lady Amelia stepped forward and fixed Lord Drakon with a reproving glare. She motioned to two servants standing nearby. "Falon, Remus, take my son to the green salon." The butlers moved quickly to do her bidding and she extended a hand to Alexandra.

"Come, my dear. We shall tend to his wounds," she offered.

Gently, Alexandra lowered Marius's head to the tile and allowed Lady Amelia to assist her to her feet. They watched as the two servants, with Lord Drakon's assistance, carefully eased Marius from the floor.

As he was carried from the oval chamber, Alexandra's attention fell to the pool of blood on the floor and her brows puckered with worry. He'd bled so much. Her hands and clothes were covered with it. She hoped to God that Marius would be okay.

She moved to follow Lady Amelia from the

room, but was suddenly assailed by a crushing pain in her chest. Gasping, she fell to her knees and gripped the place over her heart as it began to thump wildly and the air began to twist.

April raced to her side. "Alexandra, what's wrong?" she cried.

Her friend's words were barely audible beneath the torrent and the room began to spin. Alexandra shut her eyes as she fought the abrupt onset of dizziness. She covered her ears in an attempt to muffle the heinous screeching that haunted the winds about her.

Then, as it had begun, it all eased into stillness. As the pain in her chest subsided, Alexandra opened her eyes and found herself immersed in a cold darkness. She was outside, kneeling in the dirt among a thick gathering of bushes. Before her was the silhouette of a dilapidated building with a backdrop of a similarly maintained water tower. The bold letters *H.W.* were printed across the rusting white surface.

The place was unfamiliar to her, but suddenly Alexandra knew. *Mady Halman.* With all the life-altering events she'd just experienced, she'd nearly forgotten about the poor missing girl.

Somewhere on the third floor of the decaying

structure a light flickered within a single window,
and she knew that it was there she would find
Mady.

Her fingers moved to caress the charm bracelet
on her wrist and she was about to stand when two
bright headlights appeared, momentarily blinding her. Alexandra squinted into the bright beams
and the vehicle came to an abrupt halt a few feet
in front of her. She recognized the van instantly.
With the bright yellow Tweety Bird air freshener
swinging from the rearview mirror, it was unmistakable.

A tall, thin man climbed out and reached across
to the passenger side to remove a large duffel bag,
which he slung over his shoulder. He slammed the
door shut and reached into his coat pocket, pulling out a handgun. Alexandra was frozen with
fear, for she was directly in his line of vision. For
a moment she thought he would shoot her, but instead he slipped two bullets into the barrel of his
gun and replaced it.

He was shaking, she noticed. And he seemed
quite anxious. He took one hard draw from the
cigarette in his mouth before smashing it in the
dirt with a tattered sneaker. Alexandra remained
completely still as he stalked by her as if she were

invisible. As he headed toward the building, the darkness around her began to fade into the soft lighting of the oval chamber.

April's voice registered at the back of her mind, growing louder, and she realized that she'd collapsed on the floor. The huge chandelier glowed overhead and she could feel the cool mosaic tiling against her skin.

"Alexandra! Are you all right?" April appeared above her.

Alexandra blinked. She'd never experienced such an intense vision before and somehow she was sure that what she'd just witnessed hadn't yet happened. "We don't have much time," she said urgently as she sat up. "He's going to kill her!"

April frowned in confusion. "Who's going to kill who?"

"The Penn State Serial Killer. I know where he's keeping Mady, and he's going to kill her!"

Detective Beckford, who'd come to stand above her, narrowed his eyes at the mention of the serial murderer. "What do you know about the Penn State Serial Killer?" he asked.

Alexandra stood. "Not much, but I'm sure he's responsible for a missing child from the Bronx. The one that I tried to tell you about. Now he's going to kill her!" When he fixed her with an incredulous look, she decided to reveal her gift to him. "I have the gift, believe it or not. I see things, and I've seen him. I know where he's going."

His gaze became more assessing as he absorbed her declaration. Alexandra didn't think it should be so hard to believe after all he'd witnessed tonight.

April took a step toward him. "It's true, Tyrese. She's a psychic. And that apartment I took you to look at, that was the killer's residence."

His frown flitted between the two women before him, finally settling on April again. "You told me that was your ex's apartment and he was withholding some of your possessions from you. You lied," he accused.

April shrugged. "You wouldn't have gone any other way."

He was silent for a moment then nodded slowly. "True," he said, then turned to Alexandra. "Where is this killer now?"

"I'm not sure," she replied. "I've never seen the place before, but it's an old house, about three stories high. And it's near a water tower with the letters *H.W.* on it."

Detective Beckford frowned as he tried to place her description. "I couldn't begin to imagine where to start looking. I'll radio it in and have one of my men do a—"

"There's no time for that!" Alexandra interrupted. "He's going to kill her now!"

Just then one of the onlookers moved forward. "Perhaps I might be able to help you," he offered.

Alexandra looked him over. With his dark good looks, he was definitely a Drakon. He stuffed the handkerchief he'd been dabbing on his forehead into his pocket. He looked frazzled, and Alexandra guessed that the night's activities had been a bit too far removed from his daily life.

"My name is Andrew Drakon and this is my home." He introduced himself. "The place you're speaking of is a small town called Hemmingway. It's a bit of a distance from here, about an hour's drive."

Detective Beckford moved toward him as he pulled his radio from his pocket. "How do I get there?"

"You'll have to travel south on Route 92 and take Exit 21. There's no town marking, but you should be able to see the water tower from the highway," he told him.

Detective Beckford nodded and radioed his men to head out to that location instead of the mansion.

Alexandra turned worried eyes onto Andrew Drakon. "You said one hour's drive?"

He nodded.

Mady would be long dead by the time they arrived. "Is there another way?"

Detective Beckford looked at her. "Everything's going to be fine. I dispatched about twenty men out there and I'm going ahead of them," he tried to reassure her.

Alexandra shook her head. "It won't matter if you sent one hundred men if they're all too late. You don't understand. That child has only minutes left."

The oval chamber had cleared by this time save for a few people who'd remained to restore order to the room. And Nicholas and Simion, still in gargoyle form.

Nicholas, his eyes turned downward, was the first to approach. "Your gift is truly great. It would be a pity to see it rendered useless because of the mere obstacle of distance." Emerald eyes found hers then, reflecting remorse. "Please, allow me to assist you. I can fly you to this place within a few minutes."

Alexandra swallowed a lump in her throat and did her best to hide the fear she felt. April had retreated a few steps to stand beside Detective Beckford, and so she stood alone before this huge and very dangerous creature.

She had no reason to trust him, but what choice did she have? A child's life was at stake. If he was able to help her save Mady, then she was willing to put aside her mistrust.

She swallowed again. "How fast do you think you can get me there?" she asked with apprehension.

"Twenty minutes at the most."

She nodded. "I'll go with you."

April ran to her side. "Alexandra, no! It's not safe." Her gazed fixed pointedly on Nicholas.

Simion moved forward then. "She will have nothing to fear from us," he said with a hard yet repentant look. "My brother and I will also protect her with our lives. We will save this child."

Detective Beckford stepped forward, too. "I'll go with you," he offered.

Alexandra looked at Simion, who nodded his agreement. She gave a small smile of thanks, then took April's hand. "Please watch over Marius until I get back. I have to do this. I made a promise to Mady's family and I won't let them down."

Chapter 22

Everything was as she'd seen it—the building, the water tower and the light in the window. The only thing that Alexandra hadn't anticipated was not finding Mady on the third floor. The dim illumination she'd seen from outside turned out to be a single candle sitting on a wooden table that was covered with dust. A dirty mattress was pushed to one corner. Detective Beckford squatted there, wearing latex gloves as he slipped bits of evidence into a small bag.

Alexandra's attention was drawn to the mattress. She could almost feel Mady's energy lingering there. It was the very spot she'd seen in her vision.

Nicholas cast a look around. "What manner of

man would bring a child here?" His voice was laced with disgust.

"The kind that has no scruples," Detective Beckford supplied.

Alexandra moved toward the mattress, her attention riveted to the newspaper clippings taped to the wall above it. Her stomach churned as she read one of the bold headlines.

Rapist Attacks Third Victim in Bronx Area.

Slowly, she peeled the article off the wall. It was dated thirteen years ago. Realization flooded her and the clipping slipped from her fingers. The Penn State Serial Killer was Mady Halman's father.

Images flooded her then, visions of a deranged man, deeming it his right to claim a child who'd resulted from his vicious attack on a woman he didn't even know. He'd tracked down Veronica Halman and kidnapped Mady because, in his own twisted mind, he felt he was being robbed of the chance to be a father. But he was growing tired of Mady now. He hadn't considered the responsibilities of caring for a child. She was a liability, a burden, and he was ready to get rid of her, but knew he couldn't just return her to her mother. There was only one way to do away with her and prevent himself from being captured.

A feeling of desperation filled the pit of her stomach and Alexandra spun around and crossed the room to where Simion stood in the doorway. "We have to find her," she said.

Nicholas followed her to the door. "Alexandra and I will go below. You and the detective can search above," he told his brother.

Simion grunted his accord and when Detective Beckford joined him, they disappeared up the stairs.

Alexandra removed the candle from the table and turned to go with Nicholas. As they moved into the dark hallway, she remembered the day she'd climbed into the sewer with Marius. He'd been able to tell her which direction the killer had taken by picking up his scent. "Do you think you can trace Mady's scent?" she asked.

"I will try, but it is often difficult if the individual has been gone for a while. And this room has been vacant for several hours now."

They headed down the hall, Alexandra guided by the light of the candle. The place was a wreck. The wooden floors were littered with dust bunnies and bits of old cloth and they creaked beneath their weight. Cobwebs hung overhead in a decadent canopy, some wandering tendrils hanging low to shroud the way.

The stairway was even less admirable. Its dilapidated railing leaned in an awkward sway and she wondered if it would support their weight, most especially Nicholas's. As if sharing her thoughts, he leaped from the ground and disappeared somewhere above her.

She froze, her heart racing. "Where did you go?" She lifted the candle a little and made a slow turn as she searched the ceiling. The light spilled over his form, revealing that he was clinging to the wall above her.

"Keep moving," he told her. "I am at your side."

She returned her attention to the stairway and shielded the candle as it flickered in a draft. One at a time she took the stairs, carefully testing each and praying that she wouldn't fall through. In the shadows overhead Nicholas followed, moving silently.

At the bottom, she found herself facing a doorway across a narrow hall. She peered into a room filled with furniture draped in white sheets. A chill crept over her. She could feel it. Mady's energy thrived within that room. "She's here," she breathed.

Without delay, Alexandra entered and looked around. "Mady?" she called out and received no response.

Nicholas walked to one side of the room and inhaled deeply. Alexandra followed him, her trepidation rising.

"Where is she? Can you smell her?" she asked anxiously.

He gripped the end of a sheet and pulled it away, revealing a tall wardrobe. Alexandra immediately saw the length of chain draped around it, secured with a master lock. Nicholas wound it about his fist and ripped it away. There was a tiny shriek and relief flooded Alexandra.

They'd found Mady! She placed the candle on the floor as Nicholas threw open the doors. A young girl squinted up at them in fear. Her face and pink jumper were covered in dirt and her hair was tangled. Her attention focused on Nicholas and her eyes widened as she emitted a piercing scream.

Alexandra reached into the wardrobe and drew the child into her arms. "It's okay, Mady. We're not here to hurt you. We're going to take you to your mother," she told the girl in a soothing voice.

Nicholas headed for the doorway. "I will wait out here."

Alexandra nodded and helped a tearful Mady from the wardrobe. "You're safe now, sweetheart."

Mady sniffed and pointed toward the doorway. "What is that thing?"

"He…is a guardian. He's here to protect you," she reassured her. "Now tell me, did that man hurt you?"

Mady nodded. "He hit me and told me to shut up. He said he'd kill me if I didn't do what I was told." She wiped at her tears.

Alexandra gripped Mady's arms gently and looked her in the eyes. "Is that all?"

When the girl nodded, she released a sigh of relief.

Mady's mouth formed in a pitiful frown. "He said he's my dad. He's not, right?"

Alexandra squatted to look at her. "I don't know," she answered, uncertain what to say.

Mady wrapped her arms tightly around Alexandra and cried into her midsection. "I want to go home. I want my mom."

Alexandra smoothed a hand down Mady's hair. "We're going to leave soon. In just a few..." She fell silent.

She'd heard a noise that sounded like a door slamming—the door of a vehicle. She set Mady aside and raced to the window. From her vantage point she could see the tail end of the van parked in the front yard. The Penn State Serial Killer had arrived!

"What is it?" Nicholas asked from the doorway.

She crossed the room, blew out the candle and grabbed Mady's hand. "It's him," she said as calmly as possible.

Alexandra guided Mady into a corner and they faded into the shadows. Mady clung to her and Alexandra fought desperately with the fear raging inside her. He had a gun; she'd seen him load it in her vision.

Nicholas eased back into the room just as a door creaked open at the end of the hall. He, too, slipped into the shadows on the opposite end of the room.

Scuffling footsteps grew louder and a light appeared in the doorway, followed by a tall gangly figure holding a flashlight. A heavy thump resounded in the room as he dumped a duffel bag on the floor. A dark curse spilled from his lips when he pointed the light toward one end of the room. Slowly he advanced and assessed the scene: the broken chain, the candle placed on the floor and the empty wardrobe. A shaking Mady tried to hide behind her, but Alexandra stilled the child's movements. Mady's soft scuffling didn't go unnoticed. Alexandra watched as the killer reached into his jacket pocket and pulled out the handgun.

"Who's there?" he said evenly as he turned his light slowly about the room. "I know that girl ain't escaped all by her lonesome."

Alexandra held her breath as the light crept near. She knew there would be no escaping, for they were directly in its path. Her only comfort was the tall figure of the beast that was sliding from the shadows behind him.

The light passed over them then and stopped. The killer started laughing softly, a perverted wheezing that made her blood freeze.

"Well, well. Seems I got me two little rabbits in a hole," he mocked.

He trailed the light up Alexandra's body. She was still wearing the red dress and his tongue snaked out. The light fell on Mady next and he jerked his head away from the door. "Come here, girl."

Alexandra eased Mady behind her. "She stays with me," she told him determinedly.

His eyes narrowed on her. "Don't think I won't shoot you."

She stood her ground. Nicholas's figure was completely visible behind him now. "You're hardly in the position to be making threats, out-numbered as you are."

"Ain't no one else here. Now hand over the—" His thumb moved to cock the gun, but he froze as a heavy footfall sounded behind him. He tossed a look over his shoulder, his hands began to shake and the flashlight clattered to the floor.

Alexandra stepped to one side with Mady as the gargoyle's massive form emerged from the dark-ness.

The killer's eyes widened and he stumbled backward. He aimed his gun, but before he could pull the trigger, a crash resounded in the room as Simion smashed through the tall window. The killer spun around and the gun went off just as he was knocked to the ground.

From the doorway Detective Beckford raced into the room with his gun drawn. "Stay down!"

he shouted as he pulled a pair of cuffs from his pocket.

In the distance the sound of sirens could be heard and Alexandra knew that Detective Beckford's squad had arrived. She looked at the gargoyles before her. She wondered if she would ever be able to forgive them. They'd done so much wrong to her, yet on this night they'd given something back. Only time would tell.

"Thank you," she breathed softly with a shaking Mady wrapped around her waist.

Detective Beckford snatched up his prisoner and also nodded his gratitude.

Without another word, the two gargoyles disappeared into the night beyond the shattered glass of the window.

It was over. Alexandra held Mady close as a squadron of police vehicles raced into the yard. "You're safe now."

Alexandra smoothed a lock of dark hair from Marius's forehead. He'd been out for three days now, stirring in and out of a restless sleep. Miraculously, his wound had healed completely, leaving only the faintest hint of a scar. With the help of his mother, Alexandra had spent the last few days caring for him.

After the arrest of the serial killer, Alexandra had returned briefly to the city for questioning. She'd claimed that while investigating the story, she'd received an anonymous tip that had led her to the place where Mady was being held. And with Detective Beckford backing her, no one had questioned her too closely. She'd then been able to see Mady home. Ms. Halman had been over-joyed to have her daughter returned to her safely and after overcoming the shock of the motive for the kidnapping, she'd agreed to testify in court against the man who'd raped her thirteen years prior.

For Alexandra, the resolution of the case had brought her some personal peace. She'd used her mysterious talents to save a little girl from cer-tain death and a mother from the pain of losing a child. She was left with a soothing calm. She'd learned so much about herself and found love in the process.

She'd also made a name for herself in the news world. This was both a blessing and a disadvan-tage, for not only was she revered for catching the Penn State Serial Killer and rescuing his next victim, but she was also the center of the Central Park Creature investigations. As she'd feared, the entire ordeal had been the headline of every news media. The security tapes from her building had been confiscated and, along with hundreds of amateur recordings, the footage was being played daily over the Internet and the news.

Of course, when questioned, she had pretended not to know what the creatures had wanted. Again she was grateful that Detective Beckford—with some persuasion from April no doubt—had kept quiet about all he'd learned. Even April had forfeited her claim to the details that Alexandra had promised her. Instead, she'd printed a very diluted and inconclusive version of the whole ordeal. It didn't matter if the truth came out though. Any claim that members of a very wealthy and prominent family were gargoyles who changed to stone at dawn would be regarded as nonsensical. The proof simply wasn't there, for the curse had been broken. Even Marius's brothers had failed in thwarting redemption. When Simion and Nicholas had returned to the mansion and the sun had crept above the horizon, their ghastly exteriors had fallen away and, instead of stone, they'd become human.

Alexandra could only speculate that the spell Nicholas had cast had been improperly done. After all, he was hardly a witch.

The door opened and Lady Amelia entered the large bedroom. She wore a soft blue skirt suit with a pearl necklace and matching earrings and her silver hair was swept up in an elegant coiffeur. Alexandra greeted her with a smile as Amelia sat next to her on the velvet duvet.

"How is he?" his mother asked as her worried gaze flickered over him.

"His fever's broken, but he's still out of it." Alexandra smoothed the duvet over him.

Lady Amelia's hand moved to cover her fingers and Alexandra looked up at her. "You are an extraordinary woman. My son is a very lucky man." She smiled, her gray eyes twinkling with sincerity.

Alexandra shook her head. "No, I'm the lucky one. I can't believe he would've given his life to save me."

"He must truly love you." She squeezed her hand.

Alexandra looked thoughtful. "None of this should've happened. I saw the truth in my dreams. Lady Vivian lied to Necesar. She tricked her into believing that your husband got her pregnant then married you. This whole curse was based on deception."

The older woman lowered her head as she absorbed this new revelation, and Alexandra thought she glimpsed the shimmer of tears. Pity overwhelmed her. Perhaps Lady Amelia had blamed herself all these years. Perhaps she'd lived with the great burden on her shoulders, trying endlessly to compensate for her fault.

When she looked up, her face was apologetic. "Alexandra, so much wrong has been done. We have caused you and your family so much pain. I am truly sorry, and I hope that you find it in your heart to forgive us. Sometimes one can be driven to do despicable things, if only to find some peace." She sighed. "I know we can never bring your parents back, but I will always be here for you should you need a mother's comfort. I will gladly consider you one of my own."

Alexandra nodded, tears welling in her eyes. "Thank you." Alexandra understood well the motives behind the acts that Marius's family had committed against her own, but she knew it would be some time before she could forgive them, let alone trust them. However, it was something she was willing to work at. Marius was a part of the Drakon clan, but now he was also a part of her.

Lady Amelia also appeared to be fighting tears. She seemed at a loss for words. Her gaze strayed to Marius, who had begun to stir.

His eyes eased opened and squinted against the sunlight.

Alexandra leaned over him, pressing a soft kiss against his lips. "You've been sleeping," she said quietly.

He winced. "What has happened?" he groaned.

"You've been hurt, but the curse has lifted." She smiled.

Confusion crossed his face and he turned to look at his mother, who was dabbing away at her tears. "We are free at last," she told him.

His fingers touched the bandaging on his chest. "How?"

Lady Amelia sighed. "I am not certain. We assumed that there had to be a joining by marriage, but it seems that a joining of hearts was sufficient."

His eyes strayed back to Alexandra, silvery pools that reflected a deep and honest love. She offered him a smile. She still couldn't believe that he was alive and well. How she would have returned to her previous existence had he not survived, she didn't know.

Lady Amelia stood. "I will leave you two alone. I do have some matters to attend to," she said with a smile.

"Will you be staying in the States?" Alexandra asked.

She shook her head. "Romania is my home. It is a part of me. We will all be returning." She looked at Marius.

He read the unspoken question in her eyes. "I will stay here in New York, Mother. I have a new home now." His eyes riveted to Alexandra.

His mother dipped her head in an elegant gesture of approval. "As you wish."

"Where is Father?" he asked with a slightly disappointed look.

She inhaled. "He loves you, Marius. He is ashamed of himself, not you. You must give him time." She looked to Alexandra. "Both of you."

After his mother left the room, Alexandra looked at Marius. She knew that there was much she had to learn about herself, but in time such things would be revealed. For now, she was happy to be safe and with the man she loved—the man who'd risked everything, betrayed his family and given his life for her. Their eyes met in that instant and, as silent as a sunrise, they exchanged the three words that had the power to dissipate any obstacle.

I love you.

* * * * *